U0131489

FUNCTIONAL
ENGLISH

看場合
說英語

正式╳非正式的
10種說法

白安竹 (Andrew E. Bennett) 著

林錦慧　譯

眾文圖書股份有限公司

Preface

Introduction

If you're like most people, a significant amount of your daily communication involves language functions. We greet people, give and ask for help, express thanks, apologize, agree and disagree, and so on. These functions often involve set chunks of language and specific sentence patterns. A great strategy for improving your English is to make it more "functional" by learning these patterns and expressions.

It's also important to develop an awareness of the levels of formality associated with different functions, so that appropriate phrases, patterns, and sentences can be used in different contexts. *Functional English* aims to help you develop these skills. As such, it is organized in a handy, practical, and easy-to-use format.

For this book, I have analyzed, organized, and written 50 common functions. They are presented in discreet, manageable units which you can read in any order you wish. You might enjoy reading the book from the first to the last page. Or you can use it as a reference text, looking up individual functions as you need them.

Unit Structure

Each unit in *Functional English* is made up of two parts.

Part 1:

Each function contains a list of sentences and patterns used to express the function. There are 10 entries in each list. Lists are organized by levels of formality, with the most informal pattern appearing at the top of the list and the most formal pattern appearing at the bottom.

Part 2:

From the list of 10 entries in Part 1, five are chosen as target patterns for the unit. We focus on these target patterns in Part 2. For each one, three possible uses are given, so you have a rich variety of examples to consider. This set of "substitution patterns" is followed by notes related to the examples. The notes provide useful information, such as alternative expressions, usage tips, cultural notes, and sociolinguistic analyses.

Next up is a short conversation involving the target pattern. This is a dialogue showing the function used in context. Many of these dialogues are followed by notes.

Part 2 also contains an "Extra Box." This box contains words, idioms, expressions, and sentences commonly used along with the unit's target function.

Organization

Functional English starts with functions that are associated with meeting people, including Introducing Oneself (Unit 1) and Introducing Others (Unit 2). There are also units related to "making small talk": Asking about Recent Situations (Unit 3) and Asking after Someone (Unit 4).

Many of the following units are grouped into related functions. So, for instance, Offering Help (Unit 5) is followed by Requesting Help (Unit 6). Asking for Someone's Opinion (Unit 27) is followed by Expressing an Opinion (Unit 28), and so on.

Importantly, *Functional English* does not neglect "difficult" functions which, though potentially awkward, are still necessary because they come up from time to time. That's especially true when speaking English, since many native speakers are more direct and are more likely to use "aggressive" or "negative" functions. These functions include Disagreeing (Unit 15), Saying "No" (Unit 20), and Delivering Bad News (Unit 30).

Learning about language functions is interesting, but it takes time, since so many of our habits, cultural attitudes, and expectations towards others are expressed through our daily interactions.

I hope you find this book enjoyable and useful. Thank you very much, and happy reading!

Andrew E Bennett

作者序

前言

如果你和大多數人一樣，那麼你的日常語言溝通有很大一部分是功能取向，包括打招呼、求助與助人、道謝、道歉、贊同與不贊同等。這種功能取向的溝通通常會牽涉到大量的詞組和特定句型，因此增強英語能力有一個好方法，即學習這種功能性溝通的句型和說法，讓英語更具有「功能性」。

此外，還要對不同功能的正式程度培養出一種敏銳度，以便在不同的情境下使用最適當的詞組、句型和句子。《看場合說英語：正式 × 非正式的 10 種說法》的目標就是幫助你培養這些技能，因此，本書的編排方式力求方便、實用和好用。

本書分析、整理並寫出 50 種常用的功能，透過審慎編寫、便於閱讀的單元呈現出來。閱讀的順序不拘，可隨你自己的意思來學習。你可以把它當成一本有趣的書來閱讀，從第一頁讀到最後一頁；也可以把它當成一本參考書，有需要時再查找個別功能即可。

單元架構

《看場合說英語》總共收錄 50 個單元，各自介紹一個溝通功能。每個功能單元都分成兩個部分。

Part 1

每個單元針對其所介紹的功能，一開始會先列出十個例句，各自代表一種句型。這十個代表句型依照正式程度來排序，由「非正式→正式」依序排列。

Part 2

從第一部分的十個代表句型中挑選出其中五個，作為第二部分主要分析的目標句型。每個目標句型都會列舉出三個相關且多樣化的實用例句，之後再針對目標句型和實用例句提供有用的資訊，例如替換說法、使用訣竅、文化方面的注意事項、社會語言學上的分析等。

接著會提供一組簡短的 AB 對話，該目標句型會運用在對話中，以呈現其實際應用情況。另外，這裡也會視情況提供相關說明。

第二部分還會提供「相關表達」專欄，介紹該功能常用到的字彙、慣用說法、常用語句等。

編排方式

本書從打招呼的功能開始介紹，內容包括「自我介紹」（單元 1）、「介紹別人」（單元 2）等。接著是「閒聊」的功能，包括「詢問近況」（單元 3）、「透過對方問候他人」（單元 4）等。

接下來是把功能相近的單元聚集在一起，例如「提議幫忙」（單元 5）的後面是「請求協助」（單元 6）；「詢問別人的意見」（單元 27）的後面是「表達自己的意見」（單元 28）等。

重要的是，本書並未忽略「困難」功能的介紹，這一類功能儘管有可能使人尷尬，但由於不時會用到，所以仍然有介紹的必要。尤其在與英文母語者說英語時更是需要，因為許多英文母語者比較直來直往，比較有可能會使用「侵略性」或「負面」的功能。這一類功能包括「表示不贊同」（單元 15）、「表示拒絕」（單元 20）、「傳達壞消息」（單元 30）等。

學習語言的功能很有趣，卻很花時間。這是由於我們的習慣、文化涵養、對別人的期望等，有很多都是透過我們在日常生活中的互動傳達出來的。

希望你覺得這本書很有趣、很好用。非常感謝，祝你展書愉快！

白安竹 (Andrew E. Bennett)

本書使用說明

50 個功能單元
因應日常生活、社交、面試、商務、學術等各方面的溝通需要，整理出 50 個溝通功能，各以一個單元詳細介紹。

全英文錄音
每個功能單元的英文例句和英語對話都進行錄音，一個單元一軌。

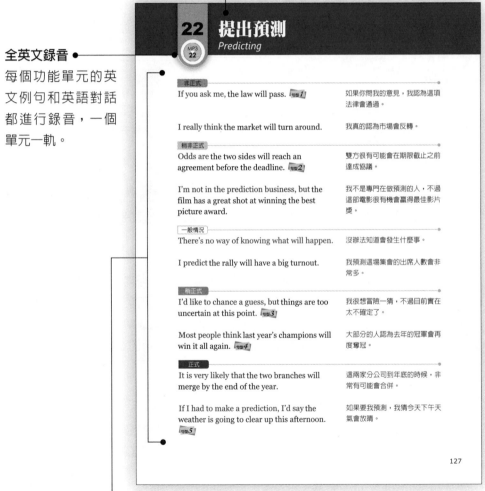

22 提出預測
Predicting

非正式

If you ask me, the law will pass. 句型*1*
如果你問我的意見，我認為這項法律會通過。

I really think the market will turn around.
我真的認為市場會反轉。

稍非正式

Odds are the two sides will reach an agreement before the deadline. 句型*2*
雙方很有可能在期限截止之前達成協議。

I'm not in the prediction business, but the film has a great shot at winning the best picture award.
我不是專門在做預測的人，不過這部電影很有機會贏得最佳影片獎。

一般情況

There's no way of knowing what will happen.
沒辦法知道會發生什麼事。

I predict the rally will have a big turnout.
我預測這場集會的出席人數會非常多。

稍正式

I'd like to chance a guess, but things are too uncertain at this point. 句型*3*
我很想冒險一猜，不過目前實在太不確定了。

Most people think last year's champions will win it all again. 句型*4*
大部分的人認為去年的冠軍會再度奪冠。

正式

It is very likely that the two branches will merge by the end of the year.
這兩家分公司到年底的時候，非常有可能會合併。

If I had to make a prediction, I'd say the weather is going to clear up this afternoon. 句型*5*
如果要我預測，我猜今天下午天氣會放晴。

127

五種正式程度
每個功能單元列出十個例句，各代表一種句型，並依「非正式→稍非正式→一般情況→稍正式→正式」順序排列。每種正式程度都提供兩個代表句型。

目標句型

從十個代表句型中選出五個較
重要的句型詳細介紹與分析。

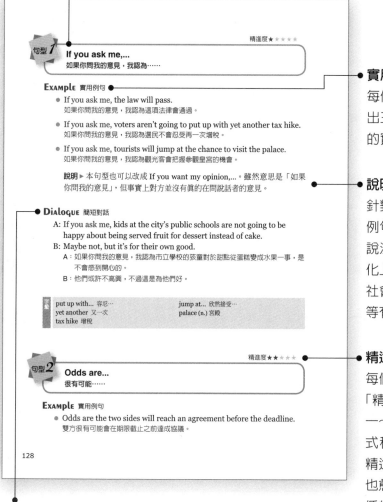

精進度 ★ ☆ ☆ ☆ ☆

句型 1

If you ask me,...
如果你問我的意見，我認為……

Example 實用例句

- If you ask me, the law will pass.
  如果你問我的意見，我認為這項法律會通過。

- If you ask me, voters aren't going to put up with yet another tax hike.
  如果你問我的意見，我認為選民不會忍受再一次增稅。

- If you ask me, tourists will jump at the chance to visit the palace.
  如果你問我的意見，我認為觀光客會把握參觀皇宮的機會。

  說明 ▶ 本句型也可以改成 If you want my opinion,...。雖然意思是「如果
  你問我的意見」，但事實上對方並沒有真的在問說話者的意見。

Dialogue 簡短對話

A: If you ask me, kids at the city's public schools are not going to be
happy about being served fruit for dessert instead of cake.
B: Maybe not, but it's for their own good.

A：如果你問我的意見，我認為市立學校的孩童對於甜點從蛋糕變成水果一事，是
不會感到開心的。
B：他們或許不高興，不過還是為他們好。

put up with... 容忍…	jump at... 欣然接受…
yet another 又一次	palace (n.) 宮殿
tax hike 增稅	

精進度 ★★ ☆ ☆ ☆

句型 2

Odds are...
很有可能……

Example 實用例句

- Odds are the two sides will reach an agreement before the deadline.
  雙方很有可能會在期限截止之前達成協議。

128

實用例句

每個目標句型都列舉
出三個相關且多樣化
的實用例句。

說明

針對目標句型及實用
例句，詳細提供替換
說法、使用訣竅、文
化上要注意的事項、
社會語言學上的分析
等有用的資訊。

精進度

每個目標句型都標示
「精進度」。精進度以
一～五顆星呈現。正
式程度愈高的句型，
精進度愈高，星星數
也愈多；正式程度愈
低的句型，精進度愈
低，星星數也愈少。

簡短對話

提供一組實際運用該目
標句型的 AB 對話。

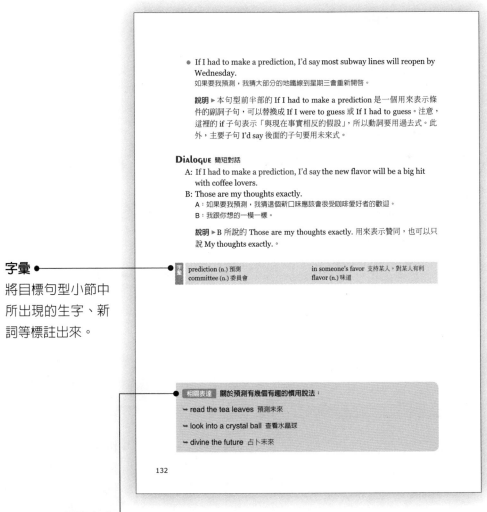

● If I had to make a prediction, I'd say most subway lines will reopen by Wednesday.
如果要我預測，我猜大部分的地鐵線到星期三會重新開啓。

說明 ▶ 本句型前半部的 If I had to make a prediction 是一個用來表示條件的副詞子句，可以替換成 If I were to guess 或 If I had to guess。注意，這裡的 if 子句表示「與現在事實相反的假設」，所以動詞要用過去式。此外，主要子句 I'd say 後面的子句要用未來式。

Dialogue 關短對話

A: If I had to make a prediction, I'd say the new flavor will be a big hit with coffee lovers.
B: Those are my thoughts exactly.
A：如果要我預測，我猜這個新口味應該會很受咖啡愛好者的歡迎。
B：我跟你想的一模一樣。

說明 ▶ B 所說的 Those are my thoughts exactly. 用來表示贊同，也可以只說 My thoughts exactly.。

字彙
prediction (n.) 預測   in someone's favor 支持某人，對某人有利
committee (n.) 委員會   flavor (n.) 味道

相關表達 關於預測有幾個有趣的慣用說法：

➥ read the tea leaves 預測未來

➥ look into a crystal ball 查看水晶球

➥ divine the future 占卜未來

132

字彙
將目標句型小節中所出現的生字、新詞等標註出來。

相關表達
每個功能單元的最後都規畫一個「相關表達」專欄，介紹該功能常用到的字彙、慣用說法、常用語句等。

Contents

Contents

Contents

自我介紹
Introducing Oneself

非正式

How's it going? I'm Ben.　　　　　你好嗎？我是班。

Hi, I'm Fred. 句型1　　　　　　　嗨，我是弗瑞德。

稍非正式

Everyone calls me Johnny.　　　　大家都叫我強尼。

I work in the banking field.　　　　我在銀行業服務。

一般情況

My name is Catherine, but you can call me
Kate. 句型2
　　　　　　　我的名字是凱瑟琳，不過你可以
　　　　　　　叫我凱特。

I work as a project manager at Burton
Securities. Here's my name card.
　　　　　　　我在伯頓證券擔任專案經理，這
　　　　　　　是我的名片。

稍正式

I am Hideki Tanaka. I am our regional sales
manager. 句型3
　　　　　　　我是田中秀樹，本公司的地區業
　　　　　　　務經理。

How do you do?　　　　　　　　你好。

正式

It's a pleasure to make your acquaintance.
句型4
　　　　　　　很高興認識你。

Please allow me to introduce myself. My
name is Jack Phillips. 句型5
　　　　　　　請容我介紹一下自己，我的名字
　　　　　　　是傑克‧飛利浦斯。

1

句型 **1**

Hi, I'm...
嗨，我是……

Example 實用例句

- Hi, I'm Fred.
  嗨，我是弗瑞德。

- Hi, I'm Emily.
  嗨，我是艾蜜莉。

- Hi, I'm Dr. Smith.
  嗨，我是史密斯醫師。

  說明▶ 雖然這是相當非正式的介紹方式，不過各行各業、各種社經地位的人都會使用。許多社會文化從衣著打扮到說話方式，都有愈來愈不拘小節的趨勢。

Dialogue 簡短對話

A: Hi, I'm Michelle.
B: How's it going? I'm Randall.

　A：嗨，我是蜜雪兒。
　B：你好嗎？我是蘭德爾。

　說明▶ 進行自我介紹時，常常會先說一句 How's it going? 或 How are you?（你好嗎？）這樣的問句，接著報上自己的名字。事實上這個問句只是作為修辭之用，不是真的在詢問、想要獲得回答。

句型 **2**

..., but you can call me ～
……，不過你可以叫我～

Example 實用例句

- My name is Catherine, but you can call me Kate.
  我的名字是凱薩琳，不過你可以叫我凱特。

● My full name is Elizabeth Jones, but you can call me Liz.
  我的全名是伊莉莎白・瓊斯，不過你可以叫我莉茲。

● I'm Jo-lin, but you can call me Lin.
  我是久琳，不過你可以叫我琳。

說明 ▶ 在許多國家中，直呼對方名字 (first name) 的情況愈來愈普遍。因此，進行自我介紹時，有人可能會以全名（即「名字 + 姓氏」）來介紹自己，或是直接介紹自己的名字。如果對方直接介紹自己的名字，表示可以直呼對方的名字。

Dialogue 簡短對話

A: Hello. My name is Theodore, but you can call me Ted.
B: Hi, I'm Samantha. Everybody calls me Sam.

　A：你好。我的名字是西爾多，不過你可以叫我泰德就好。
　B：嗨，我是珊曼莎，大家都叫我珊。

說明 ▶ 如果對方請你直呼他／她的名字或暱稱，這是一種拉近彼此距離的方式，那麼你也應該比照辦理，請對方直呼你的名字或暱稱，以維持彼此的親密關係。

精進度 ★★★★☆

句型 3

I am... I am ～
我的名字是……，職業是～

Example 實用例句

● I am Hideki Tanaka. I am our regional sales manager.
  我是田中秀樹，本公司的地區業務經理。

● I am Erika Gonzalez. I am in charge of international accounts.
  我是艾瑞卡・岡薩雷茲，負責國際客戶。

● I am Chen Li-fang. I am the lead designer for the children's department.
  我是陳麗芬，兒童部門的首席設計師。

說明▶ 在比較口語的英文中，常常會將 I am 唸成 I'm，不過有時為了表達清楚，還是會將主詞 I 和動詞 am 分開唸。另外，介紹完自己的姓名之後，通常還會把自己的職業或職位告訴對方。

Dialogue 簡短對話

A: I am Nikolai Baranov. I am a product manager.
B: It's very nice to meet you. I'm Hillary Benson.

　　A：我是尼可萊‧拜拉諾夫，產品經理。
　　B：非常高興認識你，我是希拉蕊‧班森。

in charge of... 負責…，主管…	lead (adj.) 最重要的
account (n.) 固定客戶（尤指公司）	product manager 產品經理

句型**4**　**It's a pleasure to...**
很高興……

Example 常用例句

● It's a pleasure to make your acquaintance.
很高興認識你。

● It's a pleasure to meet you.
很高興認識你。

● It's a pleasure to know you
很高興認識你。

　　說明▶ 本句型通常使用在雙方都介紹完自己的名字之後。說這句話的同時，通常會微微鞠躬示意，也有可能會伸出手與對方握手。

Dialogue 簡短對話

A: It's a pleasure to make your acquaintance.
B: Likewise. I'm glad we finally have a chance to meet face to face.

　　A：很高興認識你。
　　B：我也一樣。很高興我們終於有機會面對面相見。

說明 ▶ 為了回應對方的熱絡，一般人通常會報以相同的熱情，以 likewise 或 same here 來回答，意思是「我也一樣」，意指自己也很高興見到對方。

 字彙　acquaintance (n.) 相識，認識的人　　　　face to face 面對面

 句型5

Please allow me to introduce myself.
請容我介紹一下自己。

Example 常用例句

● Please allow me to introduce myself. My name is Jack Phillips.
請容我介紹一下自己。我的名字是傑克‧飛利浦斯。

● Please allow me to introduce myself. I'm Dr. Alicia Rossi.
請容我介紹一下自己。我是艾莉西亞‧羅西醫師。

● Please allow me to introduce myself. I am Doug McGregor Jr.
請容我介紹一下自己。我是小道格‧麥奎格。

說明 ▶ 在正式場合中，西方人常常會連名帶姓地介紹自己。如果自身有任何頭銜（例如主任、醫師等），通常也會一併說出來。另外，如果沿用父親的名字，可能會另外加上 Jr.（年紀較輕的那個），例如 Bob Jones Jr.。如果名字和父親及祖父都一樣，那就會在名字後面加上 the 3rd（第三個），例如 Marshall Fairbanks the 3rd。

Dialogue 簡短對話

A: Please allow me to introduce myself. I'm Jennifer Hurston-Tanner.
B: Nice to meet you. I'm James Smith.

A：請容我介紹一下自己。我是珍妮佛‧賀斯頓‧泰納。
B：很高興認識你。我是詹姆斯‧史密斯。

說明 ▶ 如果對方用全名介紹自己，那麼你在自我介紹時通常也要用全名。另外，有愈來愈多的西方女性婚後不再以夫姓取代原本的姓氏，而是在原本的姓氏後面加上夫姓，兩個姓氏中間通常會用連字號 (-) 隔開。

➥ Good morning. 早安。

➥ Good afternoon. 午安。

➥ Good evening. 晚安。

➥ Hello. 你好。

➥ Hi. 嗨。

介紹別人
Introducing Others

非正式

George, Tori. Tori, George.

喬治，這是托利；托利，這是喬治。

Do you know Michiko? 句型1

你認識美智子嗎？

稍非正式

Come over here and meet Theresa.

過來這裡認識一下泰瑞莎。

Have you met my friend Sam?

你見過我的朋友山姆嗎？

一般情況

I don't think you've ever met my brother. 句型2

我想你應該沒見過我弟弟。

There's someone I want you to meet. This is my good friend George. 句型3

我想介紹你認識一個人。這位是我的好朋友喬治。

稍正式

This is my business associate, Maria Dolores.

這位是我的生意夥伴，瑪莉亞·朵樂利絲。

I'd like to introduce you to my colleague, Jennifer. 句型4

我想介紹你認識我的同事，珍妮佛。

正式

Please allow me to introduce you to one of our top chemists. 句型5

請容我介紹你認識我們其中一位頂尖的化學家。

It is my (sincere) honor to introduce you to Mr. Pierre Lambert.

我很榮幸（無比榮幸）介紹你認識皮耶·藍伯特先生。

句型 1

Do you know...?

你認識……嗎？

Example 實用例句

● Do you know Michiko?
  你認識美智子嗎？

● Do you know Mr. Silver?
  你認識希爾芙先生嗎？

● Do you know my music teacher?
  你認識我的音樂老師嗎？

說明 ▶ 使用本句型來介紹別人時，通常會介紹名字、姓氏（前面會加 Mr. 之類的稱謂）、職位或與說話者的關係。一般不會介紹全名，不過某些情況下還是有可能。

Dialogue 簡短對話

A: Do you know Candice?

B: No, I don't think we've met. My name is Tori. It's good to know you.

  A：你認識坎蒂絲嗎？

  B：不認識，我想我們應該沒見過面。我的名字是托利，很高興認識你。

說明 ▶ 針對 A 所問的問題，如果以前見過 Candice 這個人，便可以回答 Yes, we've met before.（認識，我們以前見過面。）

句型 2

I don't think you've ever met...

我想你應該沒見過……

Example 實用例句

● I don't think you've ever met my brother.
  我想你應該沒見過我弟弟。

● I don't think you've ever met Lance.
  我想你應該沒見過蘭斯。

● I don't think you've ever met my mom.
我想你應該沒見過我媽媽。

說明 ▶ 如果對方要把他／她的爸爸或媽媽介紹給你，和他們第一次打招呼時通常要冠上 Mr. 或 Mrs.。之後如果對方的爸爸或媽媽要你直呼他們的名字，你就可以使用較非正式的稱呼方式。

Dialogue 簡短對話

A: I don't think you've ever met my dad.

B: Hello, Mr. Thompson. It's nice to meet you.

　A：我想你應該沒見過我爸爸。

　B：你好，湯普森先生，很高興認識你。

精進度 ★★★☆☆

句型 3

There's someone I want you to meet. This is...
我想介紹你認識一個人。這位是……

Example 實用例句

● There's someone I want you to meet. This is my good friend George.
我想介紹你認識一個人。這位是我的好朋友喬治。

● There's someone I want you to meet. This is Fanny Brawne.
我想介紹你認識一個人。這位芬妮‧布朗。

● There's someone I want you to meet. This is the person who engineered our third quarter turnaround, Chuck Reed.
我想介紹你認識一個人。這位是將我們第三季轉虧為盈的人，查克‧里德。

說明 ▶ 如果要更非正式一點，可以更動本句型的字序，變成 I want you to meet someone. This is...。此外，第三個例句提到個人背景資料：the person who engineered our third quarter turnaround，這是介紹別人時用來強調此人重要性、聲望或角色的常見方式。

Dialogue 簡短對話

A: There's someone I want you to meet. This is Bob. He's one of my oldest friends.

B: How are you? I'm Doris.

　　A：我想介紹你認識一個人。這位是鮑伯，他是我交往最久的朋友之一。

　　B：你好嗎？我是朵莉絲。

字彙

engineer (v.) 精明地處理　　　　　　　turnaround (n.)（經濟等的）突然好轉
quarter (n.) 一季

精進度★★★★☆

句型 4

I'd like to introduce you to...
我想介紹你認識……

Example 實用例句

- I'd like to introduce you to my colleague, Jennifer.
  我想介紹你認識我的同事，珍妮佛。

- I'd like to introduce you to my boss, Barbara Little.
  我想介紹你認識我的老闆，芭芭拉‧利透。

- I'd like to introduce you to Inge Lehmann.
  我想介紹你認識英格‧萊曼。

　　說明▶使用本句型時，可以先提到這個人的頭銜或與你的關係，接著再說出這個人的名字（如第一、二個例句）。直接說出這個人的名字也可以（如第三個例句）。

Dialogue 簡短對話

A: I'd like to introduce you to my accountant, Bill Walters.

B: Nice to meet you, Bill. I'm Jacob Goldstein. Please call me Jake.

　　A：我想介紹你認識我的會計師，比爾‧沃特斯。

　　B：很高興認識你，比爾。我是傑卡伯‧戈史汀，請叫我傑克。

　　說明▶本對話是另一個愈來愈不拘泥於正式禮節的例子，即聽到對方的全名之後，立刻直呼對方的名字。

精進度 ★★★★★

句型5

Please allow me to introduce you to...

請容我介紹你認識……

Example 實用例句

● Please allow me to introduce you to one of our top chemists.
請容我介紹你認識我們其中一位頂尖的化學家。

● Please allow me to introduce you to Lisa Reynolds.
請容我介紹你認識莉莎‧雷諾茲。

● Please allow me to introduce you to the vice president of operations,
Mr. Peter Olson.
請容我介紹你認識營運副總,彼德‧歐爾森先生。

說明 ▶ 可以用本句型來介紹別人的姓名、頭銜或在公司裡的職位,此時有
可能會加上 Mr. 或 Ms.,以表示正式和尊重(如第三個例句)。

Dialogue 簡短對話

A: Please allow me to introduce you to Julio Mendez. He's our Latin
American rep.

B: It's a pleasure to meet you. My name is Olivia ... Olivia Bronson.

A:請容我介紹你認識胡立歐‧門德斯,他是本公司的拉丁美洲代表。

B:很高興認識你,我的名字是奧莉維亞,奧莉維亞‧布朗森。

說明 ▶ 向別人介紹自己的姓名時,一種方式是先說出自己的名字,然後
停頓一下,接著再說出全名。很少人會像 007 系列電影的詹姆士‧龐德
(James Bond) 一樣,先講姓氏,再說出全名。

介紹別人

➥ He works with me at Geotech. 他跟我一起在吉歐科技工作。

➥ We went to school together. 我們以前都一起上學。

➥ She's been my best friend for 15 years. 她 15 年來一直是我最好的朋友。

3 詢問近況

Asking about Recent Situations

What's up? It's been a while. 句型1

最近怎麼樣呢？有好一陣子沒見面了。

What's new with you?

最近怎麼樣呢？

Where have you been hiding yourself?

最近都躲到哪裡去了呢？

How have you been keeping up?

最近怎麼樣呢？

How was your trip? 句型2

你的旅行好玩嗎？

What have you been up to recently? 句型3

你最近都在忙些什麼呢？

How's your new house coming along? 句型4

你新家的情況如何呢？

How are your wife and kids?

你的太太和小孩好嗎？

How are things with your business?

你的生意如何呢？

How have you been lately? 句型5

你最近好嗎？

句型 1

What's up?
最近怎麼樣呢？

Example 實用例句

- What's up? It's been a while.
  最近怎麼樣呢？有好一陣子沒見面了。

- What's up? I haven't seen you in ages.
  最近怎麼樣呢？好久沒看到你了。

- What's up? Long time no see.
  最近怎麼樣呢？好久不見。

  說明 ▶ 使用本句型詢問別人近況時，如果距離你們上一次見面已經有一段時間，通常會接著說 It's been a while. 或 Long time no see.，放在問句之前也可以。另外要注意，What's up? 是相當非正式的問句，通常只用於朋友之間。

Dialogue 簡短對話

A: What's up? I haven't seen you in months.
B: I've been studying hard for the GRE. I'm getting set to apply to grad school.

A：最近怎麼樣呢？好幾個月沒看到你了。
B：我最近很努力唸書準備 GRE，我要開始來申請研究所了。

說明 ▶ 如果在詢問近況的問句之後接著說 I haven't seen you in months.，通常對方會解釋他／她最近在做什麼事。

字彙

GRE 美國研究生入學考試　　　　　　　get set to V. 開始做…，著手做…
(= Graduate Record Examinations)　　grad school 研究所 (= graduate school)

句型*2*

How was...?
……如何呢？

Example 實用例句

- How was your trip?
  你的旅行好玩嗎？

- How was the meeting?
  會議進行得如何呢？

- How was soccer practice?
  足球練習得如何呢？

說明 ▶ 使用本句型時，說話者假定對方知道自己指的是什麼，所以不會進一步描述細節。

Dialogue 簡短對話

A: How was Hong Kong?
B: Pretty good. We didn't have a chance to do much sightseeing, but we ate some great dim sum.

A：香港好玩嗎？
B：相當不錯。我們沒有機會到處遊覽，不過吃了一些很棒的港式飲茶。

說明 ▶ 如果有人最近剛去旅行回來，便可以用〈How was + 城市／國家？〉這個句型來詢問對方旅行的情況。

 字彙 | sightseeing (n.) 觀光，遊覽   dim sum 點心，港式飲茶

詢問近況

句型3

What have you been up to...?

你⋯⋯都在忙些什麼呢?

Example 實用例句

● What have you been up to recently?
你最近都在忙些什麼呢?

● What have you been up to this summer?
你今年夏天都在忙些什麼呢?

● What have you been up to since getting back from Europe?
你從歐洲回來之後都在忙些什麼呢?

說明▶ 本句型 to 後面的修飾語可以是副詞(如 recently, lately)、一段尚未結束的時間(如 this summer)或副詞片語(如 since getting back from Europe)。

Dialogue 簡短對話

A: What have you been up to since leaving the army?
B: Not much. I'm still looking for a job.
A:你退伍之後都在忙些什麼呢?
B:沒什麼,我還在找工作。

army (n.) 軍隊   look for... 尋找⋯

句型4

How are things with...?

⋯⋯如何呢?

Example 實用例句

● How are things with your business?
你的生意如何呢?

● How are things with Marianne?
瑪莉安好嗎?

● How are things with the movement to turn the old courthouse into a museum?
將老舊法院改成博物館的事情進行得如何呢？

說明▶ 本句型 with 的後面通常接事情（如第一個例句）、人（如第二個例句）或狀況（如第三個例句）。

Dialogue 簡短對話

A: How are things with your auto repair shop?

B: Not bad, thanks. We're getting great word of mouth. Actually, I'm thinking of hiring another mechanic.

A：你的修車廠情況如何呢？

B：還不錯，謝謝。我們的口碑很好，其實我正在考慮再雇用一名技師。

字彙

movement (n.) 活動，行動
courthouse (n.) 法院
auto (n.) 汽車 (= automobile)

word of mouth 口碑
mechanic (n.) 技師，機械工

精進度★★★★★

句型 *5*

How have you been...?
你……怎麼樣呢？

Example 實用例句

● How have you been lately?
你最近好嗎？

● How have you been this year?
你今年好嗎？

● How have you been since graduating?
畢業之後過得如何呢？

說明▶ 本句型 been 後面的修飾語可以有多種變化，例如使用副詞（如 lately, recently）、一段時間（如 this year, the last 48 hours）、副詞片語（如 since graduating, since your move to Kaohsiung）或者副詞子句（如 since we last met）。

17

Dialogue 簡短對話

A: How have you been recently? I haven't heard from you since the Atlanta conference.

B: Things have been really busy, but all in all, I'm doing great.

A：你最近好嗎？自從亞特蘭大會議之後就沒有你的消息。

B：一直很忙，不過總體來說，我很好。

說明 ▶ 詢問對方最近過得如何之後，接下來通常會提到上一次兩人是在何時碰面的事情。

字彙	hear from... 接到…的來信、電話等	all in all 總體來說
	conference (n.) 會議	

相關表達 和許久不見的朋友見面時，可以用下面的句子來打招呼：

➥ I haven't seen you in months/years. 好幾個月／好幾年沒看到你了。

➥ It's been ages. 好久不見。

➥ It's been a while. 好一陣子沒見了。

➥ Long time no see. 好久不見。

透過對方問候他人
Asking after Someone

非正式

Tell Peter I said hi. 句型*1*　　　代我向彼德問好。

What is your youngest son up to?　　　你的小兒子在忙些什麼呢？

稍非正式

How is your mother doing?　　　你媽媽好嗎？

How is everything with your sister? 句型*2*　　　你姊姊一切都好嗎？

一般情況

I haven't seen Ms. Reynolds in a while. 句型*3*　　　我有好一陣子沒看到雷諾茲女士了。

Has your brother recovered from his operation?　　　你弟弟手術復原了嗎？

稍正式

Please say hello to your husband for me. 句型*4*　　　請代我向你先生問好。

Please give your wife my best.　　　請代我向你太太致意。

正式

I hope your father is well these days.　　　我希望你父親現在很好。

If you have a chance, please give my (best) regards to Mr. Obama. 句型*5*　　　如果你有機會，請代我向歐巴馬先生問好。

句型 *1*　**Tell ... I said hi.**
代我向……問好。

Example 實用例句

● Tell Peter I said hi.
代我向彼德問好。

● Tell your parents I said hi.
代我向你父母問好。

● Tell Ms. Keats I said hi.
代我向濟慈女士問好。

說明 ▶ 用本句型請某人代為轉達問候之意時，通常說話者並不見得期待對方真的會如實轉達，而比較像是客氣的說法，用意是讓對方知道說話者有想到口中所提到的人（如 your parents）。

Dialogue 簡短對話

A: Tell the old gang I said hi.

B: Absolutely, but wouldn't you rather tell them yourself? A bunch of us are getting together this weekend.

A：代我向大夥兒問好。

B：當然沒問題，不過你要不要自己向他們問好？我們一夥人這個週末要聚會。

說明 ▶ 如果雙方有一群共同的朋友或同事，過去常常在一起，這一群人就可以說是 the old gang。注意，雖然用了 gang 這個字，不過並沒有負面的含意。（gang 常用來指結夥的幫派。）

gang (n.) 一幫，一群	a bunch of... 一群（人）
absolutely (adv.) 毫無疑問地	get together 聚在一起

句型 2 How is everything with...?

……一切都好嗎？

EXAMPLE 實用例句

● How is everything with your sister?
你姊姊一切都好嗎？

● How is everything with the baseball team?
棒球隊一切都好嗎？

● How is everything with our old math teacher?
我們以前的數學老師一切都好嗎？

說明 ▶ 本句型 with 的後面可以接一個人、一群人或一個團體。如果是對話雙方彼此都認識的人，通常會用〈our old ＋人〉，例如 our old math teacher（我們以前的數學老師）、our old dorm mate（我們以前的宿舍室友）、our old supervisor（我們以前的主管），這裡的 old 並不是指年紀很大，而是表示「以前的，過去的」。

DIALOGUE 簡短對話

A: How is everything with the old marketing team?
B: Everyone's great. They sometimes ask about you.

A：以前的行銷團隊一切都好嗎？
B：每個人都很好。他們有時候會問起你。

 marketing (n.) 行銷

透過對方問候他人

句型 3 I haven't seen...

我沒看到……

EXAMPLE 實用例句

● I haven't seen Ms. Reynolds in a while.
我有好一陣子沒看到雷諾茲女士了。

- I haven't seen Lillian this week.
  我這星期都沒看到莉莉安。

- I haven't seen Dmitri in a long time.
  我好久沒看到迪米萃了。

  說明 ▶ 本句型 haven't seen 的後面接人（如 Ms. Reynolds, Lillian, Dmitri 等）。使用本句型，表示說話者認為對方認識他／她所提到的人，而且可能知道這個人的行蹤或近況。

Dialogue 簡短對話

A: I haven't seen our intern in a while.
B: Oh yeah, she left a few weeks ago. I think she found a job at a radio station.

A：我好一陣子沒看到我們的實習生了。
B：喔，對啊，她幾個星期前走了。我想她在電台找到工作了吧。

intern (n.) 實習生　　　　　　　　　　radio station 廣播電台

句型 **4**

Please say hello to ... for me.
請代我向……問好。

Example 實用例句

- Please say hello to your husband for me.
  請代我向你先生問好。

- Please say hello to everyone for me.
  請代我向大家問好。

- Please say hello to Janet for me.
  請代我向珍妮特問好。

說明 ▶ 如果要表現得更口語一些，可以將本句型的 hello 替換成 hi。此外，如果要像第二個例句那樣使用 everyone，則對話雙方必須有一群共同的朋友或認識的人（如同事、朋友、同班同學等）。舉例來說，說話者剛從公司離職，而對方還留在原公司工作。

Dialogue 簡短對話

A: Please say hello to Chuck for me. I think about him sometimes.
B: Sure thing.

A：請代我向恰克問好，我有時候會想到他。
B：沒問題。

說明 ▶ B 除了回答 Sure thing. 之外，也可以說 I'll be happy to.（我很樂意做。／我很高興做。）比較口語的回答則是 You bet.（當然沒問題。）

句型 5

If you have a chance, please give my (best) regards to...
如果你有機會，請代我向……問好。

Example 實用例句

● If you have a chance, please give my best regards to Mr. Obama.
如果你有機會，請代我向歐巴馬先生問好。

● If you have a chance, please give my regards to the commissioner.
如果你有機會，請代我向長官問好。

● If you have a chance, please give my best regards to your boss.
如果你有機會，請代我向你的老闆問好。

說明 ▶ 一般來說，比較正式的說法會在 please give my (best) regards to...（請代我向…問好）之外加上一個委婉的固定說法，例如 if you have a chance（如果你有機會）、if time permits（如果時間許可）、if it isn't too much trouble（如果不會太麻煩）等，讓語氣顯得比較婉轉、不唐突。但如果要問候的對象是對方的配偶，就不要使用上述這些婉轉的說法，因為對方「一定」會見到他／她的配偶，使用 if you have a chance 等說法會顯得不太合理。

透過對方問候他人

Dialogue 簡短對話

A: If you have a chance, please give my regards to Amanda.

B: Of course. In fact, I'm having lunch with her next Tuesday.

    A：如果有機會，請代我向阿曼達問好。

    B：沒問題。其實我下個星期二要和她一起吃午餐。

字彙   commissioner (n.)（政府部門的）長官

相關表達   向對方問候完某個人後，通常還會再加上下面這些話：

➥ I'd love to see him/her/them again. 我很想再見到他 / 她 / 他們。

➥ I think about him/her/them sometimes. 我偶爾會想到他 / 她 / 他們。

➥ Tell him/her to give me a call. 叫他 / 她打電話給我。

5 提議幫忙
Offering Help

Need a hand? 　　　　　　　　　　　需要幫忙嗎？

Let me open the door for you. 句型*1* 　　我來替你開門。

Do you need (any) help with that? 句型*2* 　需要幫忙你做那個嗎？

What can I do for you? 　　　　　　　　我可以幫你什麼忙呢？

I'd/I'll be happy to help you find work. 句型*3* 　我很樂意幫你找工作。

Could you use some help? 　　　　　　你需要幫忙嗎？

Is there anything I can do? 　　　　　有我可以幫忙的地方嗎？

Can I help (you) with anything? 句型*4* 　有什麼我可以幫忙（你）的嗎？

Would you like me to give you a hand? 句型*5* 　需要我幫你的忙嗎？

May I be of some assistance? 　　　　有我可以幫忙的地方嗎？

句型 *1* **Let me...**
我來⋯⋯

Example 實用例句

- Let me open the door for you.
  我來替你開門。

- Let me pour you some water.
  我來倒一些水給你。

- Let me try to find out where the package is.
  讓我來找找這個包裹在哪裡。

  說明 ▶ 這是一種向對方提議幫忙的簡單說法，清楚指出接下來馬上會做的動作（如 open the door for you），或是說話者未來願意做的事情（如 try to find out where the package is）。如果是馬上就要做的動作，通常說話者一邊提議要幫忙時，一邊就會開始採取行動，例如提議要幫你開門時就伸手去握門把。

Dialogue 簡短對話

A: Let me carry that bag for you.
B: Thanks, I could use an extra set of hands.

　A：讓我替你拿那個包包。
　B：謝謝，我正需要幫手。

---

package (n.) 包裹	an extra set of hands〔口語〕幫手
carry (v.) 提，拿，搬	(= a helper)

句型 *2*

Do you need (any) help...?

需要幫忙你……嗎？

Example 實用例句

- Do you need any help with that?
  需要幫忙你做那個嗎？

- Do you need help translating the menu?
  需要幫忙你翻譯菜單嗎？

- Do you need any help washing the dishes?
  需要幫忙你洗碗嗎？

  說明 ▶ 本句型的後面會接介系詞片語（如 with that, in the morning 等）或動名詞（如 translating the menu, posting the flyers 等）。

Dialogue 簡短對話

A: Do you need help finding anything?

B: Well, I'm looking for a watch for my father. But to be honest, I don't know anything about watches.

A：需要幫忙你找什麼東西嗎？

B：嗯，我要找一支手錶給我爸爸，不過老實說，我對手錶一竅不通。

  說明 ▶ B 所說的 to be honest（老實說）可以替換成 the truth is 或 truth be told，意思不變。說話時如果要強調自己的態度很誠懇、很老實，可以在一開頭時先說 to be honest。

 post (v.) 張貼　　　　　　　　　　　flyer (n.) 傳單

提議幫忙

句型 *3*

I'd/I'll be happy to...

我很樂意……

Example 實用例句

- I'd be happy to help you find work.
  我很樂意幫你找工作。

- I'll be happy to rehearse the play with you.
  我很樂意和你一起排練這齣戲。

- I'd be happy to write down directions if you need them.
  如果你需要,我很樂意把方向指引寫下來。

  說明 ▶ 另一個和本句型一樣正式的句型是〈(Please) let me know if you need any help + 動名詞〉,例如 Please let me know if you need any help unloading the truck.(如果需要幫忙將卡車上的東西卸下來,請告訴我。)

Dialogue 簡短對話

A: I'd like to ask about vacation packages to Ireland.

B: I'll be happy to help you with that. Please have a seat.

A:我想詢問到愛爾蘭的假期套裝行程。

B:我很樂意協助你,請坐。

find work 找工作 (= find a job)	unload (v.) 從…卸貨
rehearse (v.) 排演,排練	vacation package 假期套裝行程
play (n.) 戲劇	have a seat 坐下

句型 *4*

Can I help (you)...?

我可以幫忙(你)……嗎?

Example 實用例句

- Can I help you with anything?
  有什麼我可以幫忙你的嗎?

● Can I help unpack those boxes?
我可以幫忙打開那些箱子嗎？

● Can I help you set the table?
我可以幫你擺碗筷嗎？

說明 ▶ 本句型的後面可以接介系詞片語，例如 with anything, at the store（在店裡）等；也可以接動詞或動詞片語，例如 set the table（擺碗筷）、load the car（把東西裝上車）等。

Dialogue 簡短對話

A: Can I help you with anything?
B: Yes, please. I'm looking for the menswear department.

A：有什麼我可以幫忙你的嗎？
B：是的，麻煩你。我在找男裝部。

說明 ▶ B 除了回答 Yes, please. 外，也可以說 I'd appreciate that.（太謝謝了。）如果不需要幫忙，便可以回答 No, thanks. I'm just browsing.（不用了，謝謝。我只是隨便看看而已。）

字彙	unpack (v.) 打開（箱、盒等）	load (v.) 裝載
	set the table 擺放餐具	menswear (n.) 男裝

精進度★★★★★

Would you like me to...?
需要我……嗎？

Example 實用例句

● Would you like me to give you a hand?
需要我幫你的忙嗎？

● Would you like me to recommend a good dentist?
需要我推薦一位好的牙醫嗎？

● Would you like me to wrap that for you?
需要我幫你把那個包起來嗎？

提議幫忙

說明 ▶ 本句型 to 的後面接原形動詞，例如 give you a hand（幫你的忙）、call Mary（打電話給瑪莉）等。

Dialogue 簡短對話

A: Would you like me to help you wash the vegetables?

B: That would be a big help, thank you.

A：要我幫你洗菜嗎？

B：那就幫了大忙了，謝謝。

說明 ▶ B 所說的 a big help 也可以替換成 well appreciated。另外，也可以回答 That's very kind of you.（你真好心。）

字彙		
give ... a hand 幫…的忙		wrap (v.) 將…包裹起來
dentist (n.) 牙醫		appreciate (v.) 感激，感謝

相關表達　當別人提議幫忙時，可以怎麼回應呢？

➥ Yes, please. 是的，麻煩你。

➥ That would be a big help. 那就幫了大忙了。

➥ I certainly appreciate it. 太感謝了。

➥ I'm fine, but thanks for asking. 我來就行了，不過謝謝你。

6 請求協助
Requesting Help

MP3 06

Give me a hand, will you? 句型 1

幫我一個忙，可以嗎？

I could use some help over here.

我這裡需要幫忙。

Can you do me a favor? I need someone to watch my kids this afternoon. 句型 2

可以幫我一個忙嗎？今天下午我需要有人幫忙照顧我的小孩。

Could you please give Charles the message?

可以請你傳話給查爾斯嗎？

Would you mind closing the window? 句型 3

你介意把窗戶關起來嗎？

Sorry to bother you, but can you please open the door for me?

不好意思麻煩你，可以請你幫我開個門嗎？

Do you think you might be able to show me to the library? 句型 4

不知道你可不可以告訴我圖書館怎麼走呢？

If it isn't too much trouble, could you please hand me that bag?

如果不會太麻煩的話，可以請你把那個袋子拿給我嗎？

I was wondering if you could please give me some assistance. 句型 5

不知道你可不可以幫我個忙呢？

Could I impose on you to turn down the volume?

可以麻煩你把音量關小嗎？

句型 **1** ..., will you?
……，可以嗎？

Example 實用例句

● Give me a hand, will you?
幫我一個忙，可以嗎？

● Fold these clothes, will you?
把這些衣服摺一摺，可以嗎？

● Get me some napkins, will you?
給我一些餐巾，可以嗎？

說明 ▶ 一般來說，最非正式的請求都是簡短且直接的。在本句型中，說話者的語調也很重要。如果要讓請求聽起來比較婉轉、不像命令，語調就要輕柔一點，後面 will you 的語調往上揚。如果要讓請求比較強硬一點、比較像命令一點，will you 的語調就要往下降。

Dialogue 簡短對話

A: Tell me the sales figures again, will you?
B: We sold 225 units in June and 378 units in July.
A：再跟我講一次銷售數字，可以嗎？
B：我們在六月賣掉了 225 台，七月 378 台。

說明 ▶ 如果 A 想要更正式一點，可以把 will 改成 won't，例如 Call Mike for me, won't you?（幫我打電話給麥克，可以嗎？）。

---

fold (v.) 摺疊　　　　　　　　　　　　　　　unit (n.) 一套，一組 (= piece)
napkin (n.) 餐巾

句型2 Can you do me a favor?
可以幫我一個忙嗎？

Example 實用例句

● Can you do me a favor? I need someone to watch my kids this afternoon.
可以幫我一個忙嗎？今天下午我需要有人幫忙照顧我的小孩。

● Can you do me a favor? These buckets need to be filled with water.
可以幫我一個忙嗎？這些水桶必須裝滿水。

● Can you do me a favor? Could you fill in for me at work next Tuesday?
可以幫我一個忙嗎？下個星期二你可以代我的班嗎？

說明 ▶ 本句型是個引子，或者可說是個「定調」的問句。請別人幫忙前先說 Can you do me a favor?，這樣對方就會有個心理準備，知道接下來會聽到一個請求。這種請別人幫忙的說話方式比較婉轉。另外，提出請求時，可用直述句來表達（如第一、二個例句），也可以用問句（如第三個例句）。事實上，以直述句提出請求很常見。

Dialogue 簡短對話

A: Can you do me a favor? I need someone to water my flowers while I'm on vacation.

B: No problem. Just show me what to do.

　A：可以幫我一個忙嗎？我去度假時，需要有人幫我澆花。

　B：沒問題，告訴我怎麼做就行了。

watch (v.) 看護	water flowers 澆花
fill in for someone at work 代某人的班	be on vacation 度假

句型 *3*

Would you mind...?
你介意……嗎?

Example 實用例句

- Would you mind closing the window?
  你介意把窗戶關起來嗎?

- Would you mind explaining that one more time?
  你介意再把那個解釋一遍嗎?

- Would you mind spelling your name for me?
  你介意把你的名字拼給我聽嗎?

  說明 ▶〈Would you mind + 動名詞 + 受詞 (+ for me)?〉這個句型常用於請求別人協助時。for me 加不加都可以。

Dialogue 簡短對話

A: Would you mind talking to the building supervisor about the broken air conditioner?
B: OK, if you think it will help.
  A:你介意去向大樓管理人說空調壞了嗎?
  B:好,如果你覺得這樣有用的話。

  說明 ▶ 當說話者回應 if you think it will help 時,通常表示他 / 她抱持比較悲觀的態度,無法確定對方的提議是否確實有效。

 supervisor (n.) 管理人　　　　　　　　air conditioner 空調

句型 *4*

Do you think you might be able to...?
不知道你可不可以……呢?

Example 實用例句

- Do you think you might be able to show me to the library?
  不知道你可不可以告訴我圖書館怎麼走呢?

- Do you think you might be able to find that information for us?
  不知道你可不可以替我們找出那份資料呢？

- Do you think you might be able to send me the photo via e-mail?
  不知道你可不可以用電子郵件把照片寄給我呢？

  說明 ▶ 有別於 Can you...? 這種直接問句的形式，本句型採用間接問句的結構，通常用於比較客氣、比較正式的情況。另外，via 是個介系詞，意思是「透過，經由」，例如 via e-mail（透過電子郵件）、via regular mail（透過普通郵件）、via express courier（透過快遞）等。

Dialogue 簡短對話

A: Do you think you might be able to look over this file?
B: Sure. I'll look at it this afternoon.

　A：不知道你可不可以檢查一下這個檔案呢？
　B：沒問題，我今天下午會看。

express courier 快遞	look over... 仔細檢查…

精進度★★★★★

句型 **5**
I was wondering if...
不知道可不可以……呢？

Example 實用例句

- I was wondering if you could please give me some assistance.
  不知道你可不可以幫我個忙呢？

- I was wondering if you might be able to help me move the refrigerator.
  不知道你可不可以幫我搬這台冰箱呢？

- I was wondering if someone might be able to walk me to my car. It's dark outside.
  不知道有沒有人可以陪我走去取我的車呢？外面很暗。

說明 ► 要特別注意的是，本句型用過去時態來表達現在的狀態：〈I was wondering if + 人 + 助動詞 (could/might/may/would) + 原形動詞〉。如果是要詢問資訊，只要用過去式動詞即可：I was wondering if you knew her name.（不知道你知不知道她的名字？）。

Dialogue 簡短對話

A: I was wondering if you could tell me the price of this hat.
B: Certainly. It's 3,000 yen.

A：不知道你可不可以告訴我這頂帽子的價格呢？
B：當然可以，三千日圓。

說明 ► B 除了說 Certainly. 外，也可以回答 No problem.（沒問題。）或 Absolutely.（當然沒問題。）

字彙	
assistance (n.) 協助	walk someone to his/her car
refrigerator (n.) 冰箱 (= fridge)	陪某人走去取車

相關表達 ► 有哪些與幫忙別人相關的慣用說法呢？

↝ give/lend (someone) a hand　幫（某人）一個忙

↝ do someone a favor　幫某人一個忙

↝ impose on someone　麻煩某人幫忙

↝ help (someone) out　幫忙（某人）

7 表達感謝
Thanking Someone

非正式

Cheers! | 謝謝！

Thanks a million! I really appreciate it. 句型**1** | 萬分感謝！我真的很感激。

稍非正式

I can't thank you enough. | 感激不盡。

Much obliged. | 承蒙相助，不勝感激。

一般情況

Thank you for taking the time to meet with me. 句型**2** | 謝謝你撥出時間和我見面。

Thank you from the bottom of my heart. | 由衷感謝你。

稍正式

I'm grateful for your kind assistance. 句型**3** | 我很感謝你好心的協助。

Thank you very much (indeed). | 非常謝謝。

正式

It was very kind of you to lend me a hand. 句型**4** | 你真好心幫了我的忙。

I sincerely appreciate your putting me in touch with the paper supplier. 句型**5** | 我由衷感謝你幫我聯絡上紙張供應商。

句型 1

Thanks a million!
萬分感謝！

Example 實用例句

● Thanks a million! I really appreciate it.
萬分感謝！我真的很感激。

● Thanks a million! I hope you didn't go out of your way.
萬分感謝！希望你不是特地跑一趟。

● Thanks a million! It was very kind of you.
萬分感謝！你真好心。

說明 ▶ 另一種非正式的口語說法是 Thanks a bunch!。

Dialogue 簡短對話

A: Thanks a million! I hope it wasn't too much trouble.
B: Of course not. You'd do the same for me.
　A：萬分感謝！希望沒有給你帶來太多麻煩。
　B：當然沒有。你也一樣會這麼做的。

說明 ▶ 當對方表達感謝時，通常可以回應 You'd do the same for me.（你也一樣會這麼做的。）、You'd have done the same.（你也會做同樣的事的。）或 You've helped me out plenty of times.（你幫過我好多次了。），向對方表達「你若有機會也會比照辦理的」或「你過去也很熱心助人」。

字彙

million (n.) 百萬　　　　　　　　　　bunch (n.) 大量，大批
go out of one's way 專程去做某事

句型 **2**

Thank you for...
謝謝你……

Example 實用例句

- Thank you for taking the time to meet with me.
  謝謝你撥出時間和我見面。

- Thank you for your generosity.
  謝謝你的慷慨大方。

- Thank you for stopping by my gallery yesterday.
  謝謝你昨天順道來我的藝廊。

  說明 ▶ 如果要表達更強烈的感謝之意，可以將本句型改成 Thank you very much for... 或 Thank you so much for...。這些句型的後面如果要接動詞，必須用動名詞的形式，例如 taking, stopping by 等。

Dialogue 簡短對話

A: Thank you so much for walking me home last night. It was very thoughtful of you.

B: You're welcome. That area is so dark. They really should install more street lights.

　A：非常謝謝你昨天晚上陪我走回家，你好貼心。

　B：不客氣。那個地區很暗，真的應該多裝設一些路燈。

字彙

generosity (n.) 慷慨，大方	thoughtful (adj.) 體貼的
stop by... 順道拜訪…	install (v.) 裝設，架設
gallery (n.) 藝廊	

表達感謝

句型 **3**

I'm grateful for...
我很感謝……

Example 實用例句

- I'm grateful for your kind assistance.
  我很感謝你好心的協助。

- I'm grateful for everything you've done.
  我很感謝你所做的一切。

- I'm grateful for the way you defended my position during the meeting.
  我很感謝你在會議上為我的立場辯護。

  說明 ▶ 本句型可用於感謝對方過去、現在或未來的好心之舉。

Dialogue 簡短對話

A: I'm grateful for your hospitality. I had a wonderful time in Manila.

B: My pleasure. I hope you'll have a chance to visit again soon.

A：很感謝你的殷勤款待，我在馬尼拉玩得很愉快。

B：這是我的榮幸。希望你很快有機會再來。

說明 ▶ 到別人家作客，如果主人展現出很明確、直接的善意，例如請客人吃飯、帶領客人參觀、招待客人留宿等時，便可以用 I'm grateful for your hospitality. 來表達感謝。

| defend (v.) 為…辯護 | hospitality (n.) 款待，殷勤 |
| position (n.) 立場 | |

句型 **4**

It was very kind of you to...
你真好心……

Example 實用例句

- It was very kind of you to lend me a hand.
  你真好心幫了我的忙。

- It was very kind of you to show me around the factory.
  你真好心帶我參觀工廠。

- It was very kind of you to drive me to the airport.
  你真好心開車送我到機場。

  說明 ▶ 在對方幫你做了某件事之後，便可以用本句型來向對方表達謝意。
  to 的後面接原形動詞。

Dialogue 簡短對話

A: It was very kind of you to show my son your guitar collection.
B: I was happy to do it.

  A：你真好心，讓我兒子參觀你的吉他收藏。
  B：我很樂意。

精進度★★★★★

句型 5
I sincerely appreciate your...
我由衷感謝你……

Example 實用例句

- I sincerely appreciate your putting me in touch with the paper supplier.
  我由衷感謝你幫我聯絡上紙張供應商。

- I sincerely appreciate your taking the time to correct my essay.
  我由衷感謝你撥出時間來修改我的文章。

- I sincerely appreciate your help repairing the fence.
  我由衷感謝你幫忙修理籬笆。

  說明 ▶ 本句型 your 的後面如果要接動詞，要使用動名詞的形式，例如
  putting, taking 等（注意，第三個例句中的 help 是名詞）。

Dialogue 簡短對話

A: I sincerely appreciate your sending me a copy of the file.

B: Not at all. Please let me know if there's anything else I can do.

A：我由衷感謝你寄一份檔案給我。

B：不客氣。如果還有我做得到的地方，請告訴我。

說明 ▶ 在口語中也可以將 A 所說的 your 改成 you，至於語氣、聲調、正式程度等都沒有差別。

字彙

put someone in touch with...
讓某人與…取得聯繫

take the time (to do something)
花時間（做某事）

essay (n.) 散文，隨筆，短評

fence (n.) 籬笆，柵欄

not at all 不客氣

相關表達 向對方表達感謝之後，通常還會再加上下面這些話：

➥ I hope you didn't go out of your way. 希望你不是特地跑一趟。

➥ I really appreciate it. 我真的很感謝。

➥ It was very thoughtful/kind of you. 你真貼心 / 好心。

➥ I hope it wasn't too much trouble. 希望沒有造成你太大的麻煩。

8 表達讚美
Complimenting

非正式

That was awesome!	太厲害了！
Good job!	表現得很好！

稍非正式

What a beautiful necklace! 句型1	好漂亮的項鍊！
You're a terrific singer. 句型2	你是個很棒的歌手。

一般情況

That hat really suits you.	那頂帽子真的很適合你。
I love what you did with your house. 句型3	我很喜歡你家裡的裝潢。

稍正式

I was very impressed with your speech. 句型4	我對你的演說印象很深刻。
I must say, you did a magnificent job.	我必須說你們表現得太棒了。

正式

In all sincerity, your restaurant makes the best sushi in the city.	這是發自內心的，你們餐廳的壽司是全市最棒的。
Might I compliment you on your excellent analysis. 句型5	請讓我稱讚一下你這份優異的分析報告。

句型 *1*

What a...!
好……！

Example 實用例句

- What a beautiful necklace!
  好漂亮的項鍊！

- What a spectacular performance.
  好精采的表演。

- What a great way to get students interested in history.
  真是個讓學生對歷史產生興趣的好方法。

  說明▶ 本句型的基本結構是〈What a/an + 形容詞 + 名詞〉。不定冠詞的後面通常是一個名詞，例如 What a boat!（好棒的船！）。

Dialogue 簡短對話

A: What a unique scarf.
B: Thanks! It was a gift from my friend in Guatemala.
　　A：好特別的圍巾啊。
　　B：謝謝！這是瓜地馬拉的朋友送我的禮物。

necklace (n.) 項鍊	unique (adj.) 獨特的，獨一無二的
spectacular (adj.) 令人驚嘆的	scarf (n.) 圍巾
performance (n.) 表演	

 句型 *2*

You're a terrific...
你是個很棒的……

Example 實用例句

- You're a terrific singer.
  你是個很棒的歌手。

- You're a terrific motivational speaker.
  你是個很了不起的勵志演說家。

- You're a terrific mother.
  你是個很了不起的媽媽。

  說明 ▶ 本句型用來讚美別人的天分、職業、角色等。

Dialogue 簡短對話

A: You're a terrific teacher, and a great role model for the kids.
B: Thank you very much. That means a lot to me.

　A：你是個很了不起的老師，是這些孩子很棒的榜樣。
　B：非常謝謝，這樣的讚美對我很重要。

字彙		
terrific (adj.) 極好的		role model 榜樣，模範
motivational speaker 勵志演說家		

精進度 ★★★☆☆

句型 *3*

I love what you did with...
我很喜歡你……

Example 實用例句

- I love what you did with your house.
  我很喜歡你家的裝潢。

- I love what you did with the garden!
  我很喜歡你整理的花園！

- I love what you did with these sculptures.
  我很喜歡你做的這些雕刻品。

  說明 ▶ 本句型通常用於讚美房子、辦公室、房間、大樓或區域的設計，也可以用於稱讚其他設計，像是插花、藝術作品、圖像設計作品等。

Dialogue 簡短對話

A: I love what you did with the photos on this poster. They're gorgeous.

B: Thank you. I wanted to integrate them so that they flowed with the other design elements.

　A：我很喜歡你對這張海報上照片的處理，好美。

　B：謝謝。我想把它們整合起來，好讓它們跟其他設計元素連貫起來。

說明 ▶ 可以像 B 這樣對於受到稱讚的事物加以說明。

字彙	
sculpture (n.) 雕刻品	integrate (v.) 使整合
poster (n.) 海報	flow (v.) 連貫，流動
gorgeous (adj.) 引人入勝的，極好的	design element 設計元素

精進度★★★★☆

句型4

I was very impressed with...
我對……印象很深刻 / 感到很佩服。

Example 實用例句

● I was very impressed with your speech.
我對你的演說印象很深刻。

● I was very impressed with the cleanliness of the subway station.
我對地鐵站乾淨的程度印象很深刻。

● I was very impressed with Savanna's call for more community activism.
對於薩凡納呼籲採取更多社群行動一事，我感到很佩服。

說明 ▶ 這種表達讚美的句型不見得是直接讚美對話中的另一方（如第二個例句）。此外，本句型也可用於指涉說話者看到或聽到令他 / 她印象深刻的事物（如第三個例句）。

Dialogue 簡短對話

A: I was very impressed with the new training video. I can tell you worked hard on it.

B: Thank you very much. It's part of our push to revamp the program.

　A：我對新的訓練影片印象很深刻，看得出你們很努力。

　B：非常謝謝。那是我們努力改進訓練課程的一部分。

說明 ▶ A 所說的 I can tell... 是表示 It's clear to me...（我看得很清楚……）之意。

精進度★★★★★

句型 5

Might I compliment you on...
請讓我稱讚一下你……

表達讚美

Example 實用例句

● Might I compliment you on your excellent analysis.
請讓我稱讚一下你這份優異的分析報告。

● Might I compliment you on a very successful exhibition.
請讓我稱讚一下你這場非常成功的展覽。

● Might I compliment you on the way you improved employee morale.
請讓我稱讚一下你增強員工士氣的方法。

說明 ▶ 一聽到開頭是 might，會以為這是個問句，但其實這是個表達讚美的句子，句尾的聲調要降低，而且用句點結束。

Dialogue 簡短對話

A: Might I compliment you on a stellar first quarter. You broke a number of sales records.

B: Thank you, but it was a team effort. Everyone deserves a share of the credit.

A：請讓我稱讚一下你第一季亮眼的成績，你打破了許多銷售紀錄。

B：謝謝，不過這是團隊努力的結果，每個人都有功勞。

說明 ▶ 一個用來回應稱讚的常見說法是把功勞歸給其他人，例如 B 的回答方式。除此之外，也可以說 I couldn't have done it without everyone's hard work.（要是沒有大家的努力，我是不可能做到的。）

字彙

compliment (v.) 稱讚	team effort 團隊努力
analysis (n.) 分析報告	deserve (v.) 應得
exhibition (n.) 展覽	share (n.) 一份
morale (n.) 士氣	credit (n.) 讚揚
stellar (adj.) 傑出的，出色的	

相關表達 **讚美別人之後，通常還會再加上下面這些話：**

➥ You should be proud of yourself. 你應該要為自己感到驕傲。

➥ I can tell you worked hard on it. 我看得出來你很努力。

➥ It must have taken forever. 想必花了很久很久的時間。

9 請求許可
Asking Permission

MP3 09

Is it OK if I park here? 句型1

我把車子停在這裡可以嗎？

May I borrow your phone?

我可以借用你的電話嗎？

Are we allowed to bring our own food inside the theater? 句型2

我們可以帶自己的食物進入戲院嗎？

Would it be all right if I hung my coat here?

我把外套掛在這裡可不可以呢？

Would you mind if I took a photo of the painting? 句型3

你介意我拍這幅畫的照片嗎？

Do we have permission to walk around the mansion freely?

我們可以在這座別墅的四周自由走動嗎？

Do you think I might be able to place one of these fliers here? 句型4

我放一張傳單在這裡可以嗎？

Would anyone be against my moving these display racks?

有沒有人反對我搬動這些展示架的呢？

I wonder if it might be permissible to bring a friend along. 句型5

我想知道是否允許帶一位朋友一起來。

Would it be too much of an imposition if I watched you rehearse for a few minutes?

你們的彩排讓我看個幾分鐘，這個要求會不會太過分？

句型 *1*　Is it OK if I...?
我……可以嗎？

Example 實用例句

- Is it OK if I park here?
  我把車子停在這裡可以嗎？

- Is it OK if I leave a few minutes early today?
  我今天提早幾分鐘離開可以嗎？

- Is it OK if I use this chair?
  我用這張椅子可以嗎？

  說明 ▶ 如果要以簡短或直接的說法請求許可，可以用 Can I...?，例如 Can I park here?（我可以把車停在這裡嗎？）。在某些情況下，例如對話雙方彼此的距離比較遠時，用 Can I...? 這個句型表達最簡單，雖然是比較直接且非正式的說法，但並不會顯得無禮。

Dialogue 簡短對話

A: Is it OK if I take the bike for a test ride before I buy it?

B: I don't see why not. But you'll need to leave your license or another ID with us.

A：我買這輛腳踏車之前先試騎可以嗎？

B：我想無妨。不過，你得把你的駕照或其他身分證件留給我們。

說明 ▶ 允許別人的請求時，可以用 I don't see why not.（我想無妨。/ 我看不出有何不可。）這個說法。

字彙
test ride 試騎	ID 身分證件 (= identification)
license (n.) 駕照 (= driver's license)	

句型*2* Are we allowed to...?
我們可以……嗎？

Example 實用例句

● Are we allowed to bring our own food inside the theater?
我們可以帶自己的食物進入戲院嗎？

● Are we allowed to pet the deer?
我們可以摸這隻鹿嗎？

● Are we allowed to walk on the grass?
我們可以在這片草地上行走嗎？

說明 ▶ 本句型可以用於請求握有權力的人批准，也可以用於詢問熟悉規定的朋友、同事等。

Dialogue 簡短對話

A: Are we allowed to take buses with this pass, or just trains?
B: You can use the buses in the city center.
A：我們可以用這張通行證搭公車嗎？還是只能搭火車呢？
B：可以搭市中心的公車。

pet (v.) 撫摸	pass (n.) 通行證
deer (n.) 鹿	

請求許可

句型*3* Would you mind if I...?
你介意我去……嗎？／我去……好嗎？

Example 實用例句

● Would you mind if I took a photo of the painting?
你介意我拍這幅畫的照片嗎？

● Would you mind if I closed the window?
我去關上窗戶好嗎？

● Would you mind if I put these bags down here while I finish shopping?
你介意我買完東西時將這些袋子放在這裡嗎？

說明 ▶ Would you mind if I...? 和 Do you mind if I...? 都用於請求別人許可你做某件事，不過前者比較禮貌、客氣。表示條件的 if 子句中的動詞必須用過去式，例如上面例句中的 took a photo, closed the window, put these bags down here 等。另外，第三個例句最後的 while I finish shopping 不屬於 if 子句（即 if I put these bags down here）的一部分，用現在式來表達即可。

Dialogue 簡短對話

A: Would you mind if I invited a classmate to the beach with us?
B: Of course not. The more, the merrier!

　　A：你介意我邀請一位同學和我們一起去海邊嗎？
　　B：當然不介意。人愈多愈好玩！

 painting (n.) 畫作 　　　　　　　　　　merry (adj.) 愉快的

精進度 ★★★★☆

句型 **4**

Do you think I might be able to...?
我……可以嗎？

Example 實用例句

● Do you think I might be able to place one of these fliers here?
我放一張傳單在這裡可以嗎？

● Do you think I might be able to wait in the lobby until my friend arrives?
我在大廳等我的朋友到達可以嗎？

● Do you think I might be able to use your restroom?
我可以用你們的洗手間嗎？

說明 ▶ 將 might be able to 替換成 could 後會變得比較直接，例如 Do you think I could use your restroom?。

Dialogue 簡短對話

A: Do you think I might be able to take one of these samples?
B: Absolutely—feel free.

　A：我可以拿一份試用品嗎？
　B：當然可以，自己拿。

字彙

flier (n.) 傳單　　　　　　　　　　restroom (n.) 洗手間
lobby (n.)（大型建築的）大廳　　　feel free 請便

句型5

I wonder if it might be permissible to...
我想知道是否允許……

Example 實用例句

● I wonder if it might be permissible to bring a friend along.
我想知道是否允許帶一位朋友一起來。

● I wonder if it might be permissible to record the speech.
我想知道是否允許錄下演說內容。

● I wonder if it might be permissible to bring my bicycle onto the ferry.
我想知道把腳踏車帶上渡輪是否可行。

說明 ▶ 如果不要讓本句型顯得那麼正式，可以把 permissible 換成 all right 或 OK。另外也可以把 I wonder... 改成 I was wondering...，聽起來語氣會更婉轉。

請求許可

Dialogue 簡短對話

A: I was wondering if it might be permissible to ask the actors for autographs after they finish filming.

B: You can try, but you'll have to wait behind the rope.

A：我想知道，可不可以在演員拍攝結束之後向他們要簽名。

B：你可以試試看，不過你得在繩子的後面等待。

字彙

permissible (adj.) 可允許的	autograph (n.) 親筆簽名
ferry (n.) 渡輪	film (v.) 拍攝電影

相關表達 **當別人請求准許做某事時，常見的回答方式有下面幾種：**

➥ Absolutely./Certainly./Sure./Of course.
當然可以。

➥ I don't see why not.
我想無妨。/ 我看不出有何不可。

➥ Of course not.
當然不行。/ 當然不介意。

➥ I'm afraid that would be against our policy/the rules.
這恐怕會違反我們的政策 / 規定。

詢問別人的感受
Asking How Someone Is Feeling

非正式

How are you?

你好嗎？

How do you feel? That was a pretty big fall you took. 句型 *1*

你還好嗎？你跌了好大一跤啊。

稍非正式

Is anything wrong? There's this kind of worried look on your face.

發生什麼事了嗎？你一臉憂心忡忡的。

Are you feeling well?

你的身體還好嗎？

一般情況

Is everything all right? You look bothered about something. 句型 *2*

一切都還好嗎？你好像在為某事煩心。

Were you like me—sad that Bill and Tina split up?

你是不是和我一樣，很難過比爾和堤娜分手了？

稍正式

How did the election results make you feel? 句型 *3*

對於選舉的結果，你有什麼感想嗎？

I don't mean to pry, but I heard you were having back problems. 句型 *4*

我無意探人隱私，不過我聽說你的背有毛病。

正式

I wanted to inquire (about) how you've been (doing) since the earthquake. 句型 *5*

我想問你從地震過後過得如何。

It may not be my place to ask, but is everything all right?

或許我無權過問，不過你一切還好嗎？

句型 1

How do you feel?
你還好嗎？

Example 實用例句

- How do you feel? That was a pretty big fall you took.
  你還好嗎？你跌了好大一跤啊。

- How do you feel? I know you've been working 12-hour shifts this week.
  你還好嗎？我知道你這個星期已經輪了 12 個小時的班。

- How do you feel? Running a marathon must be exhausting.
  你還好嗎？跑馬拉松一定累壞了。

說明 ▶ 當對方遭遇到一個很明顯的逆境，例如挑戰、麻煩、疾病等，一般會用本句型詢問對方的情況如何。

Dialogue 簡短對話

A: How do you feel? I heard you were out with the flu.
B: I'm doing much better, thank you.

A：你還好嗎？我聽說你因為罹患流感而缺席了。
B：我好多了，謝謝。

take a fall 跌倒	out with (illness or injury)
shift (n.) 輪班	因為（疾病或受傷）而缺席
marathon (n.) 馬拉松	flu (n.) 流行性感冒 (= influenza)
exhausting (adj.) 筋疲力盡的	

句型 2

Is everything all right?
一切都還好嗎？

Example 實用例句

- Is everything all right? You look bothered about something.
  一切都還好嗎？你好像在為某事煩心。

- Is everything all right? You're a little pale.
  一切都還好嗎？你的臉色有點蒼白。

- Is everything all right? You look under the weather.
  一切都還好嗎？你看起來好像身體不舒服。

  說明▶ 當對方明顯出現心煩意亂或生病的徵兆時，常常會使用本句型來詢問。問完 Is everything all right? 之後，通常還會加上額外的說明，即說話者對於對方的觀察和假設，不過並不一定需要。

Dialogue 簡短對話

A: Is everything all right? You look out of sorts.
B: Is it that obvious? I broke up with my boyfriend yesterday.

  A：一切都還好嗎？你看起來心情不好。
  B：有那麼明顯嗎？我昨天和我男朋友分手了。

字彙		
bothered (adj.) 煩惱的		out of sorts 心情不好的
pale (adj.) 蒼白的		obvious (adj.) 明顯的
under the weather 身體不適，身體微恙		break up (with...)（與…）分手

精進度★★★★☆

句型 *3*

How did ... make you feel?
對於……，你有什麼感想嗎？

Example 實用例句

- How did the election results make you feel?
  對於選舉的結果，你有什麼感想嗎？

- How did all the last-minute scheduling changes make you feel?
  對於最後一分鐘才更改行程，你有什麼感想嗎？

- How did those strange jokes by the plenary speaker make you feel?
  對於特邀講者所講的那些奇怪笑話，你有什麼感想嗎？

  說明▶ 也可以把本句型的主詞（如第一個例句的 the election results）改成句型 How did you feel about...?（你對……有何感想嗎？）的受詞，例如變成 How did you feel about the election results?。

詢問別人的感受

57

Dialogue 簡短對話

A: How did Mr. Delay's decision to promote someone else make you feel?

B: At first I was disappointed, but I got over it. I'll get my chance someday.

A：帝雷先生決定擢升其他人，你有什麼感想嗎？

B：一開始我很失望，不過我釋懷了。總有一天我會有機會的。

字彙	
election (n.) 選舉	promote (v.) 擢升
last-minute (adj.) 最後的	disappointed (adj.) 失望的
plenary speaker 特邀講者	get over... 從…恢復過來

精進度 ★★★★☆

 句型 4

I don't mean to pry, but...
我無意探人隱私，不過……

Example 實用例句

● I don't mean to pry, but I heard you were having back problems.
我無意探人隱私，不過我聽說你的背有毛病。

● I don't mean to pry, but someone said you were having trouble getting adjusted.
我無意探人隱私，不過有人說你有適應不良的問題。

● I don't mean to pry, but if you want to talk to someone, I'm a pretty good listener.
我無意探人隱私，不過如果你想找人說說話，我是個很好的聆聽者。

說明 ▶ 若想詢問對方的私事，但對方不見得想說出口時，通常會使用本句型。此外，說話者通常是從別人那裡聽說對方的問題才會使用本句型，在這種情況下，but 的後面很有可能會使用過去式，不過並不意味該事件或該情況已經結束。

Dialogue 簡短對話

A: I don't mean to pry, but are you managing to keep up all right? Seriously, if you need a hand prepping for the final, I'll be happy to help.

B: Thanks! Now that you mention it, I am starting to fall behind.

> A：我無意打探隱私，不過你是不是趕不上進度？說真的，如果你需要有人幫你準備期末考，我很樂意幫忙。
>
> B：謝啦！經你這麼一說，我好像真的落後了。

說明 ▶ Now that you mention it,（既然你提起了，）是個常用的起頭句子，用來延續對方剛剛說過的話。

字彙

pry (v.) 探刺（別人的私事）	keep up 跟上進度
back (n.) 背部	prep (v.) 準備 (= prepare)
get adjusted 適應	fall behind 落後
manage to V. 設法做到…	

精進度★★★★★

句型 5

I wanted to inquire (about) how...
我想問……如何。

Example 實用例句

● I wanted to inquire about how you've been (doing) since the earthquake.
我想問你從地震過後過得如何。

● I wanted to inquire how the operation went.
我想問手術進行得如何。

● I wanted to inquire about how people are feeling about the policy changes.
我想問民眾對於這項政策的轉變有什麼感覺。

說明 ▶ 在比較正式的說法中，用過去式（例如 I wanted to inquire...）來連接一個間接問句（如第二個例句的 how the operation went）很常見。如果不要讓本句型顯得那麼正式，可以改成 I wanted to ask (about) how...。

Dialogue 簡短對話

A: I wanted to inquire how you've been dealing with this extreme weather.

B: I've been fine. Thank you for asking.

　　A：我想問你對這種極端的天氣適應得如何。

　　B：我一直很好。謝謝你的詢問。

字彙	inquire (v.) 詢問	deal with... 應付…，與…打交道
	operation (n.) 手術	extreme (adj.) 極端的
	policy (n.) 政策	

相關表達 對於別人善意的詢問或關切，要如何回應呢？

→ I appreciate your concern. 謝謝你的關心。

→ Thank you for asking. 謝謝你的詢問。

→ I'm fine, really. 我沒事，真的。／我過得很好，真的。

表達快樂的心情
Expressing Happiness

MP3
11

非正式

Hooray!	萬歲！
I'm on cloud nine.	我樂翻天了。

稍非正式

That's amazing! 句型 1	太棒了！
I still can't believe it's true.	我還不敢相信這是真的。

一般情況

I've never been happier. Moving to the countryside did me a world of good. 句型 2	我從沒這麼快樂過。搬到鄉下讓我感覺好多了。
Today is the best day of my life.	今天是我這輩子最棒的一天。

稍正式

I'm so glad (that) you can be here to share this moment with me. 句型 3	我很高興你可以在這裡和我分享這一刻。
We're very happy for you both. 句型 4	我們為你們兩位感到非常開心。

正式

I can't tell you how pleased I am with the decorations.	我無法向你形容自己對於這些裝飾品有多麼高興。
I was delighted with the turnout for the charity dinner. 句型 5	我對於這場慈善晚宴的出席人數感到很高興。

句型 1

That's...!
太……了！

Example 實用例句

- That's amazing!
  太棒了！

- That's fantastic!
  太棒了！

- That's terrific!
  太棒了！

說明 ▶ 本句型通常用來回應一則好消息。有時為了製造戲劇效果，說話者會將主詞和動詞分開，將每個字清楚且緩慢地唸出來，即唸成 That is...!。

Dialogue 簡短對話

A: One of my videos is being shown on TV. The station is even giving me some money for it.

B: That's fantastic! A spot on national TV will be great exposure for you.

A：我有一支影片在電視上播出了，電視台甚至還付我一些錢。

B：太棒了！在全國性電視上播出的話，曝光效果超棒。

字彙	
amazing (adj.) 使人驚異的	spot (n.)（節目間的）廣告插播
fantastic (adj.) 極好的	national TV 全國性電視
terrific (adj.) 極好的	exposure (n.) 曝光

句型 2

I've never been happier.
我從沒這麼快樂過。

Example 實用例句

- I've never been happier. Moving to the countryside did me a world of good.
  我從沒這麼快樂過。搬到鄉下讓我感覺好多了。

- I've never been happier. I should have quit that lousy job years ago.
  我從沒這麼快樂過。我多年前就該辭掉那個爛工作的。

- I've never been happier. It may sound corny, but Mitch is my soul mate.
  我從沒這麼快樂過。聽起來或許很老土，不過米區是我的靈魂伴侶。

  說明 ► 雖然 I've never been happier. 這種說法聽起來很武斷，不過卻相當常用。本句型可以單獨使用，也可以在後面另外加上一句話，說明感到快樂的原因。

Dialogue 簡短對話

A: I've never been happier. You were right to suggest that I follow my dreams.

B: I am so glad the salon is working out. You're an amazing stylist.

A：我從沒這麼快樂過。你建議我去追隨自己的夢想是對的。

B：真高興美容院成功了，你是很厲害的造型師。

字彙	
countryside (n.) 鄉村	soul mate 靈魂伴侶
do someone a world of good 使某人感覺好得多	follow one's dreams 追隨自己的夢想
	salon (n.) 美容院
lousy (adj.) 糟糕的，爛的	work out 成功
corny (adj.) 老土的，陳舊的	stylist (n.) 造型師

精進度 ★★★★☆

句型 *3*

I'm so glad (that)...
我很高興……

Example 實用例句

- I'm so glad that you can be here to share this moment with me.
  我很高興你可以在這裡和我分享這一刻。

- I'm so glad Jack decided to go to college nearby.
  我很高興傑克決定就讀附近的大學。

- I'm so glad that everything worked out for the best.
  我很高興每件事都有好結果。

說明 ▶ I'm so glad 的後面接一個由 that 引導的子句,說明為了什麼事情而高興。that 可以省略。

Dialogue 簡短對話

A: I'm so glad that the injury wasn't serious.

B: Same here. That was quite a scare!

A:我真高興傷害不是很嚴重。

B:我也一樣。真是嚇死了!

work out 圓滿結束	Same here. 我也一樣。
for the best 有好結果	scare (n.) 驚嚇
injury (n.) 傷害	

句型 *4*

We're very happy...
我們非常開心……

Example 實用例句

- We're very happy for you both.
  我們為你們兩位感到非常開心。

- We're very happy with the result of the IPO.
  我們為首次公開募股的結果感到非常開心。

- We're very happy to contribute to the cause.
  我們非常開心能為這個理想貢獻一己之力。

說明 ▶ 本句型的後面可以接介系詞片語〈for/with + 受詞〉,也可以接不定詞〈to + 原形動詞〉。如果要表達更開心的感受,可以把 very happy 換成 thrilled(很興奮的)。

Dɪᴀʟᴏɢᴜᴇ 簡短對話

A: We're very happy with this car. It runs smoothly and gets good mileage.

B: It's also stylish.

　　A：我們對這輛車非常滿意，跑得很平順，油耗里程數也很好。

　　B：而且很有型。

字彙	
IPO 首次公開募股 (= initial public offering)	smoothly (adv.) 平順地
contribute (v.) 貢獻	mileage (n.) 油耗里程數 (= gas mileage)
cause (n.) 理想，目標	stylish (adj.) 有型的，時髦的

精進度★★★★★

句型 5

I was delighted...

我很高興……

Exᴀᴍᴘʟᴇ 實用例句

● I was delighted with the turnout for the charity dinner.
　我對於這場慈善晚宴的出席人數感到很高興。

● I was delighted by the news that the mayor will be at the event.
　我對於市長將會出席活動的消息感到很高興。

● I was delighted to hear about the positive result.
　我很高興聽到這個正面的結果。

　　說明 ▶ delighted 的後面可以接〈with/by + 一種情況 / 一則消息〉（如第一、二個例句），也可以接不定詞（如第三個例句）。

Dɪᴀʟᴏɢᴜᴇ 簡短對話

A: I was delighted with the way the community came together to repair the boardwalk.

B: Me, too. It made me proud to live here.

　　A：整個社區一起來整修木棧道，令我很高興。

　　B：我也是，這讓我覺得住在這裡很驕傲。

字彙

delighted (adj.) 高興的
turnout (n.) 出席人數
charity (n.) 慈善
mayor (n.) 市長

event (n.) 活動
community (n.) 社區，社群
boardwalk (n.) 木棧道

相關表達　在開心的時刻，可以用哪些形容詞來表達呢？

→ thrilled　非常興奮的，極為激動的

→ ecstatic　欣喜若狂的

→ overjoyed　極度高興的

→ delighted　高興的

→ elated　興高采烈的

12 表達驚訝
Expressing Surprise

MP3 12

非正式

No kidding.　　　　　　　　　　　　　別開玩笑了。

Really?　　　　　　　　　　　　　　　真的嗎？

稍非正式

What a surprise. 句型1　　　　　　　好意外。

That's amazing!　　　　　　　　　　太令人吃驚了！

一般情況

I can't believe our vacation has been 　我不敢相信我們的假期竟然被縮
shortened to three days. 句型2　　　短成三天。

Do you mean to say nobody will be getting a　你的意思是說任何人都不會拿到
bonus? 句型3　　　　　　　　　　獎金嗎？

稍正式

I'm surprised the issue hasn't come up before.　我很驚訝這項議題以前從沒拿出
　　　　　　　　　　　　　　　　　來討論過。

That's a surprising piece of news. 句型4　那是一則出乎意料的消息。

正式

I was shocked to hear about the bank's　聽到那家銀行倒閉，我很震驚。
closure.

It came as quite a surprise that Ms. Lin left　林女士退出董事會一事令人感到
the board of directors. 句型5　　　相當意外。

句型 *1*

What a...
真是個……

Example 實用例句

- What a surprise.
  好意外。

- What a shock!
  太令人吃驚了！

- What a thing to say!
  竟然有這種事！

說明 ▶ 第一、二個例句可以用於表示驚訝或嘲諷。如果說話者要表達嘲諷之意，則通常一邊說 What a surprise. 或 What a shock! 時，會一邊誇張地轉動眼珠，同時還會搭配高低起伏的語氣。

Dialogue 簡短對話

A: Kimberly decided to sell her business and go back to school for her master's degree.
B: What a shock. She spent years building up that business.
　A：金貝莉決定把她的事業賣掉，回學校唸碩士學位。
　B：太令人吃驚了。她花了好多年才建立起那份事業。

 master's degree 碩士學位　　　　　　build up... 建立…

句型 *2*

I can't believe...
我不敢相信……

Example 實用例句

- I can't believe our vacation has been shortened to three days.
  我不敢相信我們的假期竟然被縮短成三天。

- I can't believe the bus doesn't run on Sundays.
  我不敢相信公車星期天沒開。

- I can't believe the store won't accept credit cards.
  我不敢相信這家店不收信用卡。

說明 ▶ 本句型除了有驚訝的意思，可能還帶有一點憤怒的味道。至於是不是有憤怒的意思，要看說話者的語調而定。如果語調是平的或是下降、較低，代表有驚訝，也有失望；如果語調很強烈、拉高，believe 和其他關鍵字加重音，那就代表驚訝和挫折。

Dialogue 簡短對話

A: I can't believe the price of gas is going up again.
B: Are you pulling my leg? Wow. Fortunately, living downtown, I don't need to drive too much.

A：我不敢相信油價又要上漲了。
B：你是在開我玩笑嗎？哇，幸好我住在市中心，不需要太常開車。

字彙
go up 上升　　　　　　　　　　　downtown (adv.) 市中心
pull someone's leg 開某人玩笑

精進度 ★★★ ☆ ☆

句型 3

Do you mean to say...?
你的意思是說……嗎？

Example 實用例句

- Do you mean to say nobody will be getting a bonus?
  你的意思是說任何人都不會拿到獎金嗎？

- Do you mean to say the road is closed to everyone, including residents?
  你的意思是說道路一律封鎖，包括當地居民也進不去嗎？

- Do you mean to say I actually won second place in the contest?
  你的意思是說我真的拿到比賽第二名嗎？

說明 ▸ 這種表達驚訝的說法，是說話者聽到對方的話之後所做出的反應。Do you mean to say...? 本身還帶有震驚、不敢置信的含意，也可以改說成 Are you saying...?（你是說⋯⋯？）。

Dialogue 簡短對話

A: Do you mean to say you're completely sold out of the toy robots?

B: I'm afraid so.

A：你的意思是說玩具機器人全部賣光了？

B：恐怕是如此沒錯。

說明 ▸ 肯定或確認某事時若想同時表達懊悔、不滿或不開心的感受，通常會用 I'm afraid so.。

字彙		
bonus (n.) 獎金，額外津貼		sell out of... 將⋯賣光
resident (n.) 居民		robot (n.) 機器人
second place 第二名，亞軍		

精進度★★★★☆

句型 4

That's a surprising...

那是一個出乎意料的⋯⋯

Example 實用例句

● That's a surprising piece of news.
那是一則出乎意料的消息。

● That's a surprising turn of events.
事件出現出乎意料的轉折。

● That's a surprising outcome.
那是出乎意料的結果。

說明 ▸ 聽到某個消息後若感到驚訝，便可以用本句型來表達。這個句型的後面接名詞或名詞片語，通常只有短短幾個字。

Dialogue 簡短對話

A: We're finally being allowed to telework one day a week.

B: That's a surprising change of policy. I never thought Mr. Wright would let it happen.

A：我們終於獲准一星期有一天可以在家工作。

B：政策出現出乎意料的大轉變，我從來沒想到萊特先生會答應。

字彙

piece (n.) 一則	telework (v.) 遠距工作，在家工作
turn of events 形勢的變化	policy (n.) 政策
outcome (n.) 結果	

精進度 ★★★★★

句型5 It came as quite a surprise that...
……一事令人感到相當意外。

Example 實用例句

● It came as quite a surprise that Ms. Lin left the board of directors.
林女士退出董事會一事令人感到相當意外。

● It came as quite a surprise that the country's best runner didn't try out for the Olympic team.
全國跑最快的跑者竟然沒有參加奧運代表隊的選拔，令人感到相當意外。

● It came as quite a surprise that many components of the luxury brand's watches are made of cheap plastic.
這個高級品牌的手錶竟然有許多零件是用廉價塑膠製成的，令人感到相當意外。

說明 ▶ 對過去已經發生的事情感到驚訝時，便可用本句型來表達。quite a surprise 可以改成 a big surprise。that 的後面接子句。

Dialogue 簡短對話

A: It came as quite a surprise that the taxi from the airport cost as much as the plane ticket.

B: They really do cost a fortune. The next time you're in town, call me, and I'll give you a ride.

A：從機場搭計程車所花的錢跟飛機票的錢一樣多，令人感到相當意外。

B：真的很貴。下次你進市區的時候，打電話給我，我去載你。

字彙

board of directors 董事會　　　　　　　　cost a fortune 花一大筆錢
try out 試驗，選拔（尤指運動比賽或角色甄選）

相關表達　還有哪些用於表達驚訝的有趣說法呢？

➥ You could have knocked me over with a feather. 我驚訝到不行。

　說明 ▶ 字面上的意思是「你現在用一根羽毛就足以把我敲昏了。」

➥ I was floored. 我目瞪口呆。

➥ Are you pulling my leg? 你是在開我玩笑嗎？

13 表達疑惑
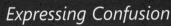
Expressing Confusion

MP3 13

That doesn't make any sense. 句型1

這不合常理。

I'm (so) confused.

我好困惑。

稍非正式

What a confusing case. 句型2

真是一個令人困惑的案子。

The message was baffling.

訊息很令人困惑。

一般情況

It's (kind of) hard to figure out who's right and who's wrong. 句型3

要搞清楚誰對誰錯有（點）困難。

Am I the only one who's confused about the instructions?

我是唯一搞不懂說明的人嗎？

稍正式

Can you help me understand what's going on? 句型4

你可以幫助我了解發生了什麼事嗎？

I'm not entirely clear what they want us to do.

我不是完全了解他們要我們做什麼。

正式

I'm not sure what to make of the situation. 句型5

我不了解這是什麼狀況。

I'm afraid I don't (quite) follow you.

我恐怕沒有聽懂你的意思。

句型 **1**

...do not make any sense.
……不合常理。

Example 實用例句

● That doesn't make any sense.
這不合常理。

● These bus schedules don't make any sense.
這些公車時刻表很不合理。

● What he said doesn't make any sense.
他的說法很不合理。

說明▶ 別人提出意見或想法時，如果要回應 That doesn't make any sense.（這不合常理。）必須很小心，因為很有可能會被認為很無禮。

Dialogue 簡短對話

A: This Robert Frost poem doesn't make any sense. Why is the rider stopping by the woods when it's snowing so hard?

B: There's a lot of symbolism in the poem. If you want, I can try and explain it.

A：羅伯特‧佛洛斯特的這首詩一點道理都沒有。雪下得那麼大，騎士幹嘛要去森林呢？

B：這首詩有很多象徵意義。如果你想知道，我可以試著解釋一下。

 字彙

poem (n.) 詩	stop by... 順便走訪…
rider (n.) 騎馬（或腳踏車、機車等）的人	symbolism (n.) 象徵意義

句型 **2**

What a confusing...
真是一個令人困惑的……

Example 實用例句

● What a confusing case.
真是一個令人困惑的案子。

- What a confusing turn of affairs.
  事件的轉折真是令人困惑。

- What a confusing situation.
  真是一個令人困惑的局面。

  說明 ▶ 這是表達對某個想法、原則、有形物件感到困惑的最簡單說法之一。

Dɪᴀʟᴏɢᴜᴇ 簡短對話

A: What a confusing menu. I'm at a loss.

B: I think you're supposed to build your own meal. Unless I'm mistaken, you can choose one item from each page. But don't quote me on that!

A：真是令人困惑的菜單，我看得一頭霧水。

B：我猜是自己組合要吃的餐點。除非我弄錯了，不然應該是從每一頁挑選一樣。不過我也不一定對！

說明 ▶ 如果對自己所說的話不是很確定，就可以說 Don't quote me on that.（不要說是我說的。）意思是「說錯了我不負責任」，萬一真的說錯了就可以免責。

字 彙	turn of affairs 事件的轉折 at a loss 茫然不知所措的	be supposed to V. 應該做… quote (v.) 引述，引用

精進度 ★★★☆☆

句型 3

It's (kind of) hard to figure out...
要搞清楚……有（點）困難。

Exᴀᴍᴘʟᴇ 實用例句

- It's kind of hard to figure out who's right and who's wrong.
  要搞清楚誰對誰錯有點困難。

- It's hard to figure out how to use this cell phone.
  要搞清楚如何使用這支手機有困難。

- It's kind of hard to figure out these directions.
  要搞清楚這些說明有點困難。

說明 ▶ figure out 的後面可以接名詞（如第三個例句）、名詞片語（如第二個例句）或名詞子句（如第一個例句）等。It's (kind of) hard to figure out. 也可以單獨當作一個句子來使用，例如你可以手裡拿著一張地圖說 It's kind of hard to figure out.（要搞懂這個有點難。）

Dialogue 簡短對話

A: It's kind of hard to figure out this dance performance.

B: I think it's supposed to be abstract. If it helps, I have no idea what's going on either.

　A：要看懂這個舞蹈表演有點困難。

　B：我想它應該是抽象的。我也看不懂在表演什麼，如果這樣會讓你好過一點的話。

figure out... 將…弄明白	performance (n.) 表演
cell phone 手機 (= cellphone)	abstract (adj.) 抽象的
directions (n.) 指示，說明	have no idea 不知道，沒意見

句型4

Can you help me understand...?
你可以幫助我了解……嗎？

Example 實用例句

● Can you help me understand what's going on?
你可以幫助我了解發生了什麼事嗎？

● Can you help me understand why renters aren't allowed to nail things to the wall?
你可以幫助我了解為什麼承租戶不可以在牆上釘東西嗎？

● Can you help me understand the directions for this form?
你可以幫助我了解怎麼填這份表格嗎？

說明 ▶ 當說話者對於某個想法、問題或特定做法（如填寫表格等）不知道該怎麼做時，就可以用本句型來詢問。本句型的後面要接名詞（如第三個例句）或名詞子句（如第一、二個例句）。

Dialogue 簡短對話

A: Can you help me understand how the ticket machine works?

B: Sure. First you put the money into the machine. Then you press the buttons of the food and drinks you want. And then you give the tickets to the server.

A：你可以幫助我了解這台售票機怎麼操作嗎？

B：沒問題。先把錢放進機器裡，接著按下你要的食物和飲料按鈕，然後把票交給服務生。

 renter (n.) 承租人　　　　　　　　　　nail (v.) 釘

 句型 **5**

I'm not sure what to make of...
我不了解……

Example 實用例句

● I'm not sure what to make of the situation.
我不了解這是什麼狀況。

● I'm not sure what to make of the announcement.
我不了解這份宣告。

● I'm not sure what to make of her decision.
我不了解她的決定。

說明 ▶ 本句型用來描述一個人對於某個狀況的矛盾感受。如果有某種情況直接對你造成衝擊，或是影響你的情緒，可以把本句型改成 I'm not sure how to deal with...（我不知道該怎麼處理……）。

Dialogue 簡短對話

A: I'm not sure what to make of the new dress code.

B: I hear you. Let's try to get some clarity from the HR office.

A：我不了解新的服裝規定是什麼。

B：我聽到你的意見了。我們去向人資部門問清楚。

14 表示贊同
Agreeing

非正式

You can say that again!

我完全贊同！/ 沒錯，就是這樣子！

I'm with you. This hotel isn't nearly as nice as it used to be. 句型 *1*

我同意你的看法。這家飯店一點也不像以前那麼好了。

稍非正式

I agree 100%.

我百分之百認同。

Hear, hear!

說得好！/ 說得對！

一般情況

My thoughts exactly. 句型 *2*

這正是我心裡的想法。/ 我正有此意。

(Very) well said.

說得（非常）好。

稍正式

I couldn't agree more. 句型 *3*

我再同意不過了。

I concur. There must be a way to lower costs without laying off staff. 句型 *4*

我同意。一定有可以不必裁員就降低成本的方法。

正式

I agree wholeheartedly.

我全心全意贊同。

I'm in complete agreement that we need to solve the quality control problem. 句型 *5*

我完全同意我們必須解決品管問題。

句型 *1*

I'm with you.
我同意你的看法。

Example 實用例句

- I'm with you. This hotel isn't nearly as nice as it used to be.
  我同意你的看法。這家飯店一點也不像以前那麼好了。

- I'm with you. I only give tips when I feel the service was good.
  我同意你的看法。只有在我覺得服務很好的時候，我才會給小費。

- I'm with you. Handmade presents are a lot better than store-bought gifts.
  我同意你的看法。自己動手做的禮物比到店裡買的禮物好多了。

  說明 ▶ 本句型 I'm with you. 也可以替換成 I'm right there with you.。另外一個相當非正式、但也是表達贊同的說法是 I feel you.。

Dialogue 簡短對話

A: We should hold our New Year's Eve party at a buffet restaurant.
B: I'm with you. That way, people can eat whatever they want.
  A：我們應該在自助式餐廳舉行除夕派對。
  B：我同意你的看法。那樣的話，大家就可以吃自己想要吃的東西。

 store-bought (adj.) 從商店買的　　　　　　buffet (n.) 自助餐

句型*2*

My ... exactly.
這正是我的……

Example 實用例句

- My thoughts exactly.
  這正是我心裡的想法。/ 我正有此意。

- My feelings exactly.
  這正是我的感受。

My sentiments exactly.
這正是我的心情寫照。

說明 ▶ 除了上面三個例句外，還可以說 Those are my thoughts exactly. 和
That's exactly how I feel.。

Dialogue 簡短對話

A: Everyone wants to make money online, but it seems like most people lose money trying.

B: My thoughts exactly. Still, we'll probably want to pay some attention to the mobile market.

A：人人都想在網路上賺錢，不過大多數嘗試的人似乎都賠錢。

B：這正是我心裡的想法。不過，我們大概會想留意一下行動裝置的市場。

字彙	sentiment (n.) 情緒，心情	mobile (n.) 行動裝置（如手機、平板電腦等）

精進度★★★★☆

 句型 *3*

I couldn't... + 比較級
我十分……

Example 實用例句

 I couldn't agree more.
我再同意不過了。

 I couldn't have said it better myself.
你說得太好了！

 I couldn't have put it (any) better if I tried.
我沒辦法說得這麼好。

說明 ▶ 這是個很有趣的句型，說話者用的是否定句，不過卻是明確表達肯定的認同。I couldn't 的後面可以接原形動詞（如第一個例句），也可以接現在完成式（如第二、三個例句）。

Dialogue 簡短對話

A: During these times of economic instability, what we need is strong leadership.

B: I couldn't have said it better myself. It's definitely what our investors want to see.

A：在這種經濟不穩定的時候，我們需要的是強勢的領導。

B：你說得太好了。這絕對是我們的投資人想要看到的。

字彙
put something better 將…說得更好	leadership (n.) 領導
economic instability 經濟不穩定	investor (n.) 投資人

精進度★★★★☆

句型4

I concur.
我同意。

Example 實用例句

● I concur. There must be a way to lower costs without laying off staff.
我同意。一定有可以不必裁員就降低成本的方法。

● I concur. Instead of looking for someone to blame, we should be looking for solutions.
我同意。與其找人來責怪，不如找出解決方法。

● I concur. Peter is the best person to lead our expansion efforts in Australia.
我同意。彼德是主導我們在澳洲擴張的最佳人選。

說明 ▶ 雖然是很簡短的說法（通常用在非正式的場合），不過 concur 這個字還是有很正式的意涵。I concur. 除了可以單獨使用外，也可以在後面接句子。

Dialogue 簡短對話

A: I concur. Let's fold the division and write it off as a loss.

B: At this point, it doesn't look like we have any other choice. It's good to know you and I are on the same page.

A：我同意。我們就把這個部門關閉，列為虧損。

B：都到這個時候了，我們似乎也沒有其他選擇。很高興知道你和我有相同的看法。

說明 ▶ write something off 可以表示除去或放棄某物，也有在帳冊上註記為財務虧損之意。另外，you and I are on the same page 表示「你和我的意見一致」。

字彙

concur (v.) 同意	fold (v.) 關閉
lay off... 將…裁員	division (n.) 部門，局處
staff (n.) 全體工作人員	write something off 承認損失（資產）
blame (v.) 責怪	on the same page 意見一致
expansion (n.) 擴展	

精進度 ★★★★★

句型 5

I'm in complete agreement that...
我完全同意……

表示贊同

Example 實用例句

● I'm in complete agreement that we need to solve the quality control problem.
我完全同意我們必須解決品管問題。

● I'm in complete agreement that our company has outgrown this tiny space.
我完全同意這個小空間已經不敷我們公司所需了。

● I'm in complete agreement that a live band would work best for the reception.
我完全同意請現場演奏樂團來這場歡迎會最適合不過了。

說明 ▶ 本句型也可以縮短成一個完整的句子：I'm in complete agreement. （我完全同意。）如果不想要表現得那麼強烈或直接，也可以改用 I agree that...（我同意⋯⋯）來表達。

Dialogue 簡短對話

A: I'm in complete agreement that brand loyalty is important to our customers.

B: Right, so our marketing should focus on the shopping experience as much as the product.

A：我完全同意，品牌忠誠度對我們的消費者很重要。

B：沒錯，所以除了產品外，我們的行銷重點應該放在購物體驗上。

字彙		
outgrow (v.) 長得比⋯快（或大）		brand loyalty 品牌忠誠度
live (adj.) 現場的，實況的		marketing (n.) 行銷
reception (n.) 歡迎會，招待會		

相關表達 若要表示贊同，有哪些好用的慣用說法呢？

➥ You're right on the money. 你說得完全正確。

➥ I think you hit the nail (right) on the head. 我覺得你一針見血。

➥ You and I are on the same page. 你和我的意見一致。

表示不贊同
Disagreeing

Are you serious?　　　　　　　　　　你是說真的嗎？

That doesn't (quite) sound right. I think the　聽起來不（太）正確。我認為比
percentage is more like 35. 句型 *1*　　　例比較像是 35。

I think we're pretty far apart on that issue.　我想我們對那項議題的看法南轅
　　　　　　　　　　　　　　　　　　北轍。

I disagree with the way the press release was　我不贊同新聞稿的處理方式。
handled. 句型 *2*

I'm not sure I agree with that.　　　　　我不是很贊同那個。

I see things a little differently. There are　我的看法有點不一樣。除了破產
other options besides bankruptcy. 句型 *3*　之外，還有其他選擇。

I have a (somewhat) different opinion.　　我有（稍微）不同的看法。

I don't quite see the issue the same way. 句型 *4*　我對這項議題的看法不太一樣。

I'm of a different mind when it comes to　說到招募新人一事，我有不同的
making new hires. 句型 *5*　　　　　　看法。

With all due respect, that's not the way I see　恕我冒昧，我不這麼認為。
it.

句型 1

That doesn't (quite) sound right.
聽起來不（太）正確。

EXAMPLE 實用例句

● That doesn't quite sound right. I think the percentage is more like 35.
聽起來不太正確。我認為比例比較像是 35。

● That doesn't sound right. I need to go back and check my notes.
聽起來不正確。我得回去查一下我的筆記。

● That doesn't quite sound right. Are you sure?
聽起來不太正確。你確定沒錯嗎？

說明 ▶ 本句型是一個很有趣的句子，說這句話時表示說話者認為對方的話可能有問題，不過自己不見得知道正確的說法。

DIALOGUE 簡短對話

A: George mentioned that more guests come here for pie than for dinner.
B: That doesn't quite sound right. But I'll go over the receipts from the last two months and see if it's true.
A：喬治提到來這裡吃派的客人比吃晚餐的客人多。
B：聽起來不太正確，不過我會去檢查一下這兩個月的發票，看看他說的對不對。

字彙 receipt (n.) 收據，發票

句型 2

I disagree with...
我不贊同……

EXAMPLE 實用例句

● I disagree with the way the press release was handled.
我不贊同新聞稿的處理方式。

● I disagree with most of the blog's ideas.
我不贊同這個部落格大部分的觀點。

● I disagree with the notion that our shareholders are unhappy.
我不贊同我們的股東並不滿意的說法。

說明 ▶ 本句型也可以替換成 I don't agree with... 或 I'm in disagreement with...，意思不變。如果要表達贊同之意，可以使用 It's hard to disagree with...（很難不贊同……）這個以雙重否定來表達的句型。

Dialogue 簡短對話

A: To tell the truth, I disagree with the decision to change distributors. I've spoken with a few other people who feel the same way.

B: I'll raise your concerns at the next management meeting.

A：說實話，我不贊同更改經銷商的決策。我和其他一些人談過，他們也有同樣的看法。

B：下一次開經營會議時，我會把你的顧慮提出來。

字彙		
press release 新聞稿		shareholder (n.) 股東
blog (n.) 部落格		distributor (n.) 經銷商，發行商
notion (n.) 想法		raise a concern 提出顧慮

精進度★★★☆☆

句型 3

I see things a little differently.
我的看法有點不一樣。

Example 實用例句

● I see things a little differently. There are other options besides bankruptcy.
我的看法有點不一樣。除了破產之外，還有其他選擇。

● I see things a little differently. Juan's suggestion was meant to be helpful, not divisive.
我的看法有點不一樣。胡安的提議是為了提供協助，而不是要引起不和。

● I see things a little differently. If we drive instead of taking the train, we'll have a lot more flexibility.
我的看法有點不一樣。如果我們不搭火車而改成開車，彈性會大很多。

表示不贊同

說明 ▶ 表示不贊同時，常會用 a little 來軟化語氣，讓所說的話比較不具強制性，也比較婉轉一點。也可以直接用 I see things differently.（我的看法不一樣。）來表達，但這樣會給人比較直接的印象。

Dialogue 簡短對話

A: I think we should close off membership for a while. We have too many members.

B: Actually, I see things a little differently. People are always coming and going, so we should keep the door open to new members.

A：我認為我們應該停止接受會員申請一陣子，我們的會員太多了。

B：其實，我的看法有點不一樣。人總是來來去去，所以我們應該繼續敞開大門接受新會員。

bankruptcy (n.) 破產
divisive (adj.) 引起不和的
flexibility (n.) 彈性

close off... 隔絕…，封鎖…
keep the door open 敞開大門

精進度 ★★★★☆

句型 **4**

I don't quite see ... the same way.
我對……的看法不太一樣。

Example 實用例句

● I don't quite see the issue the same way.
我對這項議題的看法不太一樣。

● I don't quite see things the same way.
我對事情的看法不太一樣。

● I don't quite see the situation the same way.
我對這個情況的看法不太一樣。

說明 ▶ 本句型中的 the same way 也可以替換成 that way。另外，如果拿掉 quite 這個副詞，就會變得比較沒那麼正式，不過也顯得更直接一些。

Dialogue 簡短對話

A: What's hurting us is a lack of new products. Our main lines haven't changed in two years.

B: I don't quite see the problem that way. I think it's more a question of pricing.

A：欠缺新產品才是我們的致命傷。我們的主要產品線已經兩年沒更換了。

B：我對這個問題的看法不太一樣，我覺得定價問題居多。

字彙
a lack of... 缺乏…
a question of... …的問題

pricing (n.) 定價

精進度★★★★★

 句型5

I'm of a different mind when it comes to...
說到……，我有不同的看法。

Example 實用例句

● I'm of a different mind when it comes to making new hires.
說到招募新人一事，我有不同的看法。

● I'm of a different mind when it comes to the usefulness of large POP displays.
說到大型店頭展示架的效用，我有不同的看法。

● I'm of a different mind when it comes to the best way to reach young consumers.
說到接觸年輕消費者的最佳方式，我有不同的看法。

說明 ▶ 本句型後半部的 when it comes to... 意思是「當說到…」，後面接動詞時，必須用動名詞的形式。另外，第三個例句中的〈the best way to + 原形動詞〉是一個慣用說法，意思是「…最好的方法」。

表示不贊同

Dialogue 簡短對話

A: I'm of a different mind when it comes to the effectiveness of direct mail advertising.

B: It certainly doesn't work for all products and companies, but I have seen it used successfully.

A：說到以直接郵寄來做廣告的有效性，我有不同的看法。

B：它當然不是對所有產品和公司都有效，不過我看過它運用成功的例子。

相關表達 在提出不贊同的意見之前，可用以下的開頭語來緩和語氣。

→ Actually,... 其實，……

→ To tell the truth,... 坦白說，……

→ Honestly,... 說實話，……

→ Frankly,... 老實說，……

16 提出建議
Making a Suggestion

非正式

Try driving with both hands on the wheel. 句型1

試試看把兩隻手都放在方向盤上來開車。

Let's go somewhere different for dinner.

我們去找個不一樣的地方吃晚餐吧。

稍非正式

It wouldn't hurt to eat less fried food.

少吃油炸食物不會有害。

Remember to look the audience members in the eye.

記得要注視觀眾的眼睛。

一般情況

I think you should start saving a bit more every month. 句型2

我認為你應該每個月開始多存一點錢。

Why don't you ask for a raise.

為什麼不要求加薪呢？

稍正式

If I were you, I'd buy an electric car. 句型3

如果我是你，我會買電動車。

It might be a good idea to change your sleep habits. 句型4

改變你的睡眠習慣可能會是個好主意。

正式

Maybe you could consider moving to a larger apartment.

或許你可以考慮搬到更大間的公寓。

Have you thought about bringing on more staff? 句型5

你有想過引進更多工作人員嗎？

句型 **1** **Try...**
試試看……

Example 實用例句

● Try driving with both hands on the wheel.
試試看把兩隻手都放在方向盤上來開車。

● Try breaking the ice by inviting the new guy to lunch.
試試看邀請新人吃午餐來打破僵局。

● Try these scissors. They might work better for cutting cloth.
試試看這把剪刀,用它來剪布可能會比較好用。

說明 ▶ 通常愈是非正式的句型,愈是簡短。本句型只有動詞 try 這個字,後面可以接名詞(如第三個例句)或動名詞(如第一、二個例句)。

Dialogue 簡短對話

A: Try telling Steve that his moodiness is starting to affect you.
B: I'm not sure. He's gone through a lot recently, and I don't want to upset him.
A:試著告訴史帝夫,他的喜怒無常開始影響到你了。
B:我不確定要不要耶。他最近吃了好多苦,我不想讓他心煩意亂。

說明 ▶ B 所說的 go through a lot 是「經歷很多苦難」之意,例如處理工作上的問題、從車禍中復原等。

wheel (n.) 方向盤
break the ice 舒緩緊張氣氛,打破僵局
moodiness (n.) 喜怒無常
upset (v.) 使心煩意亂

 句型 **2** **I think you should...**
我認為你應該……

Example 實用例句

● I think you should start saving a bit more every month.
我認為你應該每個月開始多存一點錢。

- I think you should hire a lawyer with at least 10 years of experience.
  我認為你應該聘請一位至少有十年經驗的律師。

- I think you should choose a career that makes you happy.
  我認為你應該選擇會讓你快樂的職業。

  說明 ▶ 提出建議時，如果想要表達得更直接一點，可以把本句型 I think you should... 替換成 You should...。

Dialogue 簡短對話

A: I think you should pick up some souvenirs for your coworkers.

B: OK. Let's look for something food-related. You can't go wrong with food.

A：我覺得你應該買一些紀念品給你的同事。

B：好的，我們去找一些和食物有關的東西吧，送吃的準沒錯。

說明 ▶ B 使用了一個很常用的句型：〈You can't go wrong with + 名詞〉，意思是「……準沒錯。」這個句型的受詞（如 food）通常是說話者覺得可行、能被認同的東西。

字彙	
career (n.) （終身的）職業	coworker (n.) 同事，同僚
souvenir (n.) 紀念品	go wrong with... …出毛病

精進度★★★★☆

 句型 **3**

If I were you, I'd...
如果我是你，我會……

Example 實用例句

- If I were you, I'd buy an electric car.
  如果我是你，我會買電動車。

- If I were you, I'd talk to the neighbor and try to work things out.
  如果我是你，我會和鄰居談一談，試著把事情解決。

- If I were you, I'd cut back on eating so much frozen food.
  如果我是你，我會減少吃那麼多冷凍食物。

說明 ▶ 本句型很常使用，前半部是一個條件句，讓說話者置身在對方的處境中。另外也可以用 If it were me, I'd...（如果是我，我會……）來表達。

Dialogue 簡短對話

A: If I were you, I'd wear one of your fancy dresses.

B: I was planning to, but the invitation said to dress casually.

    A：如果我是你，我會穿上一件你最花俏的禮服。

    B：我本來有打算這樣做，不過請帖上說要穿輕便服裝。

字彙	
work something out 把某事解決	fancy (adj.) 花俏的
cut back on... 削減…	invitation (n.) 請帖，請柬
frozen food 冷凍食物	casually (adv.) 輕便地

句型4 It might be a good idea to...
……可能會是個好主意。

Example 實用例句

● It might be a good idea to change your sleep habits.
改變你的睡眠習慣可能會是個好主意。

● It might be a good idea to shop around before buying a refrigerator.
買冰箱前先到處逛逛可能會是個好主意。

● It might be a good idea to turn your cell phone off before going into the interview.
進去面試前先把手機關機可能會是個好主意。

說明 ▶ 本句型 to 的後面要接原形動詞。另外，如果將本句型改成否定：It might not be a bad idea to...（……未嘗不是個好主意。）語氣會顯得比較沒那麼正式，也比較直接。

Dialogue 簡短對話

A: It might be a good idea to take a conversation class to brush up on your French.

B: I'd love to, but I haven't got the time. Plus, my trip to Paris is just three weeks away.

A：去上會話課複習一下你的法語，可能會是個好主意。

B：我很想去，可是我沒有時間。再說，我再過三週就要去巴黎旅行了。

字彙 shop around 到處逛街比價　　　　　　　brush up on... 複習…

精進度★★★★★

 句型 *5*

Have you thought about...?
你有想過……嗎？

Example 實用例句

● Have you thought about bringing on more staff?
你有想過引進更多工作人員嗎？

● Have you thought about buying a bike so you can exercise while commuting?
你有想過買一輛腳踏車，一邊通勤一邊運動嗎？

● Have you thought about doing a benchmark of similar products?
你有想過給類似的產品立下一個基準嗎？

說明 ▶ 提出建議時，最正式、最婉轉的說法是採取問句的形式。這是因為問句可以讓對方居於權威的地位，語氣也不會顯得那麼具有強迫性。本句型 about 的後面通常會接動名詞。

95

Dialogue 簡短對話

A: Have you thought about checking with a travel agent to see if there are any flight plus hotel package deals?

B: That's a really good idea.

A：你有想過去問旅行社，看看有沒有機加酒的套裝方案嗎？

B：真是個好主意。

字彙		
bring on... 引進…	benchmark (n.) 基準，標竿
staff (n.) 全體工作人員	travel agent 旅行社
commute (v.) 通勤	package deal 套裝方案

相關表達 對於別人的提議，有什麼常見的回應說法嗎？

→ That's a really good idea. 真是個好主意。

→ Thanks for the suggestion. 謝謝你的建議。

→ I'll think it over. 我會仔細考慮。

→ I'm not sure. 我不確定。

請求建議
Asking for a Recommendation

I'm all ears.　　　　　　　　　　　　　　　我洗耳恭聽。

Any ideas?　　　　　　　　　　　　　　　　有什麼想法嗎？

Tell me what to do. I don't want to make a mistake. 句型**1**　　　　　告訴我該怎麼做。我不想犯錯。

What's your pick for the city's best movie theater?　　　　　要你挑的話，你覺得這座城市最棒的電影院是哪一間呢？

Where do you think I should go? 句型**2**　　　你覺得我應該去哪裡呢？

Where do people around here go for good Indian food?　　　　這裡的人都到哪裡去吃好吃的印度菜呢？

Have you got any suggestions? 句型**3**　　　你有任何建議嗎？

Can you recommend a good ophthalmologist?　　　你可以推薦一位優秀的眼科醫師嗎？

If you were in my position, how would you handle things? 句型**4**　　　如果你處在我的立場，你會怎麼處理事情呢？

Do you think you might be able to recommend a reputable brand? 句型**5**　　　請問你可以推薦一個信譽良好的品牌嗎？

句型 **1**

Tell me what to do.
告訴我該怎麼做。

Example 實用例句

● Tell me what to do. I don't want to make a mistake.
告訴我該怎麼做。我不想犯錯。

● Tell me what to do. This is such a tricky situation.
告訴我該怎麼做。這種情況實在很棘手。

● Tell me what to do. You know everything about real estate.
告訴我該怎麼做。你對房地產無所不知。

說明 ▶ 不知道該怎麼做的時候（有可能是害怕犯錯，也有可能是相信對方的專業），可以說 Tell me what to do. 來請對方提供建議。不過要注意的是，說這句話時有可能會給人一種說話者很軟弱或甚至不牢靠的感覺。

Dialogue 簡短對話

A: Tell me what to do. You're the expert in all things mechanical.
B: Well, the first thing you want to do is make sure there aren't any loose or disconnected parts.

A：告訴我該怎麼做。你是機械方面的專家。
B：嗯，你要做的第一件事是確定沒有任何鬆脫或分離的零件。

說明 ▶ 如果要表達某個領域的一切事物，可以用〈all things + 形容詞〉或〈all things related to + 名詞〉，例如 all things mechanical/artistic（與機械／藝術相關的一切事物）、all things related to horses（與馬有關的一切事物）等。

tricky situation 棘手的情況   mechanical (adj.) 機械的
real estate 房地產   disconnected (adj.) 斷掉連結的

句型2

...do you think I should ～ ?
你覺得我應該……呢？

EXAMPLE 實用例句

● Where do you think I should go?
你覺得我應該去哪裡呢？

● What do you think I should do?
你覺得我應該做什麼呢？

● Who do you think I should consult with?
你覺得我應該找誰商量呢？

說明▶ 嚴格來說，第三個例句的句首應該用 Whom...?，不過，口語中很少用 whom（whom 是 who 的受格）。

DIALOGUE 簡短對話

A: When do you think I should ask for a raise?
B: Anytime, really. Just make sure your boss is in a good mood when you do it.
A：你覺得我應該在何時要求加薪呢？
B：隨時都可以，真的。只要確定當時你老闆的心情很好就行了。

字彙	consult with... 與…商量 raise (n.) 加薪	in a good mood 心情好

句型3

Have you got any...?
你有任何……嗎？

EXAMPLE 實用例句

● Have you got any suggestions?
你有任何建議嗎？

● Have you got any recommendations?
你有任何推薦嗎？

- Have you got any ideas?
  你有任何想法嗎？

  說明 ▶ 本句型有一個類似但比較正式的說法：Would you happen to have any...?（你會不會剛好有任何……？）。比較非正式的說法是 Can you give me some...?（可以給我一些……嗎？）。

Dialogue 簡短對話

A: I'm looking for a place to hold Jack's 50th birthday party. Have you got any ideas?

B: Good question. How about that piano lounge out by the riverside? It's a nice place.

A：我在找地方替傑克舉辦 50 歲生日派對，你有任何想法嗎？

B：好問題。河邊那家鋼琴酒吧怎麼樣？那是個好地方。

 piano lounge 鋼琴酒吧　　　　　　riverside (n.) 河邊

 句型 **4**

精進度★★★★★

If you were in my position,...
如果你處在我的立場，……

Example 實用例句

- If you were in my position, how would you handle things?
  如果你處在我的立場，你會怎麼處理事情呢？

- If you were in my position, what would you do?
  如果你處在我的立場，你會怎麼做呢？

- If you were in my position, would you make a different choice?
  如果你處在我的立場，你會做不同的選擇嗎？

  說明 ▶ 本句型是一個表示條件的副詞子句，另一個更簡單的說法是 If you were me,...（如果你是我，……）。比較非正式的說法是 If you were in my shoes,...（如果換作是你，……）。主要子句可以用〈wh-word/how + would + 主詞 + 動詞〉或〈would + 主詞 + 動詞〉。

Dialogue 簡短對話

A: If you were in my position, would you invest in the company?

B: That's hard to say. I'd have to see its balance sheet first.

A：如果你處在我的立場，你會投資這家公司嗎？

B：這很難說。我必須先看它的資產負債表。

字彙

position (n.) 立場，處境　　　　　　balance sheet 資產負債表
in someone's shoes 站在某人的立場

精進度★★★★★

句型5

Do you think you might be able to recommend...?
請問你可以推薦……嗎？

Example 實用例句

● Do you think you might be able to recommend a reputable brand?
請問你可以推薦一個信譽良好的品牌嗎？

● Do you think you might be able to recommend some reliable temp agencies?
請問你可以推薦一些可靠的臨時工派遣公司嗎？

● Do you think you might be able to recommend a good way to spread the word about our organization?
請問你可以推薦宣傳我們組織的好方法嗎？

說明▸動詞 recommend 的後面可以接一個簡短的名詞或名詞片語，也可以接〈a good way + 不定詞〉。另外，本句型的後面也可以接〈the best way + 不定詞〉。

Dialogue 簡短對話

A: Do you think you might be able to recommend a good limo service? I have an out of town VIP guest visiting.

B: Let me think about it... Yes, there's one out on Alameda Ave.

A：請問你可以推薦一家好的禮車服務公司嗎？我有一位外地貴客來訪。

B：我想一想……。有，阿拉米達大街上有一家。

相關表達 遇到別人請求你提供建議時，可以用下面的說法來回應：

⇨ Let me think about it. 讓我想一想。

⇨ I might have an idea or two. 我可能有一、兩個建議。

⇨ You came to the right person. 你問對人了。

⇨ That's hard to say. 這很難說。

⇨ I really don't know, sorry. 對不起，我真的不知道。

18 解釋清楚
Clarifying

非正式

You think South America should be our next target market. Is that right?

你認為南美洲應該成為我們下一個目標市場，對嗎？

What do you mean by "underrepresented"? 句型 *1*

你說的「代表性不足」是什麼意思呢？

稍非正式

Did I hear you correctly—that you won't be at the conference?

我有沒有聽錯，你將不會出席會議？

Are you saying the rates are going up? 句型 *2*

你是說價格將要上漲嗎？

一般情況

Can you please repeat that? 句型 *3*

可以請你將那個重複一次嗎？

I'm not sure what you mean.

我不知道你的意思。

稍正式

Could you say a bit more about that?

你可以多說一點那個嗎？

Forgive me. I don't fully understand you. 句型 *4*

很抱歉。我沒有完全了解你的意思。

正式

Would you mind explaining that last point? 句型 *5*

你介意將最後那一點解釋一下嗎？

Sorry, I don't completely follow you.

對不起，我沒有完全聽懂你的意思。

句型 1

What do you mean by...?

你說的……是什麼意思呢？

EXAMPLE 實用例句

- What do you mean by "underrepresented"?
  你說的「代表性不足」是什麼意思呢？

- What did you mean by "ambivalent"?
  你說的「矛盾情感」是什麼意思呢？

- What do you mean by "too young for the position"?
  你說的「以這個職位來說太年輕」是什麼意思呢？

  說明▶ 本句型有兩個用途，第一是使用於不了解對方所說的某個字或某個詞時，第二是用於確認對方是不是有其他言下之意時。

DIALOGUE 簡短對話

A: You said you misspoke when you were explaining the cause of the accident. What did you mean by "misspoke"?

B: By that I meant I made some premature statements before all the facts were in.

A：你說你解釋意外發生的原因時說錯了，你說的「說錯」是什麼意思呢？

B：我的意思是，我在掌握所有事實之前就做了草率的陳述。

underrepresented (adj.) 代表性不足的	position (n.) 職位
ambivalent (adj.)	misspeak (v.) 說錯
（對某人或某物）有矛盾情感的	premature (adj.) 不成熟的，草率的

句型 2

Are you saying...?

你是說……嗎？

EXAMPLE 實用例句

- Are you saying the rates are going up?
  你是說價格將要上漲嗎？

- Are you saying there's no way to fix the leak without ripping the wall out?
  你是說只有把牆拆掉才能修理滲漏嗎？

- Are you saying we have to wait two hours for the next bus?
  你是說下一班公車得等兩個小時嗎？

說明 ▶ 本句型用於你認為你了解對方的意思，不過想做進一步確認的時候。也可以改以 Do you mean...?（你的意思是……嗎？）來表達，意思差不多。

Dialogue 簡短對話

A: Let me see if I've got this right. Are you saying I can't check this suitcase because it's one kilogram over the maximum weight allowance?

B: I'm afraid not. Maybe you can remove something to bring the weight down.

A：讓我確認一下我是不是搞懂了。你是說這只手提箱因為超過行李限重一公斤，所以不能託運嗎？

B：恐怕是不行的。也許你可以拿些東西出來，減輕重量。

字彙	
rate (n.) 價格，費用	check (v.) 託運（行李）
go up 上升，增長	suitcase (n.) 手提箱
leak (n.)（水、瓦斯等的）漏出	maximum (adj.) 最大的，最多的
rip out... 拆…，扯破…	weight allowance 行李限重

精進度 ★★★ ☆ ☆

句型 3

Can you please repeat...?
可以請你將……重複一次嗎？

Example 實用例句

- Can you please repeat that?
  可以請你將那個重複一次嗎？

- Can you please repeat what you just said?
  可以請你將剛剛說的話重複一次嗎？

解釋清楚

● Can you please repeat the last part of that?
可以請你將最後一部分重複一次嗎？

說明▸ 這是請別人再說一次的簡單、有禮貌的說法，如果要更正式一點，可以把本句型替換成 I wonder if you might be able to repeat...（不知道你可不可以重複一次⋯⋯），這時候就不是問句，而是一個直述句了，不過用意都是請對方說清楚。

Dialoɢue 簡短對話

A: Can you please repeat those dates?

B: Sure. We're departing on June 10 and returning on June 16.
A：可以請你將那些日期重複一次嗎？
B：當然可以。我們將在 6 月 10 日出發，6 月 16 日返回。

精進度★★★★☆

句型*4*

Forgive me. I don't fully...
很抱歉。我沒有完全⋯⋯

Example 實用例句

● Forgive me. I don't fully understand you.
很抱歉。我沒有完全了解你的意思。

● Forgive me. I don't fully follow what you're saying.
很抱歉。我沒有完全聽懂你的話。

● Forgive me. I don't fully catch your point.
很抱歉。我沒有完全抓到你的重點。

說明▸ 副詞 fully 可以替換成 entirely，另外，Forgive me. 可以替換成 I'm sorry. 或 Sorry.。

Dialoɢue 簡短對話

A: Forgive me. I don't entirely follow what you're saying.

B: I'm sorry. I didn't explain it very clearly. Let me try again.
A：很抱歉。我沒有完全聽懂你的話。
B：不好意思，我沒有解釋得非常清楚，我再解釋一次吧。

| 字彙 | forgive (v.) 原諒 | catch someone's point 抓到某人的重點 |

精進度★★★★★

句型5

Would you mind explaining...?

你介意將……解釋一下嗎？

EXAMPLE 實用例句

● Would you mind explaining that last point?
你介意將最後那一點解釋一下嗎？

● Would you mind explaining what you just said?
你介意將你剛剛說的話解釋一下嗎？

● Would you mind explaining why it's a bad idea to invest in hydrothermal energy?
你介意解釋一下為什麼投資熱液能源是個糟糕的想法嗎？

說明 ▶ 本句型可用於不了解對方意思的情況下（如第一、二個例句），或用於希望對方針對某一點多做些解釋時（如第三個例句）。explaining 的後面可以接名詞或名詞子句。

解釋清楚

DIALOGUE 簡短對話

A: Would you mind explaining what you mean?

B: Sure, I mean the potential benefits of opening a new branch outweigh the risks.

A：你介意解釋一下你的意思嗎？

B：沒問題。我的意思是開一家新分店的潛在利益大於風險。

| 字彙 | hydrothermal energy 熱液能源
potential (adj.) 潛在的
benefit (n.) 利益 | branch (n.) 分店，分公司
outweigh (v.) 比…更重要或有價值
risk (n.) 風險 |

➥ Correct me if I'm wrong.
如果我錯了，請糾正我。

➥ Let me see if I've got this straight/right.
讓我確認一下我有沒有把這件事搞清楚。

➥ I want to make sure I'm clear on this.
我想確認我有把這件事搞清楚。

擬定計畫
Making a Plan

非正式

Let's do this. Call me when your bus gets in, and I'll pick you up. 句型*1*

我們這樣做好了，當你的巴士抵達時打電話給我，我會來接你。

We could visit the museum in the morning.

我們可以早上參觀博物館。

稍非正式

We should write down the pros and cons and then make a decision. 句型*2*

我們應該把利弊得失一一寫下來，然後再做決定。

Why don't we plan to meet back here in an hour.

我們何不計畫一個小時之後回到這裡碰頭。

一般情況

Taking things one step at a time may be the best plan of attack. 句型*3*

處理事情時一次一個步驟，或許是最佳的作戰計畫。

We've talked it over, and we think a summer marketing campaign would work best.

我們仔細討論過了，我們認為最可行的方式是推出一檔夏日行銷活動。

稍正式

A conservative plan would be to focus on a small number of key retailers. 句型*4*

一個保守的計畫是把重點放在少數主要的零售商。

To get things started, perhaps we should book the exhibition hall for five days.

要讓事情動起來，或許我們應該預訂展覽廳五天。

正式

This is just one idea, but we might consider sending out samples with the catalogs. 句型*5*

這只是一個想法，不過我們可以考慮連同目錄把樣品寄出去。

If I might suggest a course of action, we could put together a survey for our top customers.

如果我可以提議一項行動方案，我們可以針對忠實客戶進行一項調查。

句型 *1* Let's do this.
我們這樣做好了。

Example 實用例句

● Let's do this. Call me when your bus gets in, and I'll pick you up.
我們這樣做好了,當你的巴士抵達時打電話給我,我會來接你。

● Let's do this. We'll drive by the ice cream shop, and if it's open, we'll stop and go inside.
我們這樣做好了,我們會開車經過冰淇淋店,如果有開門營業,我們就停下來、走進去。

● Let's do this. One of us can handle the accommodations, and the other can look into local restaurants.
我們這樣做好了,我們其中一人處理住宿事宜,另一個人負責研究當地餐廳。

說明▶ 說話者透過本句型將心中已經做好的決定,以權威的口吻表達出來。本句型通常用於某件事已經討論好一陣子,而且所有相關人等都已經提出自己的想法之後。

Dialogue 簡短對話

A: Let's do this. I'll drive the truck in the morning, and you can take over after lunch.

B: That's fine with me, but I sometimes get sleepy after meals, so you'll need to keep me awake.

A:我們這樣做好了,早上由我來開卡車,然後午餐過後由你接手。

B:我沒問題,不過我有時候吃完飯後會想睡覺,所以你得讓我保持清醒。

字彙

get in 到達
pick up someone(通常指開車)接載某人
accommodations (n.) 住宿
look into... 調查⋯,研究⋯

truck (n.) 卡車
take over 接手
sleepy (adj.) 想睡的

句型 2

We should ... and then make a decision.
我們應該……然後再做決定。

Example 實用例句

● We should write down the pros and cons and then make a decision.
我們應該把利弊得失一一寫下來，然後再做決定。

● We should consider everyone's input and then make a decision.
我們應該把每個人的意見都納入考慮，然後再做決定。

● We should learn more about the situation and then make a decision.
我們應該更深入了解這個情況，然後再做決定。

說明 ▶ 本句型用於鼓勵先進行一個中間步驟，再來採取行動。這個中間步驟通常包括收集資料、將各項訊息都納入考慮等。

Dialogue 簡短對話

A: We should find out exactly what happened and then make a decision.
B: Sounds like a solid plan. We don't want to do anything hasty before the facts are all in.

A：我們應該搞清楚到底是怎麼一回事後再來做決定。
B：聽起來是個很完整的計畫。我們不希望在掌握全部事實之前就倉促行事。

字彙		
pros and cons 利弊，優缺點		solid plan 完整的計畫
input (n.) 提供的訊息、意見等		hasty (adj.) 倉促的

擬定計畫

句型 3

...may be the best plan of attack.
……或許是最佳的作戰計畫。

Example 實用例句

● Taking things one step at a time may be the best plan of attack.
處理事情時一次一個步驟，或許是最佳的作戰計畫。

● Threatening them with a lawsuit may be the best plan of attack.
以法律訴訟來威脅他們，或許是最佳的作戰計畫。

● Hiring a headhunter to recruit new talent may be the best plan of attack.

雇用獵人頭公司來網羅新的人才，或許是最佳的作戰計畫。

說明 ▶ 本句型須以動名詞開頭，作為句子的主詞。plan of attack 可以替換成 course of action（行動方案，行動方針）或 thing to do（該做的事）。

DIALOGUE 簡短對話

A: Outsourcing production, lowering costs, and slashing prices may be the best plan of attack.

B: The question is: will that be enough to convince our creditors to extend our line of credit?

A：將製造部分外包出去、降低成本、大幅降價，或許是最佳的作戰計畫。

B：問題是：那足以說服債權人提高我們的信用額度嗎？

one step at a time 一次一個步驟	outsource (v.) 外包
threaten (v.) 威脅	slash (v.) 大幅刪減
lawsuit (n.) 法律訴訟	convince (v.) 說服，使相信
headhunter (n.)	creditor (n.) 債權人
（以替人物色人才為業的）獵人頭公司	extend (v.) 擴大，延伸
recruit (v.) 網羅，招募	line of credit 信用額度
talent (n.) 人才	

精進度 ★★★★☆

句型 4

A conservative plan would be to...
一個保守的計畫是……

EXAMPLE 實用例句

● A conservative plan would be to focus on a small number of key retailers.

一個保守的計畫是把重點放在少數主要的零售商。

● A conservative plan would be to order just enough inventory to fill our current orders.

一個保守的計畫是訂購剛好足夠應付我們現有訂單的庫存。

● A conservative plan would be to put 20 percent of our profits into a rainy day fund.
一個保守的計畫是把我們 20% 的獲利放進儲備基金。

說明 ▶ conservative（保守的）可以替換成其他形容詞，端視說話者想要如何形容其計畫，比方說，計畫也許是 aggressive（積極進取的）、bold（大膽的）、cautious（謹慎的）等。

Dialogue 簡短對話

A: A conservative plan would be to ignore the fact that one of our main competitors just folded and carry on with business as usual.

B: We could do that, but I'd favor a more aggressive course of action.

A：一個保守的計畫是，我們忽視主要競爭對手之一剛剛關門大吉的事實，繼續如常進行業務。

B：我們是可以這麼做，不過我偏向採取比較積極的行動。

字彙	
retailer (n.) 零售商	ignore (v.) 忽視
inventory (n.) 庫存	competitor (n.) 競爭對手
fill an order 供應訂單	fold (v.)（事業等）失敗
rainy day fund（以備不時之需的）儲備基金	carry on with... 繼續…
aggressive (adj.) 積極進取的	business as usual 如常的業務

精進度★★★★★

句型 5

This is just one idea, but we might consider...
這只是一個想法，不過我們可以考慮……

Example 實用例句

● This is just one idea, but we might consider sending out samples with the catalogs.
這只是一個想法，不過我們可以考慮連同目錄把樣品寄出去。

● This is just one idea, but we might consider putting a freeze on wage increases as we ride out the recession.
這只是一個想法，不過我們可以考慮在安然度過經濟衰退的期間凍結薪資上漲。

● This is just one idea, but we might consider running more ads during sporting events to better reach our target demographic.
這只是一個想法，不過我們可以考慮運動賽事期間刊登更多廣告，以接觸更多我們的目標族群。

說明 ▶ 本句型前半句使用 This is just one idea，接著後半句使用〈情態助動詞 + 動詞〉(might consider)，整體顯得非常謹慎。consider 的後面通常接動名詞。

Dialogue 簡短對話

A: This is just one idea, but we might consider setting up a loyalty program with gifts and discounts for repeat customers.

B: Interesting. Go ahead and set up a cost-benefit analysis, and we'll go over it during the next planning session.

　　A：這只是一個想法，不過我們可以考慮擬定一個忠誠度方案，贈送老顧客禮物並提供折扣。

　　B：很有趣。就去做吧，然後做一份成本效益分析，在下次的企畫會議中討論。

字彙

catalog (n.) 目錄 (= catalogue)
freeze (n.) 凍結
wage (n.) 工資
ride out... 挺過（風暴或危機），安然度過…
recession (n.) 經濟衰退
demographic (n.) 特定年齡層的人口

loyalty program 忠誠度方案
repeat customer 老顧客，常客
cost-benefit analysis (CBA) 成本效益分析
go over... 認真討論…
planning session 企畫會議

相關表達 如果要擬定計畫，這裡提供幾個好用的慣用說法：

➥ plan of attack 作戰計畫

➥ course of action 行動方案，行動方針

➥ thing to do 該做的事

表示拒絕
Saying "No"

非正式

The answer is no.　　　　　　　　　　　　答案是否定的。

I think I'm going to pass. Maybe another　　我大概不去了。或許下次吧。
time. 句型 1

稍非正式

I'm afraid we have to say no.　　　　　　恐怕我們得拒絕。

We decided to go with another vendor.　　我們決定選擇另一家供貨商。

一般情況

I'm sorry. I won't be able to join the team.　很抱歉。我無法加入團隊。
句型 2

Because of the state of the economy, the　　由於目前的經濟狀況，現在這個
timing isn't right for us. 句型 3　　　　　時機對我們來說並不恰當。

稍正式

We talked it over, and we couldn't reach a　我們仔細討論過，無法達成共
consensus. I'm sorry. 句型 4　　　　　識。很抱歉。

Unfortunately, it isn't going to work out this　很可惜，這一次行不通。
time.

正式

The quality of your presentation was　　　你的報告品質非常優異，不過我
excellent, but we're in a restructuring period.　們目前處於重整階段。

As much as I regret it, we will be unable to go　非常遺憾，我們將無法繼續進行
forward with the project. 句型 5　　　　　這項計畫。

句型 1

I think I'm going to pass.
我大概不去了。

Example 實用例句

● I think I'm going to pass. Maybe another time.
我大概不去了。或許下次吧。

● I think I'm going to pass. Sorry about that.
我大概不去了。不好意思。

● I think I'm going to pass. Have you thought about asking Phil?
我大概不去了。你有想過問菲爾看看嗎？

說明 ▶ I think I'm going to pass. 的後面通常會接期待未來碰面或合作的語句，或是表示歉意、說明理由、提出藉口、提供其他選擇方案等。

Dialogue 簡短對話

A: I think I'm going to pass. I have a lot of studying to do this weekend.
B: That's OK. Don't study too hard. All work and no play makes Jack a dull boy.

A：我大概不去了。我這個週末有好多書要唸。
B：沒關係。別唸得太辛苦了。只工作不玩樂，人會變呆的。

說明 ▶ B 所說的 All work and no play makes Jack a dull boy. 是一句古諺，意思是「只工作不消遣，會使人遲鈍。」主要在鼓勵人要少工作一點、多享樂一點。這句古諺通常是用 Jack 這個名字，不過也可以替換成對方的名字。如果替換成女生的名字，則 boy 也要換成 girl。

 pass (v.) 掠過   dull (adj.) 呆滯的

句型 2　I'm sorry.

很抱歉。

Example 實用例句

● I'm sorry. I won't be able to join the team.
很抱歉。我無法加入團隊。

● I'm sorry. I can't get you free passes to the exhibition.
很抱歉。我無法讓你免費參觀展覽。

● I'm sorry. We're going with another landscaping company.
很抱歉。我們選擇另一家庭園造景公司。

說明 ▶ 使用本句型時，務必要與下一句明確地斷開，這樣才能清楚地表達出拒絕之意。此外，要明顯強調語氣時，可將 sorry 的尾音下降。

Dialogue 簡短對話

A: I'm sorry. Our plans are heading in a different direction.
B: That's too bad. I would have loved to spearhead your R&D team.

A：很抱歉。我們的計畫是完全不同的方向。

B：太可惜了。我本來很樂意擔任你們研發團隊的先鋒。

說明 ▶ 如果向對方表達雙方的計畫是 heading in a different direction（朝不同的方向），可以讓對方感受到不是因為其個人條件而遭到拒絕，而是和整個組織的大方向有關。

pass (n.) 入場券	landscaping (n.) 庭園造景
exhibition (n.) 展覽（會）	head (v.) 朝…前進
go with... 選擇…	spearhead (v.) 做先鋒

表示拒絕

句型 3

Because..., the timing isn't right for us.

由於……，現在這個時機對我們來說並不恰當。

Example 實用例句

- Because of the state of the economy, the timing isn't right for us.
  由於目前的經濟狀況，現在這個時機對我們來說並不恰當。

- Because we just launched a major new line, the timing isn't right for us.
  由於我們剛剛推出了一條重要的新產品線，現在這個時機對我們來說並不恰當。

- Because the market is still sluggish, the timing isn't right for us.
  由於市場仍然低迷，現在這個時機對我們來說並不恰當。

說明▶ 本句型用來說明拒絕的理由，如果理由是個名詞（如第一個例句），就用〈Because of + 名詞〉；如果理由比較複雜，這時就可以用副詞子句（如第二、三個例句）：〈Because + 主詞 + 動詞〉。

Dialogue 簡短對話

A: Because we just signed a large deal with another partner, the timing isn't right for us.

B: Well, let's keep the channels open. Maybe we'll have a chance to do business down the line.

A：由於我們剛剛與另一個合作夥伴簽下了一筆大交易，現在這個時機對我們來說並不恰當。

B：嗯，還是讓我們保持溝通管道暢通，也許未來我們有機會一起合作。

說明▶ B 所說的 keep the channels open 是「保持聯絡」之意。這個慣用語和 stay/keep in touch 一樣都常用在對話結束的時候，尤其是當雙方都認為接下來有好長一段時間不會再見面時。

字彙

timing (n.) 時機	sluggish (adj.) 蕭條的
launch (v.) 推出（新產品）	down the line 未來，往後

句型 **4**

We talked it over, and we couldn't reach a consensus.
我們仔細討論過，無法達成共識。

Example 實用例句

● We talked it over, and we couldn't reach a consensus. I'm sorry.
我們仔細討論過，無法達成共識。很抱歉。

● We talked it over, and we couldn't reach a consensus. Sorry things didn't work out this time.
我們仔細討論過，無法達成共識。很抱歉這次沒有成功。

● We talked it over, and we couldn't reach a consensus. We're very sorry about that.
我們仔細討論過，無法達成共識。我們非常抱歉。

說明▶ 要人解讀某些間接又婉轉的話有時是很困難的（對西方人尤其如此，因為文化與背景差異甚大），所以雖然可以不直接說 no 來表達否定意味，但是後續補上一些說明還是比較有幫助，可以減少模稜兩可的感覺。

Dialogue 簡短對話

A: We talked it over, and we couldn't reach a consensus. I'm very sorry.
B: I understand. Thank you again for your time. I hope we'll have a chance to work together in the future.

A：我們仔細討論過，無法達成共識。非常抱歉。
B：我了解。再次謝謝你撥出時間，希望我們未來有合作的機會。

句型 **5**

As much as I regret it, we will be unable to...
非常遺憾，我們將無法……

Example 實用例句

● As much as I regret it, we will be unable to go forward with the project.
非常遺憾，我們將無法繼續進行這項計畫。

表示拒絕

- As much as I regret it, we will be unable to finance the building cost.
  非常遺憾，我們將無法為這筆建築費用提供資金。

- As much as I regret it, we will be unable to renew our licensing deal.
  非常遺憾，我們將無法延續我們的授權合約。

  說明 ▶ 本句型一開頭使用了非常客氣的說法：as much as I regret it（非常遺憾），也可以改說成 unfortunately（遺憾地，可惜地）、regrettably（遺憾地，抱歉地）或者用 I'm sorry to have to tell you（很抱歉不得不告訴你）來表達。請注意，一般來說，說話者真正的用意可能不是要表達強烈的遺憾，而是要委婉地表達拒絕之意。

Dialogue 簡短對話

A: As much as I regret it, we will be unable to comply with all of your requests.

B: I see. Well, let's work through them and see if we can come to an understanding on some of them.

A：非常遺憾，你的請求我們將無法一一照辦。

B：我了解。讓我們來整個看過一遍，看看是不是能針對其中一些達成共識。

說明 ▶ B 所說的 come to an understanding 是「達成共識，取得諒解」的意思。

字彙	
go forward 前進	license (v.) 發放許可證
finance (v.) 為⋯提供資金	comply with... 遵從⋯，照辦⋯
renew (v.) 延長（合約、執照等的）有效期	

相關表達 拒絕他人後常會接著說哪些正面的話呢？

➥ I hope we'll have a chance to work together in the future.
希望我們未來有合作的機會。

➥ Best of luck in/with your future endeavors.
祝你日後的努力一切順利。

➥ I (would like to) wish you all the best going forward.
祝你一切順利向前。

提出邀請
Making an Invitation

Care to join me for a drink? 句型 *1*　　　　想跟我一起去喝一杯嗎？

Are you doing anything after work?　　　　你下班之後有什麼事嗎？

Do you want to see a movie this weekend?　　　　你週末想去看電影嗎？
句型 *2*

Are you free for dinner this Friday?　　　　這個星期五有空一起吃晚餐嗎？

Would you be interested in going to the　　　　你有興趣一起去水族館嗎？
aquarium together? 句型 *3*

I'd like to invite you to the opening of my new　　　　我想邀請你參加我的新戲首演。
play.

If you aren't doing anything tonight, would　　　　如果你今晚沒事，願意和我共進
you like to have dinner with me? 句型 *4*　　　　晚餐嗎？

I was wondering if you might like to go with　　　　不知道你願不願意和我一起去參
me to the modern art exhibit.　　　　觀現代藝術展。

I'd love for you to be my guest at the charity　　　　希望有榮幸邀請你一起參加慈善
luncheon.　　　　午宴。

Would you do me the honor of accompanying　　　　可否賞光和我一起去參加歡迎會
me to the reception? 句型 *5*　　　　呢？

句型 1　Care to join me for...?
想跟我一起去……嗎？

Example 實用例句

● Care to join me for a drink?
想跟我一起去喝一杯嗎？

● Care to join me for lunch?
想跟我一起去吃午餐嗎？

● Care to join me for a short walk?
想跟我一起去散步一會嗎？

說明 ▶ 本句型還有更隨意的說法，只要說 Join me for...? 即可。

Dialogue 簡短對話

A: Care to join me for some tea?
B: I'd love to, but I have a pile of work to finish.

A：想跟我一起去喝點茶嗎？
B：我很想，可是我有一堆工作要完成。

 a pile of work 一堆工作

句型 2　Do you want to...?
你想……嗎？

Example 實用例句

● Do you want to see a movie this weekend?
你週末想去看電影嗎？

● Do you want to spend Saturday house-sitting a friend's mansion with me?
你星期六想跟我一起去幫一個朋友的別墅看家嗎？

● Do you want to hang out with me as I film my documentary?
你想跟我一起去拍我的紀錄片嗎？

說明▶ 本句型有更口語的說法，只要說 Want to...? 即可。

Dialogue 簡短對話

A: Do you want to go horseback riding one day next week?

B: Sure! Let me check my calendar... How does Wednesday afternoon sound?

A：你想下星期找一天去騎馬嗎？

B：當然好！我看看我的行事曆……。星期三下午怎麼樣？

字彙		
house-sit (v.) 代爲照看房屋	documentary (n.) 紀錄片
mansion (n.) 獨棟別墅	horseback riding 騎馬
hang out 閒逛，逗留	calendar (n.) 行事曆，日程表
film (v.) 把…拍成電影或電視	

精進度★★★☆☆

句型 **3**

Would you be interested in...?

你有興趣……嗎？

Example 實用例句

● Would you be interested in going to the aquarium together?
你有興趣一起去水族館嗎？

● Would you be interested in taking a yoga class?
你有興趣上瑜伽課嗎？

● Would you be interested in a hot air balloon show?
你有興趣看熱氣球表演嗎？

說明▶ 本句型 in 的後面可以接動名詞（如第一、二個例句）或名詞（如第三個例句）。

Dialogue 簡短對話

A: Would you be interested in attending a lecture on astrophysics?

B: It's kind of you to ask, but I'm afraid it would be completely over my head.

A：你有興趣參加天體物理學的演講嗎？

B：謝謝你的邀請，但我恐怕是鴨子聽雷。

說明 ▶ 拒絕別人邀約的時候，通常會先表示感謝，然後再說明拒絕的原因或理由。

字彙	aquarium (n.) 水族館	lecture (n.) 演講
	yoga (n.) 瑜伽	astrophysics (n.) 天體物理學
	hot air balloon 熱氣球	over someone's head 超過某人的理解範圍

精進度 ★★★★☆

句型 **4**

If you aren't doing anything tonight, would you like to...?

如果你今晚沒事，願意……嗎？

Example 實用例句

● If you aren't doing anything tonight, would you like to have dinner with me?

如果你今晚沒事，願意和我共進晚餐嗎？

● If you aren't doing anything tonight, would you like to go for a drive?

如果你今晚沒事，願意去開車兜風嗎？

● If you aren't doing anything tonight, would you like to get together for a drink?

如果你今晚沒事，願意一起去喝一杯嗎？

說明 ▶ 如果要表達得稍微直接一些，可以把 doing anything 改成 busy。另外，tonight 也可以替換成任何一天或任何一個時間。這個句型常用於約別人外出約會時。

Dialogue 簡短對話

A: If you aren't doing anything on Sunday, would you like to take a day trip out to the vineyards? I could pick you up at your house.

B: That sounds fantastic. Let's call it 9:00 AM.

A：如果你星期日沒事，要不要去葡萄園玩一天？我可以到你家接你。

B：聽起來很棒。我們就約早上九點吧。

說明▶ B 所說的 Let's call it... 是一個很常用的句型，意思大致是 We can make it...（我們就訂在……）或 It can be...（可以訂在……）。

drive (n.) 開車旅行	vineyard (n.) 葡萄園
day trip 一日遊	pick up someone（通常指開車）接載某人

精進度★★★★★

句型5

Would you do me the honor of...?
可否賞光……呢？

Example 實用例句

● Would you do me the honor of accompanying me to the reception?
可否賞光和我一起去參加歡迎會呢？

● Would you do me the honor of joining me for dinner at the consulate?
可否賞光和我一起去參加領事館的晚宴呢？

● Would you do me the honor of being my guest at the victory celebration?
可否賞光來參加我的慶功會呢？

說明▶ 本句型非常正式，通常用於邀請別人一起參加某個特殊場合，例如典禮、婚禮、盛宴等。〈do someone the honor of + 動名詞〉是「給某人…的榮幸」之意。

Dialogue 簡短對話

A: Would you do me the honor of joining me on stage during the product demonstration?

B: Wow, that's quite an invitation, thank you. Honestly, I get stage fright, but I guess as long as I don't have to talk too much, it should be all right.

A：可否賞光和我一起在產品發表會時上台呢？

B：哇，好慎重的邀請，謝謝。說實話，我會怯場，不過只要不必講太多話，我想應該可以吧。

說明 ▶ 回答邀請時，通常會以〈Wow, that's quite a/an + 名詞〉這個句型開頭，一方面表達驚喜，一方面也是給自己一個「緩衝」，可以有時間整理一下思緒，想想該怎麼回應比較好。

字彙

honor (n.) 榮幸	victory (n.) 勝利
accompany (v.) 陪同	demonstration (n.) 示範
reception (n.) 歡迎會，招待會	stage fright 怯場
consulate (n.) 領事館	

相關表達 成功提出邀請後，如果想和對方敲定時間，可以怎麼說呢？

➥ Would 3:30 on Thursday be convenient for you?
星期四下午 3 點 30 分你方便嗎？

➥ Does Saturday work for you?
星期六你可以嗎？

➥ How does 7:00 sound?
七點怎麼樣？

提出預測
Predicting

If you ask me, the law will pass. 句型1

如果你問我的意見，我認為這項法律會通過。

I really think the market will turn around.

我真的認為市場會反轉。

Odds are the two sides will reach an agreement before the deadline. 句型2

雙方很有可能會在期限截止之前達成協議。

I'm not in the prediction business, but the film has a great shot at winning the best picture award.

我不是專門在做預測的人，不過這部電影很有機會贏得最佳影片獎。

There's no way of knowing what will happen.

沒辦法知道會發生什麼事。

I predict the rally will have a big turnout.

我預測這場集會的出席人數會非常多。

I'd like to chance a guess, but things are too uncertain at this point. 句型3

我很想冒險一猜，不過目前實在太不確定了。

Most people think last year's champions will win it all again. 句型4

大部分的人認為去年的冠軍會再度奪冠。

It is very likely that the two branches will merge by the end of the year.

這兩家分公司到年底的時候，非常有可能會合併。

If I had to make a prediction, I'd say the weather is going to clear up this afternoon. 句型5

如果要我預測，我猜今天下午天氣會放晴。

句型 *1*　If you ask me,...
如果你問我的意見，我認為……

EXAMPLE 實用例句

- If you ask me, the law will pass.
  如果你問我的意見，我認為這項法律會通過。

- If you ask me, voters aren't going to put up with yet another tax hike.
  如果你問我的意見，我認為選民不會忍受再一次增稅。

- If you ask me, tourists will jump at the chance to visit the palace.
  如果你問我的意見，我認為觀光客會把握參觀皇宮的機會。

  說明 ▶ 本句型也可以改成 If you want my opinion,...。雖然意思是「如果你問我的意見」，但事實上對方並沒有真的在問說話者的意見。

DIALOGUE 簡短對話

A: If you ask me, kids at the city's public schools are not going to be happy about being served fruit for dessert instead of cake.

B: Maybe not, but it's for their own good.

   A：如果你問我的意見，我認為市立學校的孩童對於甜點從蛋糕變成水果一事，是不會感到開心的。

   B：他們或許不高興，不過這是為他們好。

put up with... 容忍…	jump at... 欣然接受…
yet another 又一次	palace (n.) 宮殿
tax hike 增稅	

句型 *2*　Odds are...
很有可能……

EXAMPLE 實用例句

- Odds are the two sides will reach an agreement before the deadline.
  雙方很有可能會在期限截止之前達成協議。

- Odds are the baseball team will trade a star player for a handful of young prospects.
  這支棒球隊很有可能會用一位明星球員去換幾名年輕的潛力新秀。

- Odds are the things that are bothering you about working conditions are also bothering other employees.
  困擾你的工作環境很有可能也困擾著其他員工。

說明 ▶ odds 的意思是「可能性」，通常是指某個結果發生的可能性，比方說，如果你覺得某件事發生的機率會有五成，就可以說 I'd give it 50/50 odds.。

提出預測

Dialogue 簡短對話

A: Something needs to be done about the high cost of rent downtown.
B: Odds are the problem will take care of itself. People will start moving to the suburbs, driving down rental costs.

A：市區高租金的問題，必須採取一些行動來處理。
B：問題很有可能會自己解決。民眾會開始搬到郊區，導致租金下降。

說明 ▶ 說話者如果覺得某種情況會自行解決，不必採取任何行動，這時就可以說這種情況會 take care of itself（自行解決）。

字彙	
deadline (n.) 截止期限	downtown (adv.) 市中心
trade ... for ～ 用…交換～	suburbs (n.) 郊區
a handful of... 幾個…，少數的…	drive down... 使…下降
prospect (n.) 有潛力的人	

精進度 ★★★★☆

 句型 **3**

I'd like to chance a guess, but...
我很想冒險一猜，不過⋯⋯

Example 實用例句

- I'd like to chance a guess, but things are too uncertain at this point.
  我很想冒險一猜，不過目前實在太不確定了。

- I'd like to chance a guess, but I'd be concerned about getting it wrong.
  我很想冒險一猜，不過我擔心會猜錯。

- I'd like to chance a guess, but who knows what's going to happen?
  我很想冒險一猜，不過誰知道未來會發生什麼事呢？

  說明 ▶ 不想做預測時，搬出這個句型很好用。chance 當動詞時，意思是儘管不確定但願意「冒險」一試。

Dialogue 簡短對話

A: I'm no good at reading the tea leaves. What do you think will happen if the pending regulations go through?

B: I'd like to chance a guess, but right now the future is anything but clear.

  A：我不擅長預測未來。如果那項待決法規通過了，你覺得會怎麼樣呢？

  B：我很想冒險一猜，不過目前看來，未來的情況一點都不明朗。

  說明 ▶ 要表達「一點也不…」或「根本不是…」，可以用〈be anything but + 形容詞〉這個句型。

chance (v.) 冒…的險
guess (n.) 猜測，推斷
read the tea leaves 預測未來

pending (adj.) 懸而未決的
regulation (n.) 法規，規範
go through 通過

句型4

精進度 ★★★★☆

Most people think...
大部分的人認為⋯⋯

Example 實用例句

- Most people think last year's champions will win it all again.
  大部分的人認為去年的冠軍會再度奪冠。

- Most people think global warming will force governments to regulate carbon emissions more tightly.
  大部分的人認為全球暖化會迫使各國政府更嚴格地規範碳排放。

● Most people think the restaurant's home delivery service will be very popular.
大部分的人認為這家餐廳的外送到府服務會非常受歡迎。

說明 ▶ 這是比較婉轉的預測說法，因為這裡提出的是 most people（大部分的人）的想法，而不是斷然提出自己的猜測。另外，win it all 是「贏得冠軍」之意。

Dɪᴀʟᴏɢᴜᴇ 簡短對話

A: The question is, will more newspapers be able to get people to pay for online content?
B: Most people think it's an uphill battle, but I'm optimistic.

A：問題在於，未來會有更多報紙有辦法讓人付費閱讀線上內容嗎？
B：大部分的人認為那是一場非常艱困的戰役，不過我很樂觀。

說明 ▶ B 所說的 uphill battle 是指「艱困的戰鬥或挑戰」。

字彙	
champion (n.) 冠軍	carbon emissions 碳排放
force (v.) 迫使	uphill (adj.) 艱難的，費力的
regulate (v.) 規範	optimistic (adj.) 樂觀的

精進度 ★★★★★

句型 *5*

If I had to make a prediction, I'd say...
如果要我預測，我猜……

Exᴀᴍᴘʟᴇ 實用例句

● If I had to make a prediction, I'd say the weather is going to clear up this afternoon.
如果要我預測，我猜今天下午天氣會放晴。

● If I had to make a prediction, I'd say two-thirds of the committee will vote in our favor.
如果要我預測，我猜委員會有三分之二會投票支持我們。

● If I had to make a prediction, I'd say most subway lines will reopen by Wednesday.
如果要我預測，我猜大部分的地鐵線到星期三會重新開啓。

說明 ▶ 本句型前半部的 If I had to make a prediction 是一個用來表示條件的副詞子句，可以替換成 If I were to guess 或 If I had to guess。注意，這裡的 if 子句表示「與現在事實相反的假設」，所以動詞要用過去式。此外，主要子句 I'd say 後面的子句要用未來式。

Dialogue 簡短對話

A: If I had to make a prediction, I'd say the new flavor will be a big hit with coffee lovers.
B: Those are my thoughts exactly.

A：如果要我預測，我猜這個新口味應該會很受咖啡愛好者的歡迎。
B：我跟你想的一模一樣。

說明 ▶ B 所說的 Those are my thoughts exactly. 用來表示贊同，也可以只說 My thoughts exactly.。

prediction (n.) 預測	in someone's favor 支持某人，對某人有利
committee (n.) 委員會	flavor (n.) 味道

相關表達 關於預測有幾個有趣的慣用說法：

➥ read the tea leaves 預測未來

➥ look into a crystal ball 查看水晶球

➥ divine the future 占卜未來

進行談判
Negotiating

Would you take $25? | 你可以接受 25 美元嗎？

What's your best price? 句型1 | 你最便宜的價格是多少呢？

Twenty thousand yen is the best I can do. | 兩萬日圓就是我的極限了。

How does a 15 percent discount sound? | 15% 的折扣如何呢？

Can I take a few days to consider your offer? 句型2 | 可以給我幾天時間考慮你的提議嗎？

If you're willing to give us exclusive rights, I can pay a higher price. 句型3 | 如果你願意給我們獨家授權，我可以付高一點的價格。

Please feel free to make a counter-offer. | 請盡量提出還價。

What if I were to offer you free shipping? 句型4 | 要是我提供你免費運送呢？

I'm sorry, but I can't go that low. | 很抱歉，我無法接受那麼低的價格。

Would you be open to an offer of 10,000 yen? 句型5 | 你願意接受一萬日圓的報價嗎？

句型 1

What's your best...?
你最好的……是什麼呢？

Example 實用例句

● What's your best price?
你最便宜的價格是多少呢？

● What's your best offer?
你最多能出多少錢呢？

● What's your best package deal?
你最好的套裝方案是什麼呢？

說明 ▶ 有時在簡短的談判（或甚至是冗長的談判）中，其中一方想要快速確定某些條款或結束談判，這時候像這樣簡短的句型就可以 cut to the chase（直截了當，切入正題）。請注意這是一個非常直接、不委婉的句型。

Dialogue 簡短對話

A: I'm afraid I'm running short on time. Let's say I want to order 50 cases of your extra virgin olive oil. What's your best price?

B: Let me work it out... With that volume, I can do 12 euros per case.

　A：我恐怕沒時間了。假設我要訂購你的頂級冷壓初榨橄欖油 50 箱，你可以給我最便宜的價格是多少呢？

　B：讓我算一下……。以那樣的數量來說，我可以給你一箱 12 歐元的價格。

說明 ▶ A 所說的 run short on time 意思是「所剩時間不多」。另外，B 回答 do 12 euros，意思是可以把價格降到一箱 12 歐元。

offer (n.)（賣方的）報價；提議	work out... 計算出…
package deal 套裝方案	volume (n.)（生產、交易等的）量，額
run short 缺乏，不夠	euro (n.) 歐元
case (n.) 箱，盒	

句型 2

Can I ... to consider your offer?
可以給我……考慮你的提議嗎？

Example 實用例句

● Can I take a few days to consider your offer?
可以給我幾天時間考慮你的提議嗎？

● Can I have more time to consider your offer?
可以給我更多時間考慮你的提議嗎？

● Can I ask for another week to consider your offer?
可以再給我一個星期的時間考慮你的提議嗎？

說明 ▶ 協商談判常見的情況之一就是要求更多時間來考慮，這時候就可以用這個句型來表達。

Dialogue 簡短對話

A: Can I have a week or two to consider your offer?
B: Absolutely. Please take your time.

A：可以給我一、兩個星期的時間考慮你的提議嗎？

B：當然沒問題。請慢慢考慮。

 take one's time 不用急，慢慢來

句型 3

If you're willing to..., I can ～
如果你願意……，我可以～

Example 實用例句

● If you're willing to give us exclusive rights, I can pay a higher price.
如果你願意給我們獨家授權，我可以付高一點的價格。

● If you're willing to budge on the agreement length, I can compromise on other issues.
如果你願意對協議實施的時間長度做點讓步，我可以在其他問題上妥協。

進行談判

135

● If you're willing to handle packaging and shipping, I can offer a big discount.
如果你願意處理包裝和運送的部分，我可以打個大折扣給你。

說明 ▶ 本句型用於交換條件時。對話雙方的其中一方做點讓步，以換取另一方在其他方面的妥協。本句型的 If you're willing to... 可以簡化成 If you can...。

Dialogue 簡短對話

A: It looks like we're stuck on the branding issue. We'd like to have our logo on the front, back, and side of the package.

B: I've talked it over with my team. If you're willing to handle a bigger share of the marketing, I can agree to your branding needs.

A：看起來我們卡在商標刻印的問題。我們希望把我們的商標放在包裝的前、後及側邊。

B：我和我的團隊仔細討論過了。如果你們願意處理更多的行銷工作，我可以同意你們的商標需求。

字彙	
exclusive rights 獨家授權	shipping (n.) 運輸，運送
budge (v.) 讓步	stuck (adj.) 卡住的
compromise (v.) 妥協	brand (v.) 印商標於
issue (n.) 爭論的問題	talk something over 仔細討論某事

精進度★★★★☆

句型4
What if I were to offer you...?
要是我提供你……呢？

Example 實用例句

● What if I were to offer you free shipping?
要是我提供你免費運送呢？

● What if I were to offer you a ten percent discount?
要是我提供你 10% 的折扣呢？

● What if I were to offer you $33,000 for the entire contents of the warehouse?
要是我出價三萬三千美元買下倉庫裡所有的物品呢？

說明 ▶ 可以利用本句型來向對方釋放出某種誘因、折扣或金錢的資訊。本句型也可以用 What would you say if I were to offer you...?（要是我提供你……，怎麼樣呢？）來表達。

Dialogue 簡短對話

A: I'm afraid delivery by sea would take too long. Besides, other vendors ship by air.

B: What if I were to offer you our same low cost with shipping via express courier? You'll have the products in hand in three days.

A：恐怕海運花的時間會太長，再說，其他供應商都是用空運。

B：要是我提供你同樣低的價格，再加上用快遞運送呢？三天後你就可以拿到商品了。

warehouse (n.) 倉庫	vendor (n.) 供應商
delivery (n.) 遞送，運送	express courier 快遞

精進度★★★★★

句型 *5*

Would you be open to an offer of...?
你願意接受……的報價嗎？

Example 實用例句

● Would you be open to an offer of 10,000 yen?
你願意接受一萬日圓的報價嗎？

● Would you be open to an offer of 450 yen per unit, which is 5 percent more than our previous bid?
你願意接受每組 450 日圓嗎？這比我們之前的出價多了 5%。

● Would you be open to an offer of the original price plus free onsite repair for the life of the unit?
你願意接受原本的價格再加上終身免費到府維修嗎？

說明 ▶ 本句型可用於一開始提出報價或提高原先的報價時。這裡的 offer 可以包含一筆金額或是產品、服務等。本句型也可以改以 Would you be more willing to accept an offer of...? 來表達。

Dialogue 簡短對話

A: Would you be open to an offer of twenty million yen? I think that's very competitive.

B: I'll check with my boss and see if we can do that.

A：你願意接受兩千萬日圓的報價嗎？我認為這個價格很有競爭力。

B：我再向我的老闆確認一下，看看我們可不可以接受。

| 字彙 | bid (n.) 投標，出價 | onsite repair 到府維修 |
| | plus (prep.) 加 | competitive (adj.) 有競爭力的 |

相關表達 進行談判時還有幾個相當好用的說法：

➥ I'm afraid my hands are tied.
我恐怕無能為力。

➥ I'm sure we can come to an agreement.
我有把握我們能夠達成協議。

➥ I'll check with my boss and see if we can do that.
我會問我老闆，看看可不可以接受。

➥ How soon do you need to know?
需要多快給你答案呢？

說服他人
Persuading

非正式

What can I do to convince you? 句型 *1*

我該怎麼做才能讓你相信呢？

Did you consider (that) there's also a 10-day money back guarantee?

你有仔細考慮過還有十天的退款保證嗎？

稍非正式

Is there anything I can do to change your mind?

我可以做些什麼來改變你的心意嗎？

I'm certainly open to hearing other ideas. 句型 *2*

我當然很樂意聆聽其他想法。

一般情況

Another positive benefit is we'll handle the inventory management and distribution. 句型 *3*

另一個正面的好處是，我們會處理庫存管理和配銷。

Please keep in mind we have a 99 percent customer satisfaction record.

請別忘記，我們有 99% 的客戶滿意紀錄。

稍正式

I honestly believe this deal is in your best interest. 句型 *4*

我真心認為這筆交易最符合你們的利益。

What would you say your main objections are? 句型 *5*

你說說你反對的主要理由是什麼呢？

正式

If you weigh all sides, I think you'll see our service will work out the best for you.

如果你考量各個層面，我想你會看得出來，我們的服務最適合你。

I wonder if I might be able to persuade you to reconsider.

不知道我能不能夠說服你再考慮一下。

句型 1

What can I do to...?

我該怎麼做才能⋯⋯呢？

EXAMPLE 實用例句

- What can I do to convince you?
  我該怎麼做才能讓你相信呢？

- What can I do to persuade you?
  我該怎麼做才能說服你呢？

- What can I do to change your mind?
  我該怎麼做才能讓你改變心意呢？

  說明 ▶ 本句型是一個問句，也可以改成直述句，例如第一個例句可改成
  Tell me what I can do to convince you.（告訴我，我該怎麼做才能讓你相
  信。）無論是問句還是直述句，當自己所提出的觀點無法說服對方時，便
  可以使用本句型進一步向對方詢問。

DIALOGUE 簡短對話

A: What can I do to make you see things my way?

B: To be frank, I need fewer promises and more guarantees.

　A：我該怎麼做才能讓你從我的角度來看事情呢？

　B：坦白說，我需要少一點承諾，多一點保證。

字彙	convince (v.) 說服，使相信	promise (n.) 承諾
	frank (adj.) 坦白的	guarantee (n.) 保證

句型 2

I'm certainly open to hearing...

我當然很樂意聆聽⋯⋯

EXAMPLE 實用例句

- I'm certainly open to hearing other ideas.
  我當然很樂意聆聽其他想法。

- I'm certainly open to hearing alternative suggestions.
  我當然很樂意聆聽其他替代建議。

- I'm certainly open to hearing about different options.
  我當然很樂意聆聽其他不同的選項。

  說明 ▶ 本句型也可以稍微做點變化，例如將 I'm certainly open to hearing other ideas. 變成 If you have any other ideas, I'm certainly open to hearing them.（如果你有任何其他想法，我當然很樂意聽聽看。）本句型通常用於雙方在討論的過程中進展不順利時。

Dialogue 簡短對話

A: Maybe we need to bring in someone who hasn't been involved to this point.

B: I'm certainly open to hearing a fresh perspective.

A：或許我們必須邀請尚未涉入到這個程度的人加入。

B：我當然很樂意聽取全新的觀點。

alternative (adj.) 替代的，備用的	to this point 到達這個程度
bring in... 邀請…，引入…	perspective (n.) 觀點

精進度 ★★★☆☆

句型 *3*

Another positive benefit is...
另一個正面的好處是……

Example 實用例句

- Another positive benefit is we'll handle the inventory management and distribution.
  另一個正面的好處是，我們會處理庫存管理和配銷。

- Another positive benefit is our headquarters is in the same city as yours, so we can provide immediate service.
  另一個正面的好處是，我們的總部與你們的總部位於同一座城市，所以我們可以提供立即的服務。

- Another positive benefit is our sunglasses appeal to consumers in several key age groups.
  另一個正面的好處是，我們的太陽眼鏡對好幾個重要年齡層的消費者很有吸引力。

  說明 ▶ 如果要提出具體且詳細的好處來說服對方，可以使用本句型來表達。

Dialogue 簡短對話

A: We'll match any competitor's offer. Another positive benefit is our lighting systems meet the highest energy efficiency standards.
B: That is helpful. Our energy bills are getting out of hand.

A：我們會比照任何競爭對手所開出的條件來辦理。另一個正面的好處是，我們的照明系統符合最高的節能標準。
B：那很有幫助。我們的能源帳單愈來愈失控了。

字彙
positive (adj.) 正面的，積極的	competitor (n.) 競爭對手
inventory management 庫存管理	energy efficiency 節能
distribution (n.) 配銷	standard (n.) 標準
headquarters (n.)（企業、機構等的）總部	energy bill
appeal to... 吸引…	能源帳單（指電費、冷暖氣等的帳單）
consumer (n.) 消費者	get out of hand 失去控制
age group 年齡層	

句型 4

精進度★★★★☆

I honestly believe this deal...
我真心認為這筆交易……

Example 實用例句

- I honestly believe this deal is in your best interest.
  我真心認為這筆交易最符合你們的利益。

- I honestly believe this deal benefits us both.
  我真心認為這筆交易對我們雙方都有利。

- I honestly believe this deal meets all of your needs.
  我真心認為這筆交易可以滿足你們所有的需求。

說明 ▶ 本句型使用於企圖說服對方相信這筆交易是有利、有益時。副詞 honestly 可以替換成 truly。

Dialogue 簡短對話

A: I honestly believe this deal works well for both parties.

B: I'm still not entirely convinced, but I'm willing to give it another look.

A：我真心認為這筆交易對雙方都有好處。

B：我仍然不完全相信，不過我願意再考慮看看。

字彙

interest (n.) 利益	party (n.)（契約等的）當事人，一方
benefit (v.) 有益於	entirely (adv.) 完全地
meet someone's needs 符合某人的需求	

精進度★★★★☆

句型5

What would you say ... are?
你說說⋯⋯是什麼呢？

Example 實用例句

- What would you say your main objections are?
  你說說你反對的主要理由是什麼呢？

- What would you say the chief stumbling blocks are?
  你說說主要的障礙是什麼呢？

- What would you say your areas of concern are?
  你說說你的顧慮是什麼呢？

說明 ▶ 像第一個例句這樣的問題，另一個更直接的問法是 What are your main objections?（你反對的主要理由是什麼呢？）。也可以在本句型的開頭加上 From your point of view,（依你來看，），例如第二個例句可改成 From your point of view, what are the chief stumbling blocks?。

說服他人

Dialogue 簡短對話

A: What would you say the remaining sticking points are?

B: The biggest one is the reporting issue. We'd like to have something approaching real-time reporting of the daily sales figures.

A：你說說還剩下哪些困難之處呢？

B：最大的一個是通報問題。我們希望有一個接近即時的通報制度，報告每天的銷售數字。

說明 ► A 所說的 sticking point(s) 是「困難點，瓶頸」之意；相對地，如果解決了一個問題，就可以用 smooth it over。

字彙

objection (n.) 反對的理由
chief (adj.) 主要的
stumbling block 障礙物，絆腳石
concern (n.) 顧慮

real-time (adj.) 即時的
figure (n.) 數字
smooth over... 平息…，紓解…

相關表達　這裡進一步提供其他用來說服別人的好用說法：

➥ Here's something else to consider.
還有其他必須考慮的事項。

➥ We'll match any competitor's offer.
我們會比照任何競爭對手所開出的條件來辦理。

➥ I've got something that might convince you.
我有東西或許能說服你。

➥ Please don't make a decision too quickly.
請不要太快下決定。

提出理由／說辭
Giving Reasons/Making Excuses

What happened was we got stuck in traffic.
句型1

原因是我們塞車了。

The QC problems were caused by a batch of inferior components.

品管問題起因於一批次級零件。

Not to make excuses, but we were understaffed.

不是找藉口,而是我們的人手不夠。

A problem with the electrical wiring is to blame. 句型2

原因要歸咎於電線問題。

There were a number of reasons behind the decision to raise prices.

漲價的決策背後有許多理由。

As far as I can tell, all the applicants faced the same difficulties. 句型3

就我所了解,所有應徵者都面臨到相同的難題。

I accept full responsibility for the mix-up.

我為搞混承擔所有責任。

The reason for the delay was a software glitch. 句型4

延誤的原因是軟體發生小故障。

Due to unseasonably hot weather, many grapes died on the vine.

由於反常的炎熱天氣,使得葡萄藤上有很多葡萄枯掉。

We've come to the conclusion that population shifts have led to a shrinking market. 句型5

我們做出了結論,人口流動導致了市場萎縮。

句型 1

What happened was...
原因是⋯⋯

Example 實用例句

- What happened was we got stuck in traffic.
  原因是我們塞車了。

- What happened was my phone couldn't get reception up in the mountains.
  原因是我的電話在山上收不到訊號。

- What happened was I left my laptop at home, so I couldn't get any work done.
  原因是我把筆電留在家裡了,所以無法做任何工作。

  說明 ▶ 本句型在口語中很常用,後面接一個子句,進行說明。其他類似的句型還有 What went wrong was... (問題出在⋯⋯)。

Dialogue 簡短對話

A: We waited for you for 30 minutes. What happened?
B: I am so sorry. What happened was I got the dates mixed up in my calendar. I thought we were meeting tomorrow.
  A:我們等了你半小時,發生了什麼事?
  B:很對不起。我把日期搞混了,我以為我們明天才見面。

 字彙

reception (n.) 接收效果	get ... mixed up 把⋯弄混淆
laptop (n.) 筆記型電腦	

句型 2

...be to blame.
原因要歸咎於⋯⋯

Example 實用例句

- A problem with the electrical wiring is to blame.
  原因要歸咎於電線問題。

- A lack of accounting oversight was to blame.
  原因要歸咎於欠缺會計監督。

- A number of mistakes with the original design specs were to blame.
  原因要歸咎於原始設計規格出現了許多錯誤。

  說明 ▶ 本句型用於直接表達問題發生的原因，be 動詞可以用現在式或過去式。

Dialogue 簡短對話

A: Did they ever find out what started the fire?

B: They did. Apparently, some rats chewing on the power lines were to blame.

A：他們有找出起火的原因嗎？

B：有，很顯然，要歸咎於一些老鼠把電源線啃食掉了。

字彙

blame (v.) 責怪	apparently (adv.) 顯然地
electrical wiring 電線	rat (n.) 老鼠
accounting oversight 會計監督	chew (v.)（人或動物）咬，啃
specs (n.) 規格 (= specifications)	

精進度 ★★★ ☆ ☆

句型 3　As far as I can tell,...
就我所了解，……

Example 實用例句

- As far as I can tell, all the applicants faced the same difficulties.
  就我所了解，所有應徵者都面臨到相同的難題。

- As far as I can tell, the garage filled up and guests couldn't find anywhere to park.
  就我所了解，車庫停滿了，客人找不到地方停車。

- As far as I can tell, we were supposed to bring our receipts to the 7th floor for a tax refund.
  就我所了解，我們應該帶著收據到七樓退稅。

提出理由／說辭

說明 ▶ 本句型用於不完全確定發生了什麼事的時候，句首的 as far as I can tell 具有緩衝的作用，萬一說話者最後證明說錯了也不會受到責難。

Dialogue 簡短對話

A: As far as I can tell, the server crashed when too many people tried to log on at the same time.

B: If that's the case, we need to get the problem taken care of. We can't afford for it to happen again.

A：就我所了解，太多人同時登入的時候，伺服器就會當機。

B：如果是這樣，我們就必須把問題解決。我們承擔不起這種事情再度發生。

說明 ▶ 如果必須馬上解決某個嚴重問題，或是避免再度發生，這時就可以用 We can't afford...（我們承擔不起……）這個句型，例如 Every day that we're closed, we're losing money. We can't afford for this situation to continue much longer.（我們每天打烊休息時就虧錢，我們承擔不起這種情況再繼續下去了。）

字彙	
applicant (n.) 應徵者，申請人	server (n.) 伺服器
garage (n.) 車庫	crash (v.) 當機
tax refund 退稅	

精進度 ★★★★☆

句型 **4**

The reason for the ... was ～
……的原因是～

Example 實用例句

● The reason for the delay was a software glitch.
延誤的原因是軟體發生小故障。

● The reason for the malfunction was an operator error.
發生故障的原因是操作人員的失誤。

● The reason for the recession was a real estate bubble.
經濟衰退的原因是房地產泡沫化。

說明 ▶ 在本句型中，發生的事件（通常是負面的事情）要放在 The reason for the 的後面，發生的原因則放在動詞 was 的後面。for 也可以替換成 behind，變成 The reason behind the ... was ～。

Dialogue 簡短對話

A: A lot of people are grumbling about the higher coffee prices.

B: I know. The reason behind the hike was a sharp increase in the price of beans. My hands were tied.

A：很多人在抱怨咖啡價格變貴。

B：我知道。漲價背後的原因是咖啡豆價格大漲，我也束手無策啊。

字彙

glitch (n.) 小故障
malfunction (n.) 故障
operator (n.) 操作人員
recession (n.) 經濟衰退
real estate bubble 房地產泡沫化

grumble (v.) 發牢騷
hike (n.)（價格）上升
sharp (adj.) 急遽的
someone's hands were tied 某人束手無策

精進度★★★★★

句型 *5*

We've come to the conclusion that...
我們做出了結論……

Example 實用例句

- We've come to the conclusion that population shifts have led to a shrinking market.
  我們做出了結論，人口流動導致了市場萎縮。

- We've come to the conclusion that nothing could have prevented the landslide.
  我們做出了結論，這次山崩完全無法避免。

- We've come to the conclusion that social media, though potentially lucrative, is changing too fast for our purposes.
  我們做出了結論，社群媒體雖然有獲利潛力，但是對我們的目標來說變化太快了。

提出理由／說辭

說明 ▶ 如果要強調是經過深思熟慮之後才做出結論，可以在本句型的一開頭加上 After due consideration（經過充分的思考之後），變成 After due consideration, we've come to the conclusion that...。

Dialogue 簡短對話

A: What was the result of your team's analysis?

B: We've come to the conclusion that the store closure was inevitable. There was nothing we could have done to stop it.

A：你們團隊分析的結果是什麼？

B：我們做出的結論是，關閉這家門市是不可避免的事，我們無法事先做什麼來阻止它的發生。

字彙		
population shift 人口流動		lucrative (adj.) 獲利多的
shrink (v.) 萎縮		due (adj.) 充分的
landslide (n.) 山崩		analysis (n.) 分析
social media 社群媒體		closure (n.)（企業、工廠等的）永久性關閉
potentially (adv.) 有潛力地		inevitable (adj.) 不可避免的

相關表達 要如何表達錯不在己呢？

➥ There was nothing we could do about it. 我們無能為力。

➥ It was out of my hands. 超出我所能掌控的地步了。

➥ My hands were tied. 我束手無策。

➥ We did our best. 我們盡力了。

提供建言或忠告
Giving Advice

非正式

Why not install brighter lights? 句型1

為什麼不安裝比較明亮的燈呢？

You'd better spend two or three months preparing for the TOEIC.

你最好花兩、三個月的時間準備多益測驗。

稍非正式

You need to find another agent.

你必須再另外找個仲介。

I recommend spending a bit more for a washing machine that will last longer. 句型2

我建議多花一點錢買一台可以使用比較久的洗衣機。

一般情況

If I were you, I'd go to Korea in October instead of November.

如果我是你，我會十月去韓國，而不是十一月去。

If you ask me, it might be time to cut your losses and close the business.

如果你問我的意見，我認為該是減少虧損、結束生意的時候了。

稍正式

My advice would be to look for an apartment near your job. 句型3

我的建議是在你工作地點的附近找一間公寓。

It wouldn't be a bad idea to diversify your investments.

分散你的投資準沒錯。

正式

You might want to consider boarding up your windows before the storm hits. 句型4

你或許可以考慮在暴風雨來襲之前把窗戶用木板封好。

I'm not sure (if) I'm qualified to give advice, but a conservative approach might be best. 句型5

我不知道我夠不夠資格給你建言，不過採取保守的做法或許是最好的。

句型 *1*

Why not...?

為什麼不……呢？

Example 實用例句

- Why not install brighter lights?
  為什麼不安裝比較明亮的燈呢？

- Why not have one party with your work friends and another with your relatives?
  為什麼不辦一個給工作友人的派對，並辦另一個給親戚的派對呢？

- Why not get some rechargeable batteries so you don't have to keep buying new ones?
  為什麼不買一些可重複充電的電池，這樣就不必一直買新的電池了？

說明 ▶ Why not...? 是一個很有趣的句型，有時候是個問句，有時候是個直述句。Why not...? 作問句時可用來提供建議，此時句尾語調要上揚。用本句型來提供建議，不僅可降低衝擊，又能給對方回答的空間。

Dialogue 簡短對話

A: I'm never going to get all my shopping done by Christmas.

B: Why not do some of it online? A lot of places will even ship for free.

　　A：我從來沒在耶誕節之前把所有我要的東西採買完畢。

　　B：為什麼不在網路上買呢？很多地方甚至還免運費。

relative (n.) 親戚	ship (v.) 運送
rechargeable battery 可重複充電的電池	for free 免費

句型 *2*

I recommend...

我建議……

Example 實用例句

- I recommend spending a bit more for a washing machine that will last longer.
  我建議多花一點錢買一台可以使用比較久的洗衣機。

● I recommend starting with light exercise like jogging before doing anything strenuous.
我建議開始做一些輕量運動，像是慢跑，然後才開始做激烈運動。

● I recommend following some top designers on Twitter if you want to catch up on fashion trends.
如果你想跟上時尚潮流，我建議你在推特上追蹤一些頂尖設計師。

說明▶ 如果要提供建言或忠告，這是一個非常簡單但相當有效的說法。若要顯得更正式一點，可以說 I would recommend...，或更加正式的 I might recommend...。recommend 的後面若要接另一個動詞，必須用動名詞。

Dialogue 簡短對話

A: I don't know how I'm going to get out from under this mountain of debt.

B: I've been in your shoes before. I recommend consolidating your credit card payments so you only have to make one payment per month.

A：我不知道該如何擺脫堆積如山的債務。

B：我以前也曾陷入和你一樣的處境。我建議把你的信用卡付款整合起來，每個月只要付一筆就好。

說明▶ A 所說的 get out from under... 意思是「脫離…的困境」，意即擺脫某種負擔，像是沉重的工作負荷、債務等。另外，如果有人說自己 have been in your shoes before，表示這個人以前也有過類似的經驗。

strenuous (adj.) 激烈的
catch up on... 趕上…
trend (n.) 趨勢

mountain of debt 堆積如山的債務
consolidate (v.) 將…合併

精進度★★★★☆

句型 *3*

My advice would be to...
我的建議是……

Example 實用例句

● My advice would be to look for an apartment near your job.
我的建議是在你工作地點的附近找一間公寓。

● My advice would be to try to relax and stop taking work home with you.
我的建議是試著放鬆一下，不要再把工作帶回家。

● My advice would be to confront Stephanie with what you heard and see how she reacts.
我的建議是把你所聽到的，拿去和思黛芬妮當面對質，看看她的反應如何。

說明 ▶ 可以在 advice 的前面加 best，變成 My best advice would be to...。
to 的後面用原形動詞。另外，advice 可以替換成 suggestion。

Dialogue 簡短對話

A: I've put so much money into this old car. It's like a giant sink hole.

B: My advice would be to start shopping for a new car. It's time you let this one go.

A：我已經在這輛舊車上花了好多錢，它就像一個巨大的錢坑。

B：我的建議是開始去採購新車。該是放掉這輛舊車的時候了。

說明 ▶ 如果在房屋、汽車、船等東西上投入很多金錢，可用〈put + 金錢 + into + 事物〉表達，例如 Mario put his life savings into the business.（馬力歐把畢生積蓄投入事業中。）

| relax (v.) 放鬆 | react (v.) 做出回應 |
| confront (v.) 與…當面對質 | let something go 放掉某物 |

精進度 ★★★★★

句型 4　You might want to consider...
你或許可以考慮……

Example 實用例句

● You might want to consider boarding up your windows before the storm hits.
你或許可以考慮在暴風雨來襲之前把窗戶用木板封好。

● You might want to consider scheduling your vacation during the off-peak season.
你或許可以考慮把假期安排在淡季。

● You might want to consider taking a class to help prepare for the TOEFL.
你或許可以考慮去報名上課，準備托福考試。

說明 ▶ 本句型還有一個類似說法：Maybe you could consider...（或許你可以考慮……）。另一個類似但比較直接有力的說法是 You really should consider...（你真的應該考慮……）。consider 的後面通常接動名詞。

Dialogue 簡短對話

A: The roofer said this whole section needs to be replaced.
B: Can I give you some advice? You might want to consider getting a second opinion.

A：裝修屋頂的人說這整個部分都需要換掉。
B：我可以給你一些建議嗎？你或許可以考慮徵詢第二個意見。

說明 ▶ 碰到醫療、汽車修護、房屋修繕等問題時，建議對方去尋求 second opinion（第二個意見）是很常見的。second opinion 是指徵詢另一名專業人士的看法或建議。

字彙	board up... 將…木板封住	off-peak season 淡季
	hit (v.) 襲擊	roofer (n.) 裝修屋頂的人

精進度 ★★★★★

句型 5

I'm not sure (if) I'm qualified to give advice, but...
我不知道我夠不夠資格給你建言，不過……

Example 實用例句

● I'm not sure if I'm qualified to give advice, but a conservative approach might be best.
我不知道我夠不夠資格給你建言，不過採取保守的做法或許是最好的。

- I'm not sure I'm qualified to give advice, but the fall is usually a good time to release new toys.
  我不知道我夠不夠資格給你建言，不過秋天通常是推出新玩具的好時機。

- I'm not sure if I'm qualified to give advice, but I've heard that learning a musical instrument can help children improve their math.
  我不知道我夠不夠資格給你建言，不過我聽說學樂器可以幫助孩童增進數學能力。

  說明 ▶ 本句型是一個比較謙虛、保守的說法。另一個類似且常見的說法是 I don't know if I should be giving anyone advice, but...（我不知道我應不應該給人建言，不過……），通常用於說話者覺得自己有缺點或不適合給別人建言時。

Dialogue 簡短對話

A: My computer is running slower and slower.

B: I'm not sure if I'm qualified to give advice, but uninstalling and reinstalling the operating system might speed it up.

A：我的電腦愈跑愈慢了。

B：我不知道我夠不夠資格給你建言，不過將作業系統移除之後再重新安裝，可能會讓它跑快一點。

字彙	
conservative (adj.) 保守的	musical instrument 樂器
approach (n.) 方法，做法	run (v.) 運作
release (v.) 推出，發行	operating system 作業系統

相關表達　提供建言或忠告之前的開場白有哪些呢？

➥ Can I give you some advice?　我可以給你一些建言嗎？

➥ Take it from me.　相信我。

➥ I've been in a similar position.　我有過類似的處境。

➥ I've been in your shoes before.　我以前也遇過跟你一樣的情況。

詢問別人的意見
Asking for Someone's Opinion

非正式

What do you think? Should the lunch break be extended by 30 minutes? 句型 *1*

你是怎麼看的呢？午休時間應該延長半小時嗎？

Are you on board with Cathy's suggestion?

你贊成凱西的提議嗎？

稍非正式

Do you support the decision to close one of the branches? 句型 *2*

你贊成關閉其中一家分店的決定嗎？

How do you feel about hiring someone to redo our website?

請人來重弄我們的網站，你覺得如何？

一般情況

I'd love to hear your thoughts on the new design. 句型 *3*

我很想聽聽你對這個新設計有何看法。

What would you say if I told you we're relocating to another city?

如果我告訴你我們要搬到另一座城市，你有什麼看法呢？

稍正式

Your assessment would be invaluable.

你的評估很寶貴。

I wonder what your take is on the proposal to change our logo. 句型 *4*

針對更改我們商標的提議，我想知道你的看法如何。

正式

Would you mind sharing your point of view with us?

你介意和我們分享你的看法嗎？

If you don't mind my asking, were you in agreement with the board's decision? 句型 *5*

如果不介意我問的話，你贊同董事會的決定嗎？

句型 **1**

What do you think?

你是怎麼看的呢？/ 你的看法如何？

Example 實用例句

● What do you think? Should the lunch break be extended by 30 minutes?

你是怎麼看的呢？午休時間應該延長半小時嗎？

● What do you think? Is there a better way to reduce childhood obesity rates?

你的看法如何？有更好的方法來降低兒童肥胖症的比例嗎？

● What do you think? Does the prime minister deserve to stay in power?

你的看法如何？總理應該繼續掌權嗎？

說明 ▶ 本句型可以替換成 What's your opinion?（你的意見是什麼？），或更口語的說法：Where do you stand?（你是怎麼看的？）。

Dialogue 簡短對話

A: What do you think? Will we ever get over our dependence on fossil fuels?

B: I sure hope so. We can't ignore climate change forever.

A：你的看法如何？我們有可能克服對化石燃料的依賴嗎？

B：我當然希望如此。我們無法永遠忽視氣候變遷的事實。

字彙	
lunch break 午休時間	get over... 克服…
extend (v.) 延長	dependence (n.) 依賴
childhood obesity 兒童肥胖症	fossil fuel 化石燃料
prime minister 總理，首相	ignore (v.) 忽視
deserve (v.) 值得，應得	climate change 氣候變遷

句型2

Do you support...?
你贊成……嗎？

Example 實用例句

● Do you support the decision to close one of the branches?
你贊成關閉其中一家分店的決定嗎？

● Do you support the union's call for a strike?
你贊成工會的罷工呼籲嗎？

● Do you support a temporary tax to pay for harbor repairs?
你贊成繳交臨時稅來支應港口整修嗎？

說明 ▶ 本句型的 support（贊成，支持）也可以替換成 agree with（贊同……的意見）。

Dialogue 簡短對話

A: I've been meaning to ask you. Do you support the switch to fair trade cinnamon?

B: I do, as long as it doesn't impact our bottom line.

　A：我一直想問你。你贊成改用公平貿易肉桂嗎？

　B：我贊成，只要不影響我們的盈虧就行了。

字彙	
branch (n.) 分店，分公司	fair trade 公平貿易
union (n.) 工會	cinnamon (n.) 肉桂
call (n.) 呼籲	impact (v.) 衝擊，影響
strike (n.) 罷工	bottom line 盈虧總額
harbor (n.) 港口	

句型3

I'd love to hear your thoughts on...
我很想聽聽你對……有何看法。

Example 實用例句

● I'd love to hear your thoughts on the new design.
我很想聽聽你對這個新設計有何看法。

詢問別人的意見

- I'd love to hear your thoughts on my presentation.
  我很想聽聽你對我的簡報有何看法。

- I'd love to hear your thoughts on these drawings.
  我很想聽聽你對這些素描有何看法。

  說明 ▶ on 的後面要接名詞。另外，your thoughts on 可以替換成 how you feel about，整個句型就變成 I'd love to hear how you feel about...。

Dialogue 簡短對話

A: Can I ask you something? I'd love to hear your thoughts on the building's "no pets" policy.

B: Well, on the one hand, I can understand the landlord wanting to protect his property. On the other hand, it would be nice to be able to have a cat.

  A：我可以問你一件事嗎？我很想聽聽你對這棟大樓的「禁養寵物」政策有何看法。

  B：嗯，一方面，我可以了解房東希望保護他自己的財產，但是話又說回來，如果可以養貓會很好。

drawing (n.) 素描　　　　　　　　　landlord (n.) 房東
on the one hand ... on the other hand ～　　property (n.) 財產
從一方面來看……從另一方面來看～

精進度★★★★☆

句型 *4*　**I wonder what your take is on...**
針對……，我想知道你的看法如何。

Example 實用例句

- I wonder what your take is on the proposal to change our logo.
  針對更改我們商標的提議，我想知道你的看法如何。

- I wonder what your take is on the revisions to the immigration laws.
  針對移民法的修訂，我想知道你的看法如何。

I wonder what your take is on corporate's decision to redo the employee uniforms.
針對公司決定重做員工制服，我想知道你的看法如何。

說明 ▶ 雖然本句型是直述句，但其實是在問對方的意見。如果要把直述句改成直接問句，便可以說 What's your take on...? 。take 是「看法，觀點」的意思。

Dialogue 簡短對話

A: I wonder what your take is on the theater's upcoming schedule.
B: It's pretty good. I'm really looking forward to seeing *Macbeth*.

A：我想知道你對戲院即將實施的時刻表有何看法。
B：那個時刻表相當好。我很期待去看《馬克白》。

take (n.) 看法，觀點　　　　immigration (n.) 移民
logo (n.) 商標　　　　　　　corporate (n.) 公司
revision (n.) 修訂　　　　　uniform (n.) 制服

精進度★★★★★

句型*5*

If you don't mind my asking,...?
如果不介意我問的話，……？

Example 實用例句

● If you don't mind my asking, were you in agreement with the board's decision?
如果不介意我問的話，你贊同董事會的決定嗎？

● If you don't mind my asking, was a full review of our safety procedures really necessary?
如果不介意我問的話，真的有必要全盤檢討我們的安全流程嗎？

● If you don't mind my asking, did you like the way the parade turned out?
如果不介意我問的話，你喜歡這場遊行最後的結果嗎？

161

說明 ▶ 徵詢對方的意見時若不想過於唐突,可以使用本句型來表達。副詞子句 if you don't mind my asking 也可以替換成 if it's all right to ask(如果可以問的話)。主要子句則是一個問句。

Dialogue 簡短對話

A: If you don't mind my asking, would you have handled the crisis differently?

B: Not at all. Your team did a magnificent job.

A:如果你不介意我問的話,你會用不同的方式來處理這個危機嗎?

B:完全不會。你的團隊表現得非常好。

字彙		
board (n.) 董事會 (= board of directors)	handle (v.) 處理
safety procedure 安全流程	crisis (n.) 危機
parade (n.) 遊行	magnificent (adj.) 令人印象深刻的
turn out... 結果…	

相關表達 詢問別人的意見之前,有哪些常用的開場白呢?

⇥ I've been meaning to ask you. 我一直想問你。

⇥ I wanted to get your opinion (about/on…). 我想聽聽你(對……)的意見。

⇥ Can I ask you something? 我可以問你事情嗎?

⇥ Would you mind if I picked your brain? 你介意我請教你一下嗎?

說明 ▶ pick someone's brain 的意思是「向某人詢問事情」。

I think the spa's service is top notch.

我認為這個水療服務是一流的。

In my opinion, the soup is a bit salty. 句型 1

在我看來,這湯有點鹹。

The way I see it, customer service should be a top priority. 句型 2

我是這麼看的,客戶服務應該是第一優先才對。

If you ask me, the curtains are too dark.

如果你問我的意見,我認為這窗簾太暗了。

From my perspective, nothing needs to be changed. 句型 3

從我的觀點看來,不需要做任何改變。

Maybe we should consider hiring a consultant.

或許我們應該考慮聘請一位顧問。

We need to proceed with caution would be my take. 句型 4

我們必須謹慎繼續進行,這是我的意見。

It might be useful to set up a customer hotline.

成立一條消費者專線或許會有幫助。

I'm not an expert, but it seems to me the windows could be slightly wider. 句型 5

我不是專家,不過在我看來這扇窗戶可以再稍微寬一點。

If I may venture an opinion, I'd say we need to be careful about spending too much on new technology.

如果我可以大膽提出我的看法,我認為我們必須謹慎小心,不要花太多錢在新科技上。

句型 1

In my opinion,...
在我看來，……

EXAMPLE 實用例句

- In my opinion, the soup is a bit salty.
  在我看來，這湯有點鹹。

- In my opinion, Doris would make an excellent supervisor.
  在我看來，桃瑞絲會是很優秀的主管。

- In my opinion, we should repair the forklift instead of getting a new one.
  在我看來，我們應該把堆高機修一修，而不是買一輛新的。

說明▶ 這是表達意見時最簡單、最常用的說法。表達意見前先說 In my opinion,...，可以軟化語氣，比較不會那麼咄咄逼人。

DIALOGUE 簡短對話

A: In my opinion, this wool is too abrasive. I wouldn't want to use it for our scarves.

B: Maybe not for our high-end scarves, but I can see the potential for a new, low-end line.

A：在我看來，這種羊毛太粗糙了，我不會想用在我們的圍巾上。

B：或許不適合用於我們的高檔圍巾，不過我看有潛力成為一個新的低階產品線。

forklift (n.) 堆高機 (= forklift truck)	scarf (n.) 圍巾
wool (n.) 羊毛	potential (adj.) 有潛力的，可能的
abrasive (adj.) 粗糙的	low-end (adj.) 低階的

句型 2

The way I see it,...
我是這麼看的，……

EXAMPLE 實用例句

- The way I see it, customer service should be a top priority.
  我是這麼看的，客戶服務應該是第一優先才對。

● The way I see it, losses from shoplifting are inevitable in the retail sector.
我是這麼看的，順手牽羊的損失在零售業是不可避免的。

● The way I see it, a rooftop garden would be perfect for small get-togethers and performances.
我是這麼看的，屋頂花園最適合小型聚會和表演。

說明 ▶ 本句型還有另外兩個類似的說法：The way I look at things,... 和 The way I see the situation,... 。

Dialogue 簡短對話

A: The way I see it, the more we spend on R&D, the more we'll benefit in the future.
B: I'd like to increase our R&D budget, but that's going to have to wait until we're in the black again.

A：我是這麼看的，我們在研發上的花費愈多，未來獲利也會愈多。
B：我也想增加研發預算，不過那得等到我們轉虧為盈。

說明 ▶ 公司如果有賺錢，就是 in the black（有盈餘）；如果處於虧損狀態，就是 in the red（有赤字，負債）。

表達自己的意見

字彙	top priority 第一優先，當務之急	retail sector 零售業
	shoplifting (n.) 順手牽羊	rooftop (n.) 屋頂
	inevitable (adj.) 不可避免的	get-together (n.) 聚會

精進度 ★★★☆☆

句型 3

From my perspective,...
從我的觀點看來，……

Example 實用例句

● From my perspective, nothing needs to be changed.
從我的觀點看來，不需要做任何改變。

- From my perspective, we need to speed up the response time to customers' e-mails.
  從我的觀點看來,我們必須加快回應客戶電子郵件的速度。

- From my perspective, the volatility in f/x markets creates an earning opportunity.
  從我的觀點看來,外匯市場的多變創造了賺錢的機會。

  說明 ▶ 本句型中的名詞 perspective（觀點,看法）也可以替換成其他說法,例如 point of view（觀點,見解）。另外,本句型也可以替換成 To my mind,...（依我看,……）。

Dialogue 簡短對話

A: From my perspective, there's no downside to buying earthquake and flood insurance.

B: Well, there is the cost. But I like your proactive thinking.

  A：從我的觀點看來,購買地震和水災保險沒有什麼不好。

  B：嗯,是有成本負擔啦,不過我喜歡你這種積極主動的想法。

response time 回應時間 volatility (n.) 多變 f/x 外匯市場 (= foreign exchange)	earning (n.) 收入 downside (n.) 缺點,負面 proactive (adj.) 積極主動的

精進度 ★★★★☆

 句型4

...would be my take.
……,這是我的意見。

Example 實用例句

- We need to proceed with caution would be my take.
  我們必須謹慎繼續進行,這是我的意見。

- A lower entrance fee could attract more visitors would be my take.
  門票價格降低一點可以吸引更多遊客,這是我的意見。

- Just one or two security cameras may deter thieves would be my take.
  只要裝設一或兩台保全攝影機就可以嚇阻竊賊,這是我的意見。

說明 ▶ would be my take 有軟化語氣的作用，放在意見之後，強調說話者只是在表達意見而已，而不是在發表強勢的談話、建議或命令。如果要製造更強勢一點的效果，可以在表達意見之後稍微停頓一下，再接 would be my take。

Dialogue 簡短對話

A: Most people won't notice a three percent subscription rate hike would be my take.

B: I hope you're right. We're not in a position to start shedding subscribers.

A：大多數的人不會注意到訂閱價格增加了 3%，這是我的意見。

B：我希望你是對的。我們禁不起開始流失訂戶啊。

說明 ▶ 如果要表達無法允許或承受不起某件事的發生，可以用〈be not in a position to + 原形動詞〉。

字彙

proceed (v.) 繼續進行
caution (n.) 謹慎
deter (v.) 嚇阻
subscription (n.) 訂閱

hike (n.) 上漲
shed (v.) 流失
subscriber (n.) 訂戶

精進度 ★★★★★

句型5

I'm not an expert, but it seems to me...
我不是專家，不過在我看來……

Example 實用例句

● I'm not an expert, but it seems to me the windows could be slightly wider.
我不是專家，不過在我看來這扇窗戶可以再稍微寬一點。

● I'm not an expert, but it seems to me we should use thicker insulation.
我不是專家，不過在我看來我們應該使用更厚的隔熱層。

● I'm not an expert, but it seems to me a larger font would draw more attention to the package.
我不是專家，不過在我看來比較大的字體可以吸引人更注意到這個包裝。

說明 ▶ 本句型有另一個比較非正式的說法：I'm no expert, but it seems to me...。另外，but it seems to me 的後面接子句。如果想要比較和緩地提出意見，助動詞可以用 could（如第一個例句）；如果想要強勢一點，則助動詞可以用 should（如第二個例句）。至於 must 就太過強勢了，不適合用在這裡。

Dialogue 簡短對話

A: I'm not an expert, but it seems to me we'd be better off using a higher percentage of nylon.

B: That would make the garments more wrinkle resistant.

A：我不是專家，不過在我看來尼龍的比例更高一點會更好。

B：那會讓衣服更加抗皺。

字彙

insulation (n.) 隔熱層，隔熱材料	nylon (n.) 尼龍
font (n.) 字體	garment (n.) 衣服
draw attention to... 引起對…的注意	wrinkle resistant 抗皺的
package (n.) 包裝袋（盒、箱）	

相關表達 下面提供表達意見時常用的說法：

➞ perspective 觀點，看法

➞ point of view 觀點，見解

➞ vantage point 觀點，看法

➞ way of thinking 思考方式

29 傳達好消息
Delivering Good News

Check this out. I got a raise at work.

來看！我獲得加薪了。

Guess what? I got the job! 句型1

你知道嗎？我找到工作了！

You aren't going to believe it. I'm getting married!

你絕對不會相信的，我要結婚了！

Good news! My cousin is visiting me next month. 句型2

好消息！我表哥下個月要來看我了。

Listen to this bit of good news. My company is sending me to a conference in Paris.

仔細聽這個好消息。我公司要派我去巴黎參加會議。

I want you to be the first to know. I'm going to be a father!

我想第一個告訴你，我要當爸爸了！

I have some wonderful news. We're buying a house. 句型3

我有很棒的消息要告訴你。我們要買房子了。

I'm happy to be able to tell you (that) your entry to the poetry contest is a top-five finalist.

我很高興能告訴你這個消息，你參加詩歌比賽的作品是最後決選前五名。

You'll be pleased to know (that) you were selected to be the team leader. 句型4

你一定會很高興得知你被選為隊長了。

It is my great honor to announce the winner of the scholarship. 句型5

我非常榮幸來宣布獎學金的得主。

169

句型 1　Guess what?
你知道嗎？

EXAMPLE 實用例句

● Guess what? I got the job!
你知道嗎？我找到工作了！

● Guess what? We're hiring a movie star to be our spokesperson, and I get to be his assistant!
你知道嗎？我們聘請一位電影明星來擔任我們的代言人，而且我是他的助理！

● Guess what? My parents are getting a new car, and they're giving me their old one.
你知道嗎？我父母要買新車，他們要把舊車給我。

說明 ▶ Guess what? 這個問句的後面，通常會馬上接著敘述詳情，說話者並非真的要對方回答 Guess what? 這個問句。像這樣的問句稱為 rhetorical question（修辭性問句），雖然是問句，但並不是真的要對方回答。

DIALOGUE 簡短對話

A: Guess what? I entered my name in a drawing for a new TV, and I won!
B: Wow, you have the luck of the Irish!

A：你知道嗎？我參加一個電視機抽獎，結果抽中了！
B：哇，你運氣很好耶！

說明 ▶ B 所說的 have the luck of the Irish，字面上的意思是「有愛爾蘭人的運氣」，實際上的意思則是「運氣非常好」，這是因為從前傳說愛爾蘭人有好運。

 spokesperson (n.) 發言人　　　　　　the luck of the Irish 運氣非常好
drawing (n.) 抽籤

句型 *2*

Good news!
好消息！

EXAMPLE 實用例句

● Good news! My cousin is visiting me next month.
好消息！我表哥下個月要來看我了。

● Good news! One of my friends is starting a business, and he wants me to be his partner.
好消息！我有一位朋友要創業，他希望我和他合夥。

● Good news! They cleared the mountain pass, so our ski trip is back on!
好消息！他們清理了山路，所以我們的滑雪之旅又復活了！

說明 ▶ Good news! 通常用於很興奮的情況下，所以才會以驚嘆號結尾。通常說完 Good news! 之後，會接著陳述到底是什麼消息。

DIALOGUE 簡短對話

A: Good news! I passed the bar exam.
B: I am so happy for you! You're going to be a terrific lawyer.

A：好消息！我通過律師資格考試了。
B：我為你感到好開心喔！你一定會是個很棒的律師。

mountain pass 山路	bar exam 律師資格考試
back on 再度啟動	terrific (adj.) 極好的

傳達好消息

句型 *3*

I have some wonderful news.
我有很棒的消息要告訴你。

EXAMPLE 實用例句

● I have some wonderful news. We're buying a house.
我有很棒的消息要告訴你。我們要買房子了。

- I have some wonderful news. My patent for a self-cleaning stove went through!
  我有很棒的消息要告訴你。我的自動清潔爐取得專利了！

- I have some wonderful news. Our son Kyle is moving back to New Orleans.
  我有很棒的消息要告訴你。我們的兒子凱爾要搬回紐奧良了。

  說明 ▶ 本句型另外有兩個類似的說法：I have something wonderful to tell you. 及 I've got some great news.。

Dialogue 簡短對話

A: I have some wonderful news. Do you remember how I auditioned for a car commercial? I got the part!

B: That's fantastic! You're on your way up!

  A：我有很棒的消息要告訴你。你記得我去參加了一部汽車廣告的試鏡嗎？我雀屏中選了！

  B：太棒了！你更上一層樓了！

  說明 ▶ A 所說的 get a part 是指獲選擔綱某部廣告、電影、戲劇等的角色。on one's way up 是指在事業上或技能發展方面等取得進展。

patent (n.) 專利	audition (v.) 試鏡
stove (n.) 火爐	commercial (n.) 商業廣告
go through（法律、協議等）被通過	

精進度★★★★★

句型4

You'll be pleased to know (that)...
你一定會很高興得知……

Example 實用例句

- You'll be pleased to know that you were selected to be the team leader.
  你一定會很高興得知你被選為隊長了。

● You'll be pleased to know we're nearly finished, and we're coming in under budget.
你一定會很高興得知我們就快完成了，而且在預算範圍內。

● You'll be pleased to know that your application was approved.
你一定會很高興得知你的申請通過了。

說明 ▶ 本句型中的 pleased 也可以替換成 happy。You'll 也可以替換成 You may。

Dialogue 簡短對話

A: You'll be pleased to know that we recruited a top chef to take over in the kitchen. I just found out today.

B: That's a relief. Thank you for letting me know so soon.

　A：你一定會很高興得知我們網羅到一位頂尖主廚來接管廚房。我也是今天才知道的。

　B：那我就放心了。謝謝你這麼快就讓我知道。

說明 ▶ 如果聽到一個可以讓你解除顧慮的消息，就可以用 That's a relief.（那我就放心了。）來表達。

字彙		
team leader 隊長		recruit (v.) 網羅，招募
come in 完成		take over 接管
under budget 在預算之內		

精進度 ★★★★★

句型 5

It is my great honor to...
我非常榮幸……

Example 實用例句

● It is my great honor to announce the winner of the scholarship.
我非常榮幸來宣布獎學金的得主。

● It is my great honor to tell you about a breakthrough by our engineers.
我非常榮幸來告訴你本公司工程師所取得的突破性進展。

● It is my great honor to deliver some amazing news from our Himalayan research mission.
我非常榮幸來傳達我們喜瑪拉雅山研究任務幾個很棒的消息。

說明 ▶ 本句型通常用於發表演說時。另一個類似的說法是 I'm honored to be able to...（我很榮幸能夠……）。

Dialogue 簡短對話

A: It is my great honor to present you with an award for outstanding achievement in literature.

B: Thank you very much. I am indeed honored.

A：我非常榮幸來頒發文學傑出成就獎給你。

B：非常感謝。我真的很榮幸。

字彙	
scholarship (n.) 獎學金	outstanding (adj.) 傑出的
breakthrough (n.) 突破性進展	achievement (n.) 成就
engineer (n.) 工程師	literature (n.) 文學
Himalayan (adj.) 喜瑪拉雅山的	indeed (adv.) 確實
research mission 研究任務	

相關表達 聽到好消息時，可以善用下面的說法來回應：

➥ That's fantastic! 太棒了！

➥ I am so happy for you! 我替你感到好開心！

➥ Good for you! 恭喜你！

傳達壞消息
Delivering Bad News

非正式

Sadly, the school isn't offering pottery classes anymore.

令人遺憾的是，學校不再開設陶藝課了。

The bad news is I can't go to New York with you.

壞消息是我不能跟你去紐約了。

稍非正式

I'm afraid (that) the speech was cancelled because of the weather. 句型*1*

恐怕由於天氣的因素，演說取消了。

It's a real shame (that) only a few people volunteered to help with the parade.

太可惜了，只有少數人自願幫忙遊行的事。

一般情況

Unfortunately, we couldn't get tickets to the concert. 句型*2*

很遺憾，我們買不到音樂會的門票。

Please don't take this the wrong way, but we're going with another ink supplier.

請別誤會我的意思，不過我們決定選擇另一家碳粉供應商。

稍正式

Sorry to be the bearer of bad news, but the expansion plan might not go forward. 句型*3*

很抱歉有個壞消息要告訴你，擴張計畫可能不進行了。

We're very sorry to have to tell you (that) we have to let you go. 句型*4*

我們很抱歉得告訴你，我們必須請你走人。

正式

It is with a heavy heart that I announce the closure of this branch.

我以沉重的心情宣布這家分店要關閉了。

I regret to inform you (that) your submission to our journal was not accepted. 句型*5*

我很遺憾通知你，你投稿我們期刊並未獲得接受。

句型 1

I'm afraid (that)...
恐怕……

EXAMPLE 實用例句

- I'm afraid that the speech was cancelled because of the weather.
  恐怕由於天氣的因素，演說取消了。

- I'm afraid the restaurant is already fully-booked.
  恐怕這家餐廳的訂位已經滿了。

- I'm afraid that our Russian interpreter is out of town until the 23rd.
  恐怕我們的俄語口譯員出差去了，要到 23 日才會回來。

  說明 ▶ 另一個和擔心、害怕、憂慮有關的負面句型是 I fear (that)...，這種用法通常代表說話者的顧慮很有可能會成真，例如 I fear there may not be enough time to visit both Disneyland and Universal Studios.（如果迪士尼樂園和環球影城都去的話，我擔心時間可能會不夠。）

DIALOGUE 簡短對話

A: Will it be possible to camp out on the mountain top?
B: I'm afraid camping is allowed only in certain areas at the base of the mountain.
  A：有可能在山頂露宿嗎？
  B：恐怕在山腳下某些區域才能露營。

fully-booked 訂位滿了	camp out 搭帳篷露宿，野營
interpreter (n.) 口譯人員	base (n.) 底部，基座
out of town 去外地，不在城裡	

句型 2

Unfortunately,...
很遺憾／令人失望的是／可惜的是，……

EXAMPLE 實用例句

- Unfortunately, we couldn't get tickets to the concert.
  很遺憾，我們買不到音樂會的門票。

● Unfortunately, I wasn't able to get any answers when I called the helpline.
令人失望的是，我打電話給客服專線，還是沒辦法獲得任何答案。

● Unfortunately, the jacket only comes in red or blue, not green.
可惜的是，這件外套只有紅色和藍色，沒有綠色。

說明 ▶ unfortunately（很遺憾，令人失望的是，可惜的是）可以替換成各種帶有負面意涵的副詞，例如 sadly 或 regrettably。

Dialogue 簡短對話

A: I've got some bad news. Unfortunately, the shipping container is too small for all our furniture.

B: That leaves us with two choices. Either we can get rid of some stuff or find a courier with larger containers.

A：我有壞消息要說。很遺憾，船運貨櫃太小，裝不下我們所有的家具。

B：那我們就只剩下兩個選擇，要不是丟掉一些東西，就是找一家有更大貨櫃的貨運公司。

| helpline (n.) 客服電話專線，熱線服務電話 | get rid of... 拋棄…，丟掉… |
| shipping container 船運貨櫃 | courier (n.) 快遞公司；快遞員 |

精進度 ★ ★ ★ ★ ☆

 句型 **3**

Sorry to be the bearer of bad news, but...
很抱歉有個壞消息要告訴你，……

Example 實用例句

● Sorry to be the bearer of bad news, but the expansion plan might not go forward.
很抱歉有個壞消息要告訴你，擴張計畫可能不進行了。

● Sorry to be the bearer of bad news, but we lost the bid to another contractor.
很抱歉有個壞消息要告訴你，標案被另一家承包商標走了。

傳達壞消息

● Sorry to be the bearer of bad news, but our factory failed the health department inspection.
很抱歉有個壞消息要告訴你,我們工廠沒通過衛生部門的檢查。

說明 ▶ bearer 是指「傳達消息、口信等的人」。另一個類似但比較不那麼正式的說法是 Sorry to be the one to break it, but...,break 在這裡是「(消息在報紙、電視或電台)發布,傳播」的意思。break news 就是「報告消息」之意。

Dialogue 簡短對話

A: Sorry to be the bearer of bad news, but we couldn't get more than 100 cases of the new lenses.

B: That should be enough to get us going with the first batch of cameras.

A:很抱歉有個壞消息要告訴你,我們頂多只能拿到一百箱新鏡頭。
B:那應該足夠我們開始處理第一批照相機。

expansion plan 擴張計畫	inspection (n.) 檢查
go forward 前進	case (n.) 箱,盒
bid (n.) 投標,出價	lens (n.) 鏡頭
contractor (n.) 承包商	batch (n.) 一批(生產量)

精進度 ★★★★☆

句型4 We're very sorry to have to tell you (that)...
我們很抱歉得告訴你……

Example 實用例句

● We're very sorry to have to tell you that we have to let you go.
我們很抱歉得告訴你,我們必須請你走人。

● We're very sorry to have to tell you the building is going to be demolished.
我們很抱歉得告訴你,這棟大樓要拆除了。

● We're very sorry to have to tell you that if you want to keep your apartment, you'll have to give up your cats.
我們很抱歉得告訴你,如果你還想保有你的公寓,你就必須放棄你的貓。

說明 ▶ 本句型有一個稍微沒那麼正式的說法是 I'm sorry to have to tell you (that)...。另一個類似的說法是 Sorry to be the one to tell you (that)...。

Dialogue 簡短對話

A: We're very sorry to have to tell you the dress you ordered won't be here until next week.

B: But my sister's wedding is this Sunday!

A：我們非常抱歉必須告訴你，你訂購的洋裝要下星期才會到貨。

B：但是這個星期日就是我姊姊的婚禮了！

字彙
let someone go 請某人離職　　　　　　give up... 放棄⋯
demolish (v.) 拆除

精進度 ★★★★★

句型**5**

I regret to inform you (that)...
我很遺憾通知你⋯⋯

Example 實用例句

● I regret to inform you that your submission to our journal was not accepted.
我很遺憾通知你，你投稿我們期刊並未獲得接受。

● I regret to inform you there are no internship opportunities available at this time.
我很遺憾通知你，現在並沒有開放實習的機會。

● I regret to inform you that due to budgetary cutbacks, we aren't pursuing any new research projects.
我很遺憾通知各位，由於預算刪減，我們不會進行任何新的研究計畫了。

說明 ▶ 本句型常見於正式的英文口語及書寫中，尤其是信件。

傳達壞消息

Dialogue 簡短對話

A: I regret to inform you that the Evergreen Shopping Complex is shutting down permanently in June of next year.

B: Wow, that's quite a shock. Well, at least you've given us a lot of advance notice. Thank you for that.

A：我很遺憾通知各位，長青購物商場將於明年六月永久關閉。

B：哇，好震撼的消息。嗯，至少你們這麼早就先通知我們，謝謝。

字彙		
submission (n.) 投稿	shopping complex 購物商場
journal (n.) 期刊	shut down 關閉
internship (n.) 實習	permanently (adv.) 永久地
budgetary cutback 預算刪減	advance notice 事先通知，預告
pursue (v.) 進行，從事	

相關表達 要告知別人壞消息之前，可以先說哪些話讓對方有所準備呢？

→ I've got some bad news. 我有個壞消息要告訴你。

→ Brace yourself. 你要有心理準備。

→ You might want to sit down. 你可能坐下來聽比較好。

非正式

One positive point is the wide reach of their sales force.

一個優點是，他們的銷售人員可以接觸到的範圍很廣。

In particular, retailers love the new POS displays.

零售商特別喜歡這個新的店頭陳列架。

稍非正式

My favorite thing about the new coffee blend is its aroma. 句型*1*

我最喜歡這款新調豆咖啡的地方就是它的香氣。

The building plan's key strength is the design of its façade. 句型*2*

這項興建計畫具有一個關鍵的優勢，即建築物正面的設計。

一般情況

Your ability to clearly communicate ideas is impressive. 句型*3*

你有清楚表達意見的能力，令人印象深刻。

I must commend the team's focus on improving the car's safety features.

我必須稱讚這個團隊對於改進汽車安全性能的執著。

稍正式

We couldn't find a single flaw in the report.

這份報告我們連一個瑕疵都找不到。

I especially like the ad's use of bright colors. 句型*4*

我特別喜歡這個廣告對亮色系的運用。

正式

Something I really appreciate is the quality of the photos in the brochure.

我很欣賞的地方是小冊子裡的照片品質。

I was very impressed by your attention to detail. 句型*5*

你對細節的注重令我印象非常深刻。

句型 *1*　**My favorite thing about ... is ～**
我最喜歡……的地方就是～

Example 實用例句

● My favorite thing about the new coffee blend is its aroma.
我最喜歡這款新調豆咖啡的地方就是它的香氣。

● My favorite thing about this band is its sense of rhythm.
我最喜歡這支樂團的地方就是它的節奏感。

● My favorite thing about Seoul was the food.
我最喜歡首爾的地方就是它的食物。

說明 ▶ 如果最喜歡的東西不只一個,便可以將 My favorite thing about...
改成 One of my favorite things about...。about 的後面接說話者想要談論
的主題,之後再接 be 動詞 is 或 was,然後再說出最喜歡的那一個。

Dialogue 簡短對話

A: My favorite thing about cross-country skiing is the quiet solitude.
B: I can imagine. It must feel like you're worlds away from the city.

A：我最喜歡越野滑雪的地方就是它相當孤寂。
B：我可以想像,感覺一定很像遠離城市好幾個世界。

說明 ▶ worlds away(或用 a world away)的意思是距離另一個地方非常遙
遠,無論身體和心靈都是。

---

blend (n.) 混合　　　　　　　　　cross-country skiing 越野滑雪
aroma (n.) 香氣　　　　　　　　　solitude (n.) 孤寂
rhythm (n.) 韻律,節奏

句型*2* ...'s key strength is ～

……具有一個關鍵的優勢，即～

Example 實用例句

● The building plan's key strength is the design of its façade.
這項興建計畫具有一個關鍵的優勢，即建築物正面的設計。

● This proposal's key strength is its analysis of our main competitors.
這個企畫案具有一個關鍵的優勢，即對我們主要競爭對手的分析。

● Theodore's key strength is his aptitude for using many kinds of software.
西爾多具有一個關鍵的優勢，即他有使用多種軟體的才能。

說明 ▶ 本句型的第一個部分是一個所有格（人、東西、公司等的所有格），第二個部分的 key strength 可以替換成 best attribute（最佳特質），第三個部分則說明一項正面特質。

Dialogue 簡短對話

A: First, let's look at the plus side. The harbor's key strength is its ability to accommodate ships of every size.

B: It's also just minutes from a major highway.

A：首先，我們來看看有利的一面。這個港口具有一個關鍵的優勢，即可以容納各種大小的船隻。

B：距離主要的公路也只有幾分鐘的距離。

 façade (n.) 建築物的正面　　　　　accommodate (v.) 容納
aptitude (n.) 才能，天資　　　　　highway (n.)（尤指城市間的）公路
harbor (n.) 港口

句型 *3*　**...is impressive.**

……令人印象深刻。

Example　實用例句

● Your ability to clearly communicate ideas is impressive.
你有清楚表達意見的能力，令人印象深刻。

● These brooches are especially impressive.
這些胸針特別令人印象深刻。

● The marching band's precision is impressive.
這支軍樂隊的演奏精準無誤，令人印象深刻。

說明 ▶ 本句型以陳述優點來開頭，作爲主詞。優點的陳述可以用一個簡短的名詞或一個較長的名詞片語。至於 impressive（令人印象深刻的），可以替換成其他正面的形容詞，例如 superb（非常棒的，上乘的）或 marvelous（了不起的，令人讚嘆的）。

Dialogue　簡短對話

A: Ms. Winter's skill in handling classrooms full of screaming children is impressive.

B: No argument here. I wouldn't last five minutes.

A：溫特爾女士有辦法控制住一整間在教室尖叫的小孩，令人印象深刻。
B：同意。我撐不了五分鐘。

說明 ▶ B 所說的 No argument here. 是表達贊同的口語說法，表示贊同 A 所說的話，沒有異議。

字彙　brooch (n.) 胸針　　　　　　　　　　precision (n.) 精準
　　　marching band 軍樂隊　　　　　　　screaming (adj.) 尖叫的

句型 **4**　**I especially like...**
我特別喜歡……

EXAMPLE 實用例句

● I especially like the ad's use of bright colors.
我特別喜歡這個廣告對亮色系的運用。

● I especially like your suggestion to pack more vegetables into the lunch boxes.
我特別喜歡你的提議——在便當盒裡多放一些蔬菜。

● I especially like the way the pattern looks like a snowflake.
我特別喜歡這個看起來像雪花的圖案。

　　說明 ▶ 本句型的後面常常會接〈the way + 主詞 + 動詞〉，例如第三個例句的 the way the pattern looks like a snowflake。

DIALOGUE 簡短對話

A: Let's begin by looking at the positive areas. I especially like the airport's inclusion of a daycare center.
B: Absolutely. We think it's going to be a big hit with parents traveling with children.
　A：我們先從優點部分開始看。我特別喜歡這座機場還設有日間托育中心。
　B：一點也沒錯。我想帶孩子旅行的父母會很愛這個的。

pack (v.) 將…打包，把…裝箱	inclusion (n.) 納入，包含
pattern (n.) 圖案，花樣	daycare center 日間托育中心
snowflake (n.) 雪花	hit (n.) 成功而風行一時的事物

句型 *5*　**I was very impressed by...**
……令我印象非常深刻。

Example　實用例句

- I was very impressed by your attention to detail.
  你對細節的注重令我印象非常深刻。

- I was very impressed by Ms. Lin's résumé.
  林女士的履歷表令我印象非常深刻。

- I was very impressed by the creativity that went into the display.
  這場展覽的創意令我印象非常深刻。

  說明 ▶ 本句型用過去式，是因為說話者表達的是他 / 她初次的感受。但除非另有說明，不然通常都表示說話者至今仍有相同的感受。此外，句型中的 by 可以替換成 with。

Dialogue　簡短對話

A: I was very impressed by the movie's cinematography.
B: So was I. The camera work was breathtaking.

　A：我對這部電影的拍攝技巧印象非常深刻。
　B：我也是。影像部分令人屏息。

	résumé (n.) 履歷表 creativity (n.) 創意，創造力	cinematography (n.) 電影攝影術 breathtaking (adj.) 令人屏息的，令人讚嘆的

相關表達　在指出優點之前，常常會先用哪些話來開頭呢？

➥ I always like to start with the good points. 我一向喜歡從優點開始講起。

➥ Let's begin by looking at the positive areas. 我們先從優點部分開始看起。

➥ First, let's look at the plus side. 首先，我們來看有利的一面。

　說明 ▶ the plus side 的意思是「好的 / 有利的 / 樂觀的方面」。

指出缺點
Identifying Weaknesses

非正式

I'm not crazy about the amount they charge to join the gym. 句型1

對於他們的健身房入會費用，我不敢恭維。

There's a problem with the battery life.

電池壽命有問題。

稍非正式

It's a great home electronics store, but the customer service could be better. 句型2

這是一家很棒的家電行，不過顧客服務還可以更好。

There's room for improvement with the material used for the camera's neck strap. 句型3

相機頸帶的材質還有進步的空間。

一般情況

To me, the biggest shortcoming was the size of the exhibition hall.

在我看來，最大的缺點就是展覽廳的大小。

The only weak point I found was the length of the screenplay. 句型4

我唯一找到的缺點就是這部電影劇本的長度。

稍正式

Some people have pointed out (that) the handle is too small.

有些人已經指出來，就是這個把手太小了。

Please don't take this the wrong way, but it might be difficult for a new hotel to succeed in this economy.

請別誤會我的意思，不過在這種經濟情勢之下，一家新飯店要成功可能很困難。

正式

At the risk of sounding negative, there are a lot of similar products on the market. 句型5

或許聽起來很負面消極，不過市場上有很多類似產品。

One area you might want to consider improving is the pricing structure.

有一個部分你可能會想要考慮改進，就是定價結構。

句型 *1*
I'm not crazy about...
對於……，我不敢恭維。

Example 實用例句

● I'm not crazy about the amount they charge to join the gym.
對於他們的健身房入會費用，我不敢恭維。

● I'm not crazy about the acoustics of the auditorium.
對於禮堂的音響效果，我不敢恭維。

● I'm not crazy about this summer's catalog.
對於這份夏季目錄，我不敢恭維。

說明 ▶〈(be) crazy about + 某事物〉是一種口語說法，表示非常喜歡某事物。如果要表達不是很喜歡某事物，則用〈(be) not crazy about + 某事物〉。about 的後面可以接名詞或動名詞。

Dialogue 簡短對話

A: I'm not crazy about having to fill in so many forms. We're renting rock climbing equipment, not buying the mountain.
B: Tell me about it. We'll be here all morning.

A：對於必須填這麼多表格，我不敢恭維。我們是要租攀岩設備，而不是要把山買下來。
B：就是說嘛！我們整個早上都要待在這裡了。

說明 ▶ B 所說的 Tell me about it. 是一個口語說法，用來表示認同，意思是「就是說嘛。」一般是用來認同不愉快的事，說這句話時並不是真的要對方告訴自己什麼內容。

字彙
charge (v.) 收費	catalog (n.) 目錄 (= catalogue)
acoustics (n.) 音響效果	form (n.) 表格
auditorium (n.) 禮堂	

句型*2* ...could be better.
……還可以更好。

Example 實用例句

- It's a great home electronics store, but the customer service could be better.
  這是一家很棒的家電行，不過顧客服務還可以更好。

- We loved the swimming pool, but the weight room could be better.
  我們很喜歡這座游泳池，不過重量訓練室還可以更好。

- Everyone agrees their pasta is delicious, but the soup could be better.
  每個人都同意他們的義大利麵很好吃，不過湯還可以更好。

說明▶ 使用本句型時一般先陳述優點，之後再提出缺點來做對比。better 可以替換成其他的形容詞，端視上下文及討論的東西而定。

Dialogue 簡短對話

A: Well, intermission lasts another 10 minutes. How do you like the opera so far?

B: It's pretty good. The singing is fantastic, but the set design could be better.

A：好，中場休息還有十分鐘。你覺得這齣歌劇到目前為止怎麼樣？

B：相當不錯。歌唱的部分非常棒，不過布景設計還可以更好。

字彙	
weight room 重量訓練室	last (v.) 持續
pasta (n.) 義大利麵	opera (n.) 歌劇
intermission (n.)（電影、音樂會等的）中場休息	fantastic (adj.) 極好的
	set design 布景設計

指出缺點

句型 3

There's room for improvement with...

……還有進步的空間。

Example 實用例句

● There's room for improvement with the material used for the camera's neck strap.
相機頸帶的材質還有進步的空間。

● There's room for improvement with the way the tables and chairs are arranged.
桌椅排列的方式還有進步的空間。

● There's room for improvement with the placement of the volume control buttons.
音量控制鈕的位置安排還有進步的空間。

說明 ▶ room for improvement 是一種用來陳述缺失的婉轉說法，更直接的說法是 There's something wrong with...（……出了差錯。）或 There's a problem with...（……有問題。）

Dialogue 簡短對話

A: Did you find any drawbacks with the information pamphlet?
B: In general, it's excellent. Still, there's room for improvement with the color contrast.

　A：你有發現這本資訊小手冊有任何缺點嗎？
　B：大致來說很棒，不過顏色對比還有進步的空間。

---

neck strap 頸帶，背帶	drawback (n.) 缺點，不利條件
placement (n.) 放置	pamphlet (n.) 小手冊（如宣傳用的各類傳單）
volume (n.) 音量	color contrast 顏色對比

句型 4

The only weak point I found was...

我唯一找到的缺點就是……

Example 實用例句

● The only weak point I found was the length of the screenplay.
我唯一找到的缺點就是這部電影劇本的長度。

● The only weak point I found was a lack of diversity in the company's workforce.
我唯一找到的缺點就是這家公司的員工缺乏多元性。

● The only weak point I found was the flimsiness of the carrying case.
我唯一找到的缺點就是這個收納盒太脆弱了。

說明 ▶ 本句型用於對某件事情做過分析後,或看過、讀過、體驗過某樣東西後,指出這件事情或這樣東西的缺點。雖然本句型是用來表達負面之處(即缺點),不過由於只有一個缺點被挑出來,所以被討論的事情或東西基本上仍然是很好的。

Dialogue 簡短對話

A: What did you think of the blueprints?

B: The only weak point I found was the narrowness of the hallways.

A:你對這份藍圖有何看法?

B:我唯一找到的缺點就是走廊太狹窄了。

字量	
screenplay (n.) 電影劇本	carrying case 收納盒
diversity (n.) 多元性	blueprint (n.)(建築、設計的)藍圖
workforce (n.) 全體員工	narrowness (n.) 狹窄
flimsiness (n.) 脆弱	hallway (n.) 走廊

指出缺點

191

句型 5

At the risk of sounding negative,...
或許聽起來很負面消極，……

Example 實用例句

● At the risk of sounding negative, there are a lot of similar products on the market.
或許聽起來很負面消極，不過市場上有很多類似產品。

● At the risk of sounding negative, the plan is a little risky.
或許聽起來很負面消極，不過這項計畫有點冒險。

● At the risk of sounding negative, drilling wells in this area may not be profitable.
或許聽起來很負面消極，不過在這個地區鑽井可能無利可圖。

說明 ▶ 如果不想讓人感覺太過負面消極，可以使用本句型來表達。另外也可以使用 At the risk of being negative,... ，意思不變。無論是西方還是東方社會，一般人都希望獲得正面積極的鼓勵。

Dialogue 簡短對話

A: What's your assessment of the strategy?

B: At the risk of sounding negative, I'm not sure we should be targeting college-aged consumers.

A：你對這個策略的評估為何？

B：或許聽起來很負面消極，不過我不確定我們是否應鎖定大學年齡層的消費者。

字彙

risky (adj.) 冒險的	profitable (adj.) 有利可圖的
drill (v.) 鑽探	assessment (n.) 評估
well (n.) 井	

相關表達 要討論缺點時，有哪些好用的語彙呢？

→ shortcoming(s) 缺點

→ deficit 缺陷，不足

→ drawback 缺點，不利之處

→ area/point of weakness 弱點

33 表達含糊籠統的意見
Making Vague Comments

非正式

I'm not sure right now.　　　　　　　　　　　我目前無法確定。

The speech was very thoughtful. 句型1　　　　這場演說非常發人深思。

稍非正式

It isn't bad, but it could be better.　　　　　不算差,不過還可以更好。

I'm sorry I can't be more specific. 句型2　　很抱歉我不能講得更具體了。

一般情況

We need more time to reach a consensus. 句型3　　我們需要更多時間來達成共識。

I'd say we're more or less happy with the
situation.　　　　　　　　　　　　　　　我覺得我們或多或少對於這個情
　　　　　　　　　　　　　　　　　　　　　況是滿意的。

稍正式

At this time I haven't got an answer (for you).　　我到現在還沒找出答案(給你)。

We're going to look into the suggestion in the
near future.　　　　　　　　　　　　　　　我們不久之後會研究一下這個建
　　　　　　　　　　　　　　　　　　　　　議。

正式

Generally speaking, it was an interesting
presentation. 句型4　　　　　　　　　　　整體來說,這是一場很有趣的簡
　　　　　　　　　　　　　　　　　　　　　報。

Without being too specific, I'd say things are
moving in a positive direction. 句型5　　　　不要說得太具體,我可以透露事
　　　　　　　　　　　　　　　　　　　　　情正在往正面的方向邁進。

句型 1

...was very thoughtful.
……非常發人深思。

EXAMPLE 實用例句

● The speech was very thoughtful.
這場演說非常發人深思。

● I found the gesture to be very thoughtful.
我發現這個舉動非常發人深思。

● Allyson's proposal was very thoughtful.
艾莉森的提案非常發人深思。

說明▶ 本句型使用了一個相當模糊籠統的字眼：very thoughtful，讓說話者避開具體的用字。這是政治人物和謹慎小心的人常用的說話技巧。除了 thoughtful，其他常見的籠統字眼包括 well-thought out（經過深思的）、nicely presented（巧妙呈現的）、carefully done（謹慎完成的）。

DIALOGUE 簡短對話

A: How did you like Dr. Hansen's presentation about antique hair pins?
B: Mostly, I thought it was very thoughtful.

A：你喜歡漢森博士對於古代髮簪的報告嗎？
B：大致上喜歡，我覺得非常發人深思。

gesture (n.) 舉動　　　　　　　　　hair pin 髮簪
antique (adj.) 古代的，古董的

句型 2

...can't be more specific.
……不能講得更具體了。

EXAMPLE 實用例句

● I'm sorry I can't be more specific.
很抱歉我不能講得更具體了。

● I wish I could be more specific.
我希望我可以講得更具體，但是不行。

● I apologize for not being more specific.
很抱歉我不能講得更具體了。

說明▶ 說話者可以在表達完含糊籠統的意見之後使用本句型，為不能提供更具體的資訊道歉。一旦碰到必須把話說得比較含糊籠統時，本句型就相當好用。

Dialogue 簡短對話

A: The land value analysis may take anywhere from three to six weeks. I'm sorry I can't be more specific.

B: I understand. I'd rather you take your time and get it right the first time.

A：土地價值分析可能要花三到六個星期不等。很抱歉我不能講得更具體了。

B：我了解。我寧願你慢慢來，第一次就做好。

說明▶ B 所說的 get something right the first time 是指第一次就做出精準的報告或分析，沒有錯誤，不必來來回回修改或重做。

 land value analysis 土地價值分析

精進度★★★☆☆

 句型3

We need more time to...
我們需要更多時間來……

Example 實用例句

● We need more time to reach a consensus.
我們需要更多時間來達成共識。

● We need more time to make a decision.
我們需要更多時間來做決定。

● We need more time to formulate a response.
我們需要更多時間來想出回應方式。

說明 ▶ 如果要拖延做出回應的時間，只要用本句型含糊籠統地說出還需要更多時間即可。more time 也可以替換成其他表達時間的說法，例如 a few more weeks, at least another month 等。

Dialogue 簡短對話

A: Have you decided yet?

B: Not quite yet. We need more time to talk things over.

A：你做了決定沒？

B：還不算。我們需要更多時間來討論。

說明 ▶ B 所說的 talk things over 是「討論事情」之意。

consensus (n.) 共識	formulate (v.) 規畫，想出

精進度★★★★★

句型 4

Generally speaking,...

整體來說 / 一般來說，⋯⋯

Example 實用例句

● Generally speaking, it was an interesting presentation.
整體來說，這是一場很有趣的簡報。

● Generally speaking, the farmer's market is a great place to get fresh produce.
一般來說，農夫市集是購買新鮮農產品的好地方。

● Generally speaking, our franchisees are adapting nicely to the new ordering system.
整體來說，我們的經銷商對這套新的訂貨系統適應得很好。

說明 ▶ 本句型是一個簡單總結看法但不深入談論細節的說法，generally speaking 還可以替換成 in general（一般來說，大致來說）。

Dialogue 簡短對話

A: Would you recommend the clinic?

B: I would, yes. Generally speaking, their physical therapists are all good.

　A：你會推薦這家診所嗎？

　B：是的，我會。整體來說，他們的物理治療師都很不錯。

字彙	farmer's market 農夫市集 produce (n.) 農產品 franchisee (n.) 經銷商	adapt (v.) 適應 physical therapist 物理治療師

精進度★★★★★

句型 5

Without being too specific, I'd say...
不要說得太具體，我可以透露……

Example 實用例句

● Without being too specific, I'd say things are moving in a positive direction.
不要說得太具體，我可以透露事情正在往正面的方向邁進。

● Without being too specific, I'd say we're on track to have an excellent year.
不要說得太具體，我可以透露我們正朝著豐收的一年循序漸進。

● Without being too specific, I'd say our investors are feeling good about our prospects.
不要說得太具體，我可以透露我們的投資人看好我們的前景。

說明 ▶ 若要表達不具體的意見，無論是說話者沒有很多細節可以講，或是說話者不想透露太多細節，都可以用本句型表達，非常好用！

Dialogue 簡短對話

A: What can you tell me about this year's turnout for the computer show?

B: Without being too specific, I'd say we're happy with the gate receipts.

　A：可以說說今年電腦展的參觀人數嗎？

　B：不要說得太具體，我可以透露我們對門票收入很滿意。

specific (adj.) 具體的，明確的
on track 在軌道上漸進
prospects (n.) 前景，前途

turnout (n.) 出席人數
gate receipts 門票收入

相關表達 表達意見時有時要含糊籠統些，不妨視情況來使用下面的字眼：

➥ generally speaking 整體來說，一般來說

➥ more or less 或多或少，差不多，大約

➥ somewhat 有點，稍微

➥ mostly 大部分，主要地，多半

➥ unclear 不清楚的，不確定的

非正式

Who are you trying to reach? 句型*1*　　　你要找誰呢？

Would you like her to call you back?　　　要請她回電給你嗎？

稍非正式

I'll connect you now. Just a moment, please. 句型*2*　　　我現在就為你轉接，請稍等。

Thank you. I'll make sure she gets the message.　　　謝謝。我一定會把訊息轉給她。

一般情況

He isn't at his desk right now. Should I tell him you called? 句型*3*　　　他現在不在座位上，要我告訴他你來電嗎？

May I take a message?　　　需要我幫你留言嗎？

稍正式

Mr. Lee isn't in. Would you like to leave a message? 句型*4*　　　李先生現在不在。你要留言嗎？

I'm afraid she's in a meeting. 句型*5*　　　恐怕她正在開會。

正式

Just a moment, please. I'll put you through to him.　　　請稍等一下，我幫你轉接給他。

Please wait a moment while I connect you.　　　請稍等一下，我替你轉接。

句型 1

...are you trying to reach?
你要找……呢？

Example 實用例句

● Who are you trying to reach?
你要找誰呢？

● Which department are you trying to reach?
你要找哪個部門呢？

● What extension are you trying to reach?
你要找幾號分機呢？

說明▶ 本句型通常出現在電話不是打給本人的時候。辦公室有時候會因為電話系統的緣故，員工會隨機接到不是打給本人的電話。

Dialogue 簡短對話

A: Which Mr. Smith are you trying to reach?

B: Oh, sorry. Larry Smith. He's in the accounts receivable department.

A：你要找哪位史密斯先生呢？

B：噢，不好意思，是賴瑞·史密斯。他是應收帳款部門。

說明▶ 本句型適合用在同一個辦公室裡，有兩位以上姓氏相同的人（例如對話中都姓 Smith 的人），這種情況相當常見。

reach (v.)（通常指透過電話）聯絡   accounts receivable 應收帳款
extension (n.) 電話分機

句型 2

I'll connect you now.
我現在就為你轉接。

Example 實用例句

● I'll connect you now. Just a moment, please.
我現在就為你轉接，請稍等。

● I'll connect you now. Please wait a moment.
我現在就為你轉接，請稍候。

● I'll connect you now. Please stay on the line.
我現在就為你轉接，請不要掛斷。

說明▶轉接電話時，還可以向對方說 I'll put you through.（我為你轉接過去。）

Dialogue 簡短對話

A: Good morning. I'm trying to reach Brian Wilson at extension 393.
B: Thank you. I'll connect you now. Please hold the line.

　　A：早安。我要找分機 393 的布萊恩‧威爾森。
　　B：謝謝。我現在就為你轉接，請不要掛斷。

說明▶B 所說的 hold the line 是「在電話上稍候，不掛斷電話」的意思。

字彙	connect (v.) 為…接通電話	on the line 在電話線上，通話中

精進度★★★☆☆

He isn't at his desk right now.
他現在不在座位上。

Example 實用例句

● He isn't at his desk right now. Should I tell him you called?
他現在不在座位上，要我告訴他你來電嗎？

● He isn't at his desk right now. Have you tried calling his cell phone?
他現在不在座位上，你打過他的手機嗎？

● He isn't at his desk right now. I'm not sure where he is.
他現在不在座位上，我不知道他人在哪裡。

說明▶本句型用在說話者轉接了電話、但本人沒有接聽的情況。另外，也可用在說話者可以直接看到本人不在座位上的時候。

Dialogue 簡短對話

A: Michael isn't at his desk right now. I'm not sure where he is.

B: Oh, I see. Well, could you please give him a message for me?

> A：麥可現在不在座位上，我不知道他人在哪裡。
>
> B：噢，我知道了。可以請你幫我留言給他嗎？

說明 ▶ A 提到 Michael 不在座位上，不過並沒有提供任何資訊，也沒有說要幫忙傳話，這時候就看來電者要不要主動提出請求。

 message (n.) 訊息，留言，口信

精進度 ★★★★☆

句型 4

...isn't in.

……現在不在（辦公室）。

Example 實用例句

● Mr. Lee isn't in. Would you like to leave a message?
李先生現在不在。你要留言嗎？

● She isn't in. I'd be happy to take a message.
她現在不在。我很樂意幫你留言。

● He isn't in. Can you call back in a few hours?
他現在不在。可以請你幾個小時之後再打來嗎？

說明 ▶ 本句型通常用在辦公環境中，意思是「……現在不在辦公室。」至於打電話到某人家裡找某人，如果本人不在，則接電話的人可能會說 Jake isn't here.（傑克不在。）

Dialogue 簡短對話

A: Mr. Hemingway isn't in. Is there anything I can do for you?

B: Maybe. I believe there's a conference call scheduled for tomorrow afternoon. I'm trying to find out exactly what time that will be.

> A：海明威先生現在不在。有什麼我可以為你效勞的嗎？
>
> B：或許你知道。明天下午排定了一場電話會議，我想知道到底是幾點鐘。

說明 ▶ 有時候接電話的人會詢問來電者有沒有需要協助的地方，除了 Is there anything I can do for you? 外，另一個常見的說法是 Can I help you with anything?。

 conference call 電話會議

精進度★★★★☆

 句型5 **I'm afraid...**
恐怕……

EXAMPLE 實用例句

● I'm afraid she's in a meeting.
恐怕她正在開會。

● I'm afraid Mr. Cameron is busy at the moment.
恐怕卡麥隆先生正在忙。

● I'm afraid he isn't free right now.
恐怕他現在沒空。

說明 ▶ 可以用本句型向來電者說明某人無法接聽電話的原因。通常之後會接著問對方要不要留言。

DIALOGUE 簡短對話

A: I'm afraid Ms. Brightman is on the other line. May I take a message?
B: No thank you. I'll call back later.
A：恐怕布萊曼女士正在講電話。需要我幫你留言嗎？
B：不用了，謝謝。我稍後再打過來。

說明 ▶ 如果某人正在講電話，通常可以說 He/She is on the other line.，意思是「他／她正在講電話。」

轉接電話與接受留言

203

→ I think you have the wrong number. 我想你打錯電話了。

→ Can you call back in a few minutes? 你可以幾分鐘之後再打過來嗎？

→ Let me get a pen and paper. 我去拿一下紙筆。

→ Can you please spell your name for me? 可以請你把名字拼給我聽嗎？

→ Can I put you on hold for a moment? 可以請你稍等一下嗎？

→ Do you know her extension? 你知道她的分機幾號嗎？

35 打電話與留言
Making Phone Calls and Leaving a Message

非正式

Is Ken there? 句型1　　　　　　　　　肯在嗎？

Is this Fresh Field Foods?　　　　　　是鮮田食品嗎？

稍非正式

Reed Jennings, please. 句型2　　　　　麻煩請接里德‧詹寧斯。

I need to speak with the person in charge of media relations.　　　　　　　我要找負責媒體關係的人。

一般情況

I'm trying to reach extension 315. 句型3　　我要找分機 315。

Would it be all right if I left a message?　我可以留言嗎？

稍正式

Can you please take a message? 句型4　　可以請你幫我留言嗎？

May I speak with Samantha, please?　　請問珊曼莎在嗎？

正式

Would you mind telling Mr. McGregor that I will be 15 minutes late?　　　　　可以麻煩你告訴麥奎格先生，我會晚 15 分鐘嗎？

If it isn't too much trouble, could you please tell her John Ellis called? 句型5　　如果不會太麻煩的話，可以請你轉告她約翰‧艾里斯來電嗎？

句型 1　**Is ... there?**
……在嗎？

Example 實用例句

- Is Ken there?
  肯在嗎？

- Is my cousin there?
  我表哥在嗎？

- Is the head pastry chef there?
  糕點主廚在嗎？

說明▶ 這是詢問某人在不在最直接的方法，因為非常口語，所以比較常用於打電話到家裡或小店。如果要打電話給有多位員工的公司，用其他比較正式的句型會比較適合。

Dialogue 簡短對話

A: Is the chief mechanic there?
B: Sorry, you have the wrong number. This is a dance studio.

A：總技師在嗎？
B：抱歉，你打錯號碼了，這裡是舞蹈工作室。

說明▶ 發現對方打錯電話時，便可以說 You have the wrong number. 或 You have dialed the wrong number. （你撥錯號碼啦。）

字彙

pastry chef 糕點主廚　　　　　　　　　　studio (n.) 工作室
chief mechanic 總技師

句型*2* ..., please.
麻煩請接……

EXAMPLE 實用例句

- Reed Jennings, please.
  麻煩請接里德・詹寧斯。

- Human resources, please.
  麻煩請接人資部。

- Extension 22, please.
  麻煩請接分機 22。

  說明▶ 這是詢問某人在不在最簡單的說法，雖然非常簡短，但並不會沒有禮貌，只是相當直接。另外，本句型只用於公事上的電話，不會用在私人電話或打到別人家裡去時。

DIALOGUE 簡短對話

A: Charlotte Jones, please.
B: Just a moment. I'll connect you.
  A：麻煩請接夏洛特・瓊斯。
  B：稍等一下，我幫你轉接。

字彙 human resources (HR) 人力資源部，人資部 connect (v.) 為…接通電話

句型*3* I'm trying to reach...
我要找……

EXAMPLE 實用例句

- I'm trying to reach extension 315.
  我要找分機 315。

- I'm trying to reach Betty Reynolds.
  我要找蓓蒂・雷諾茲。

打電話與留言

- I'm trying to reach the person in charge of the Paper & More stationery account.

  我要找負責 Paper & More 文具公司這家客戶的人。

  說明 ▶ 可以用本句型來找特定的人（如第二個例句）、電話分機（如第一個例句）或部門，也可以用來找負責某項職務或業務的人（如第三個例句）。

Dialogue 簡短對話

A: I'm trying to reach someone who can answer a question about getting connected to the Internet.

B: I might be able to help you with that.

　　A：我要找可以回答上網問題的人。

　　B：我或許可以幫得上忙。

 stationery (n.) 文具　　　　　　　　　　account (n.) 固定客戶（尤指公司）

精進度★★★★☆

句型 **4**

Can you please...?

可以請你……嗎？

Example 實用例句

- Can you please take a message?

  可以請你幫我留言嗎？

- Can you please transfer me to William Clinton?

  可以請你幫我轉接威廉‧柯林頓嗎？

- Can you please give me an idea when he might be back?

  可以請你告訴我他可能何時會回來嗎？

  說明 ▶ 可以利用本句型來提出各式各樣的問題，就像上述三個例句一樣。give someone an idea 是「給予大致的看法」之意。

Dialogue 簡短對話

A: Can you please let me know where she'll be this afternoon?

B: I'm afraid I don't know.

A：可以請你告訴我，她今天下午會在哪裡嗎？

B：恐怕我也不知道。

字彙　message (n.) 訊息，留言，口信　　　　　transfer (v.) 使轉移

精進度★★★★★

句型 *5*

If it isn't too much trouble, could you please...?
如果不會太麻煩的話，可以請你⋯⋯嗎？

Example 實用例句

● If it isn't too much trouble, could you please tell her John Ellis called?
如果不會太麻煩的話，可以請你轉告她約翰‧艾里斯來電嗎？

● If it isn't too much trouble, could you please ask Ms. Chen to call me back?
如果不會太麻煩的話，可以請你請陳女士回電給我嗎？

● If it isn't too much trouble, could you please let him know I'm on my way?
如果不會太麻煩的話，可以請你告訴他我在路上了嗎？

說明 ▶ 如果要請人幫忙傳話，本句型算是比較正式的說法，另外也可以說 Do you think you might be able to...?。

Dialogue 簡短對話

A: If it isn't too much trouble, could you please give her my name and number?

B: Sure, I'll be happy to.

A：如果不會太麻煩的話，可以請你把我的名字和電話號碼轉告給她嗎？

B：沒問題，我很樂意。

講電話時，還有哪些可以派上用場的句子呢？

➥ Sorry, I (must) have the wrong number. 抱歉，我（一定是）打錯了。

➥ Sorry, you (must) have the wrong number. 抱歉，你（一定是）打錯了。

➥ Do you know when he'll be back? 你知道他什麼時候會回來嗎？

➥ Would you happen to know where she is? 你會不會剛好知道她人在哪裡？

非正式

Just a sec.　　　　　　　　　　　　等一下。

Check back with me a bit later. 句型*1*　　稍後再來找我。

稍非正式

Hold on a minute.　　　　　　　　　等一下。

Give me just a bit more time.　　　　再多給我一點時間。

一般情況

Can I send you the samples on the 29th? 句型*2*　我可以 29 日那天再把樣本寄給你嗎？

It's going to take me another week, at the soonest. 句型*3*　我最快也要再花一個星期的時間。

稍正式

Could you give me a few more days?　可以再多給我幾天的時間嗎？

I'm afraid I'll need more time to complete the project. 句型*4*　我恐怕需要更多時間才能完成這項計畫。

正式

If you aren't in too much of a hurry, can I please get back to you Friday afternoon?　如果你不是很趕，我可以星期五下午再回覆你嗎？

Would it be all right if I let you know in a few days? 句型*5*　如果我過幾天再告訴你，可以嗎？

句型 *1*

Check back with me...
……再來找我。

Example 實用例句

● Check back with me a bit later.
稍後再來找我。

● Check back with me after the holidays.
假期過後再來找我。

● Check back with me in a day or two.
一、兩天後再來找我。

說明 ▶ check back with someone 是指「稍後再與某人聯繫」。the holidays 通常是指耶誕假期，也就是 12 月底到新年這段時間。

Dialogue 簡短對話

A: Did you figure out what's causing our network slowdown?
B: Not yet, but I'm getting there. Check back with me in a bit.
A：你弄清楚網路變慢的原因了嗎？
B：還沒，不過快了。稍後再來找我。

字彙 | figure out... 弄清楚…   get there 完成
slowdown (n.) 減速，怠工

句型 *2*

Can I ... on the 29th?
我可以 29 日那天再……嗎？

Example 實用例句

● Can I send you the samples on the 29th?
我可以 29 日那天再把樣本寄給你嗎？

● Can I e-mail the file to you on the 29th?
我可以 29 日那天再把檔案寄到你的電子信箱嗎？

- Can I get back to you with an answer on the 29th?
  我可以 29 日那天再給你回覆嗎？

  說明 ▶ 本句型前半部的 can I 也可以替換成 is it all right if I，變成 Is it all right if I ... on the 29th?。除了 on the 29th 外，還可以使用其他時間點，例如 at 10:30, on Saturday 等；也可以是一段時間，例如 in a month or two（一、兩個月後）、a few weeks from now（幾個星期之後）等。

Dialogue 簡短對話

A: Can I give you the laid-out catalog on Friday?
B: I'd prefer it if you could get it to me by Wednesday, if possible.
　　A：我可以星期五再給你排版好的目錄嗎？
　　B：如果可以的話，星期三之前給我比較好。

字彙		
get back to... 回覆…		catalog (n.) 目錄 (= catalogue)
lay out... 安排…，設計…		prefer (v.) 寧願（選擇），更喜歡

精進度 ★ ★ ★ ☆ ☆

句型 *3*

It's going to take me another..., at the soonest.
我最快也要再花……的時間。

Example 實用例句

- It's going to take me another week, at the soonest.
  我最快也要再花一個星期的時間。

- It's going to take me another month, at the soonest.
  我最快也要再花一個月的時間。

- It's going to take me another hour, at the soonest.
  我最快也要再花一個小時的時間。

  說明 ▶ 向對方請求延長時間之後，可以再用本句型向對方明確地提出一段時間。at the soonest（最快）可以視情況替換成 at least（至少）或 if not longer（不超過）等說法。

213

Dialogue 簡短對話

A: How much longer will it take to finish sewing the buttons onto the costumes?

B: It's going to take me another hour or two, at least.

A：還要多久才能把戲服上的鈕扣縫好？

B：我至少還要花一到兩個小時。

字彙	sew (v.) 縫紉 button (n.) 鈕扣	costume (n.)（戲劇或電影的）服裝

精進度★★★★☆

句型4

I'm afraid I'll need more time...
我恐怕需要更多時間⋯⋯

Example 實用例句

● I'm afraid I'll need more time to complete the project.
我恐怕需要更多時間才能完成這項計畫。

● I'm afraid I'll need more time to get everything ready.
我恐怕需要更多時間才能將一切都準備好。

● I'm afraid I'll need more time if I'm to produce an accurate analysis.
如果要我做出精準分析的話，我恐怕需要更多的時間。

說明 ▶ 本句型 time 的後面通常會接不定詞（如第一、二個例句），不過也可以接副詞子句（如第三個例句）等其他形式的內容。另外，如果要表達得更直接，可以說 I need more time...（我需要更多時間⋯⋯）。

Dialogue 簡短對話

A: I'm afraid I'll need more time to determine whether the DNA samples match.

B: Understood, but please hurry. Time is of the essence.

A：我恐怕需要更多時間，才能判定這些 DNA 樣本是否一致。

B：了解，不過請快一點。時間寶貴。

214

說明 ▶ 如果某人在趕時間，可能會說 Time is of the essence.，意思是時間寶貴，必須儘快完成某事。

accurate (adj.) 精確的，精準的　　　　　　　essence (n.) 精髓
determine (v.) 判定

精進度★★★★★

句型 5

Would it be all right if I let you know...?
如果我……再告訴你，可以嗎？

EXAMPLE 實用例句

● Would it be all right if I let you know in a few days?
　如果我過幾天再告訴你，可以嗎？

● Would it be all right if I let you know next week?
　如果我下星期再告訴你，可以嗎？

● Would it be all right if I let you know after our planning meeting?
　如果我開完企畫會議之後再告訴你，可以嗎？

說明 ▶ 本句型另外有一個同樣正式的說法：Would it be possible for me to let you know...?。此外，還有兩個比較沒那麼正式的說法：Can I let you know...? 及 Would it be OK if I let you know...?。

DIALOGUE 簡短對話

A: I apologize for the delay. Would it be all right if I let you know by next Tuesday?
B: That should be fine. I look forward to hearing from you.
　A：我為延誤一事致歉。如果我下個星期二之前告訴你，可以嗎？
　B：應該沒問題。期待你的回音。

delay (n.) 延誤，耽擱　　　　　　　　　　　hear from... 收到…的信；從…得到消息
look forward to... 期待…

➥ Time is of the essence. 時間寶貴。／刻不容緩。

➥ I want to do the best job possible. 我希望盡可能做到最好。

➥ I apologize for the delay. 我為延誤一事致歉。

➥ Please let me know as soon as possible. 請儘快讓我知道。

➥ I look forward to hearing from you. 我期待你的回音。

非正式

I hope I can find out what happened. 句型1

我希望我可以弄清楚到底發生了什麼事。

I only want to avoid any misunderstandings.

我只是想避免任何誤解。

稍非正式

We are passionate about creating environmentally friendly skincare products. 句型2

我們充滿熱情,想要製造出對環境友善的護膚產品。

Basically, we're looking to prevent future accidents from happening.

基本上,我們希望避免未來發生意外事故。

一般情況

We'd like to make it easier for senior citizens to order medication online.

我們希望讓年長者更容易在網路上訂購藥品。

The group is focusing on raising awareness about childhood poverty. 句型3

這個團體的重點是提高大眾對兒童貧窮的認識。

稍正式

Our purpose is to find a way to reduce the crime rate. 句型4

我們的目的是找到方法來降低犯罪率。

We're here to do whatever you need to help you reach your goals.

我們來這裡是要做任何可以幫助你達成目標的事。

正式

Increasing brand awareness is our primary mission. 句型5

提高品牌知名度是我們的首要任務。

The program's chief aim is to get more students involved in community volunteering.

這項計畫的主要目標是讓更多學生參與社區志工服務。

句型 1

I hope I can...
我希望我可以……

Example 實用例句

● I hope I can find out what happened.
我希望我可以弄清楚到底發生了什麼事。

● I hope I can convince you that I'm telling the truth.
我希望我可以讓你相信我說的是真的。

● I hope I can get all these presents wrapped by 5:00.
我希望我可以在五點之前把這些禮物全部包好。

說明 ▶ 本句型也可以替換成 I'm hoping to be able to...。

Dialogue 簡短對話

A: I hope I can book a block of adjoining rooms, but I'll have to check with the hotel to see if it's possible.

B: That would be perfect.

A：我希望可以訂下一整區相鄰的房間，不過我得問一下飯店，看看有沒有可能。

B：那就太好了。

convince (v.) 說服，使相信	block (n.) 街區
wrap (v.) 包，包裹	adjoining (adj.) 相鄰的

句型 2

We are passionate about...
我們充滿熱情，想要……

Example 實用例句

● We are passionate about creating environmentally friendly skincare products.
我們充滿熱情，想要製造出對環境友善的護膚產品。

- We are passionate about publishing DIY books that can turn anyone into a carpenter.
  我們充滿熱情，想要出版可以讓任何人都變成木匠的 DIY 書籍。

- We are passionate about getting fans involved in decisions about the TV show.
  我們充滿熱情，想要讓粉絲參與這個電視節目的製作決策。

  說明 ▶ passionate about 也可以替換成 firmly committed to（堅定致力於）、completely dedicated to（完全致力於）等具有正面含意的用語。另外，about 的後面接動名詞。

Dɪalogue 簡短對話

A: We're passionate about developing clean energy solutions for homes and businesses.

B: I can tell. I've never been in an office powered entirely by renewable energy.

A：我們充滿熱情，想要為一般家庭和企業開發出乾淨能源的解決方案。

B：我看得出來。我從來沒看過一間辦公室完全以再生能源來發電。

字彙	
passionate (adj.) 熱情的	DIY 自己動手做 (= do it yourself)
environmentally friendly 　對環境友善的，環保的	carpenter (n.) 木匠
skincare (adj.) 護膚的	clean energy 乾淨能源 solution (n.)（問題、困難等的）解決辦法
publish (v.) 出版	renewable energy 再生能源

精進度 ★★★☆☆

句型 *3*

...is focusing on ～
……的重點是～

Example 實用例句

- The group is focusing on raising awareness about childhood poverty.
  這個團體的重點是提高大眾對兒童貧窮的認識。

表達目的／意圖

- The group is focusing on retraining workers in the manufacturing sector.
  這個團體的重點是再訓練製造業的勞工。

- The group is focusing on finding new retail channels for our cosmetics.
  這個團體的重點是為我們的化妝品找到新的零售通路。

  說明 ▸ 本句型中的 focusing 常常可以替換成 focused，變成 ...be focused on ～；on 的後面一般接動名詞。另外，上面三個例句中的 The group is focusing on... 也可改成 The group's focus is on... 或 The group's attention is squarely on...（這個團體的注意力很明確地放在⋯⋯）來表達。

Dᴉᴀʟᴏɢᴜᴇ 簡短對話

A: What are you working on?

B: Well, these days I'm focusing on completing the integration of a company we recently acquired.

  A：你在忙什麼呢？

  B：嗯，我們公司近來剛收購一家公司，我最近忙著完成整合工作。

awareness (n.) 察覺，認識	squarely (adv.) 直截了當地
poverty (n.) 貧窮	work on... 忙於…，致力於…
manufacturing sector 製造業	integration (n.) 整合
retail channel 零售通路	acquire (v.) 收購，購得
cosmetics (n.) 化妝品	

精進度★★★★☆

句型4

Our purpose is...
我們的目的是⋯⋯

Eхᴀᴍᴘʟᴇ 實用例句

- Our purpose is to find a way to reduce the crime rate.
  我們的目的是找到方法來降低犯罪率。

- Our purpose is to shorten the time between R&D breakthroughs and product roll-outs.
  我們的目的是縮短研發出現突破性進展到產品上市之間的時間。

● Our purpose is to educate the public about the dangers of carbon monoxide poisoning.
我們的目的是教育大眾一氧化碳中毒的危險性。

說明 ▶ purpose（目的，目標）也可替換成 objective 或 goal，意思不變。另外，is 的後面接〈to + 原形動詞〉。

Dialogue 簡短對話

A: What are you hoping to achieve?

B: Our purpose is to map this section of the ocean floor to better understand the local ecosystem.

A：你希望達到什麼目的呢？

B：我們的目的是畫出這片海床區域的地圖，以便更了解當地生態。

字彙	R&D 研究和發展，研發 　(= research and development) breakthrough (n.) 突破性進展 roll-out (n.)（新產品、服務等）首次展示 carbon monoxide (CO) 一氧化碳	poisoning (n.) 中毒 achieve (v.) 達成 map (v.) 繪製（某地區的）地圖 floor (n.)（海洋或山谷的）底部 ecosystem (n.) 生態系統

精進度★★★★★

句型 5

...is our primary mission.
……是我們的首要任務。

Example 實用例句

● Increasing brand awareness is our primary mission.
提高品牌知名度是我們的首要任務。

● Fostering cross-cultural understanding is our primary mission.
促進跨文化了解是我們的首要任務。

● Switching to more "best practice" procedures is our primary mission.
轉換到更符合「最佳作業」流程是我們的首要任務。

說明 ▶ 本句型的主詞通常以動名詞開頭。另外，mission（任務，使命）可以指公司的任務，也就是公司的經營哲學；也可以指某項工作任務，此時 mission 可以替換成 function 或 goal。

Dialogue 簡短對話

A: How would you categorize the NPO's mission?

B: Administering vaccines to rural communities is our primary mission.

A：你會如何歸類這項非營利組織的任務呢？

B：提供疫苗給鄉下社區是我們的首要任務。

字彙

brand awareness 品牌知名度
primary (adj.) 首要的
mission (n.) 任務，使命
foster (v.) 促進
cross-cultural (adj.) 跨文化的
procedure (n.) 流程

categorize (v.) 把…歸類，把…列作
NPO 非營利組織 (= non-profit organization)
administer (v.) 提供，給予
vaccine (n.) 疫苗
rural (adj.) 鄉下的
community (n.) 社區

相關表達 有哪些用來詢問目的或目標的好用句呢？

➥ How would you categorize your purpose/mission?
你會如何歸類你的目的 / 任務呢？

➥ What would you say your primary goal is?
你的主要目標是什麼呢？

➥ What are you hoping to achieve?
你希望達到什麼目標呢？

➥ What are you working on?
你在忙什麼呢？

➥ What's your top objective?
你的首要目標是什麼呢？

非正式

Well done.　　　　　　　　　　　　　表現得很好。

Great job!　　　　　　　　　　　　　幹得好！

稍非正式

I'm really happy for you. 句型 *1*　　　我真的很替你高興。

I was thrilled to hear the news.　　　我很興奮聽到這個消息。

一般情況

Congratulations on your promotion. 句型 *2*　　恭喜你升職了。

Let me be the first to shake your hand. 句型 *3*　　讓我第一個來和你握手道賀。

稍正式

I want to applaud you on your hard work leading the division to profitability.　　對於你勤奮努力地帶領這個部門獲利，我要向你表示讚許。

May I congratulate you on a stunning victory.　　恭喜你取得漂亮的勝利。

正式

You are to be commended for never quitting despite the tall odds. 句型 *4*　　儘管勝算不大，不過你從未放棄，值得讚揚。

I'd like to extend my congratulations on the success of your sales campaign. 句型 *5*　　你們的銷售活動辦得很成功，我想要表達祝賀之意。

句型 *1* **...for you.**
替你……

Example 實用例句

- I'm really happy for you.
  我真的很替你高興。

- I'm thrilled for you.
  我替你感到興奮。

- We're all tickled pink for you.
  我們全都替你高興極了。

  說明 ▶ 本句型 for you 的前面可以用各種表達正面意思的說法。以第一個例句來說，really happy 還可以替換成 delighted（欣喜的）或 overjoyed（欣喜若狂的）。

Dialogue 簡短對話

A: Can you believe it? I won a full scholarship to Stanford!
B: I'm so happy for you. It couldn't have happened to a nicer person.
  A：你相信嗎？我拿到史丹佛大學的全額獎學金了！
  B：我替你感到好開心。沒有人比你更有資格拿到了。

thrill (v.) 使極度興奮	scholarship (n.) 獎學金
tickled pink 高興極了，樂不可支	Stanford 美國史丹佛大學

句型 *2* **Congratulations on...**
恭喜……

Example 實用例句

- Congratulations on your promotion.
  恭喜你升職了。

● Congratulations on coming in first.
恭喜你獲得了第一名。

● Congratulations on finishing your dissertation.
恭喜你完成了學位論文。

說明 ▶ 如果是朋友之間要用本句型來互道恭喜，通常會將 congratulations 縮短說成 congrats。congratulations 也可以替換成 kudos（獎賞，榮譽），只不過這種說法非常不正式。

Dialogue 簡短對話

A: Congratulations on the race. Your time was amazing.
B: It was my personal best. I've never pushed myself that hard.

A：恭喜你完成了比賽。你所花的時間真是令人稱奇。
B：這是我個人最佳成績，我從來沒那麼努力鞭策過自己。

說明 ▶ 如果要表達自己創造了一項紀錄，可以用 personal best（個人最佳成績）。這個說法通常用於田徑運動上，不過也可以指其他競賽或嗜好。

字彙	congratulations (n.) 恭喜 (= congrats)	dissertation (n.) 學位論文
	promotion (n.) 升職，擢升	kudos (n.) 獎賞，榮譽
	come in first 比賽時獲得第一名	push (v.) 督促，鼓勵

精進度 ★★★☆☆

句型 *3*

Let me be the first to...
讓我第一個來……

Example 實用例句

● Let me be the first to shake your hand.
讓我第一個來和你握手道賀。

● Let me be the first to congratulate you.
讓我第一個來恭喜你。

● Let me be the first to offer my well wishes.
讓我第一個來獻上祝福。

說明 ▶ 本句型用於非常急切地想向對方道賀時，也可以用 I wanted to be the first to...（我想第一個……）來表達。

Dialogue 簡短對話

A: Let me be the first to say congratulations. You really earned the appointment, and I think you'll make an excellent trade minister.

B: I appreciate it. I hope I'm up for the task.

A：讓我第一個來說聲恭喜。這項任命是你努力得來的，我想你一定會成為優秀的貿易部長。

B：謝謝。希望我能勝任這份工作。

說明 ▶ B 使用了〈be up for + 工作、任務〉這個句型，意思是「夠資格或準備好要執行某項工作、達成某項任務等」。

congratulate (v.) 向（某人）道賀	trade minister 貿易部長
wishes (n.) 祝頌	appreciate (v.) 感激，感謝
appointment (n.) 任命，指派	be up for... 為…做好準備

精進度★★★★★

句型4

...to be commended for ～
……值得讚揚，因為～

Example 實用例句

● You are to be commended for never quitting despite the tall odds.
儘管勝算不大，不過你從未放棄，值得讚揚。

● Your team is to be commended for setting a terrific example.
你的團隊立下很棒的榜樣，值得讚揚。

● Jackie and you are to be commended for sticking to your principles.
你和傑奇堅守原則，值得讚揚。

說明 ▶ 本句型一般由位高權重的人來使用。另有一個比較沒那麼正式，可以用在很多種情況下的說法：〈It's really commendable the way + 主詞 + 動詞〉。另外，stick to one's principles 是「堅守原則」的意思。

Dialogue 簡短對話

A: You are to be commended for scoring a perfect score on the qualification exam.

B: Thank you, sir. I still can't believe it myself.

　A：你的資格考拿到滿分，值得讚揚。

　B：謝謝老師。我自己都還不敢相信。

字彙
commend (v.) 讚揚	commendable (adj.) 值得讚美的，可欽佩的
tall (adj.) 難以置信的	perfect score 滿分
odds (n.) 勝算，可能性	qualification exam 資格考
set an example 立下榜樣	

精進度★★★★★

句型 **5**

I'd like to extend my congratulations on...
我想要對⋯⋯表達祝賀之意。

Example 實用例句

● I'd like to extend my congratulations on the success of your sales campaign.
你們的銷售活動辦得很成功，我想要表達祝賀之意。

● I'd like to extend my congratulations on what you were able to accomplish on a shoestring budget.
對於你能以微薄的預算完成任務，我想要表達祝賀之意。

● I'd like to extend my congratulations on your being selected for the task force.
對於你獲選為本任務小組的一員，我想要表達祝賀之意。

說明 ▶ extend（給予）可以替換成 offer。on 的後面可以接名詞（如第一個例句）或名詞子句（如第二個例句），也可以接〈代名詞所有格 + 動名詞〉（如第三個例句）。

Dialogue 簡短對話

A: I'd like to extend my congratulations on the positive reviews your art show got.

B: Thank you! To be honest, I didn't expect the critics to be so kind.

A：你的藝術展獲得好評，我想要表達祝賀之意。

B：謝謝！坦白說，我沒想到評論家這麼仁慈。

相關表達　向對方道賀時，通常還會說些什麼應景的話呢？

➥ You really earned it/the promotion/the award.
這個／這次升遷／這個獎是你努力贏來的。

➥ You deserve it.
這是你應得的。

➥ It couldn't have happened to a better/nicer person.
沒有比你更適合／更有資格的人選了。

提出警告 / 告誡
Issuing a Warning/Caution

非正式

Watch your head.

小心你的頭。

Word of warning: they'll charge you extra if you use a credit card. 句型1

提醒一句：如果你使用信用卡，他們將會收取額外的費用。

稍非正式

Pay attention to the temperature gauge.

注意這支溫度計。

Don't take any unnecessary chances.

不要冒不必要的風險。

一般情況

Acting too fast could be risky. 句型2

急於行動可能會有風險。

It can be an unpredictable market.

那是個無法預測的市場。

稍正式

You might want to be careful with those wires. 句型3

你最好小心那些電線。

Has anybody warned you about the potential risk of exchange rate losses?

有人警告你可能會有匯差損失的風險嗎？

正式

I'd caution against producing too many units in the initial run. 句型4

我想提醒你不要在剛開始運轉時就生產太多套。

If I might issue a word of caution, be careful what you say around Mario. 句型5

如果願意聽我提醒一句，馬力歐在的時候說話要小心。

句型 1 Word of warning:...
提醒一句：……

Example 實用例句

● Word of warning: they'll charge you extra if you use a credit card.
提醒一句：如果你使用信用卡，他們將會收取額外的費用。

● Word of warning: a lot of tourists get cheated by local jewelers.
提醒一句：很多觀光客被當地珠寶商詐騙。

● Word of warning: the engine gets very hot after an hour or two.
提醒一句：引擎運轉一、兩個小時後會變得非常熱。

說明 ▶ 本句型有一個類似但長度比較長的說法：Let me give you a word of warning:...。冒號的後面接子句。

Dialogue 簡短對話

A: This has been a fantastic trip. We're thinking of taking a train into the city for dinner.

B: Nice plan. Word of warning: the last train leaves the main station at about midnight. If you miss it, it will be an expensive taxi ride back.

A：這是一段很棒的旅行。我們正在考慮搭火車到市區吃晚餐。

B：很好的計畫。提醒一句：最後一班火車大約午夜離開中央車站，如果錯過了，搭計程車回去會很貴。

charge (v.) 索價	jeweler (n.) 珠寶商
cheat (v.) 欺騙	engine (n.) 引擎

句型 2 ...could be risky.
……可能會有風險。

Example 實用例句

● Acting too fast could be risky.
急於行動可能會有風險。

● Buying stocks in this market could be risky.
買這塊市場的股票可能會有風險。

● Trusting someone you just met could be risky.
信任剛認識的人可能會有風險。

說明 ▶ 本句型用來警告一個人做某件事可能會有某種程度的風險。可以用動名詞開頭作主詞。如果語氣要更強烈一點，可以把 could be risky 替換成 is very risky 或 would be very risky。

Dialogue 簡短對話

A: Letting an inexperienced person run your South American operations could be risky. Keep a close eye on things.

B: Don't worry. It will be fine.

A：讓一個缺乏經驗的人負責南美的營運可能會有風險。要隨時保持密切關注。

B：不要擔心，沒事。

說明 ▶ A 所說的 keep a close eye on... 是「密切關注…」之意。

字彙 risky (adj.) 有風險的   operation (n.) 運作

精進度 ★★★★☆

 句型 3
You might want to be careful with...
你最好小心……

提出警告／告誡

Example 實用例句

● You might want to be careful with those wires.
你最好小心那些電線。

● You might want to be careful with that electric saw.
你最好小心那把電鋸。

● You might want to be careful with the reptile cage.
你最好小心這個爬蟲類動物的籠子。

說明 ▶ 如果要更直接一點，might want to 可以替換成 should；如果還要更強勢一點，可以說 really should 或 have to。

Dialogue 簡短對話

A: You might want to be careful with that tea pot. It's an antique.

B: Oh, sorry. I'll put it down.

A：你最好小心那只茶壺。那是古董。

B：噢，對不起。我把它放下來。

精進度★★★★★

句型4

I'd caution against...

我想提醒你不要……

Example 實用例句

- I'd caution against producing too many units in the initial run.

  我想提醒你不要在剛開始運轉時就生產太多套。

- I'd caution against using components from too many different suppliers.

  我想提醒你不要使用太多不同供應商的零件。

- I'd caution against taking the highway unless you want to be stuck in traffic.

  我想提醒你不要走公路，除非你想塞車。

  說明 ▶ 本句型直接提出具體的警告，提醒對方不要做某事，against 的後面通常以不要對方做的事情開頭，採用動名詞的形式，或者也可以直接接 it 或 that。

Dialogue 簡短對話

A: Do you think I should buy a watch from the guy? He's got great prices.

B: I'd caution against it. His feedback isn't very good.

A：你覺得我應該向那個人買手錶嗎？他的價錢很便宜。

B：我想提醒你不要。他的評價不是非常好。

說明 ▶ 本對話通常出現在網路購物或網路拍賣的情境。

精進度★★★★★

句型*5*

If I might issue a word of caution,...

如果願意聽我提醒一句，……

Example 實用例句

● If I might issue a word of caution, be careful what you say around Mario.

如果願意聽我提醒一句，馬力歐在的時候說話要小心。

● If I might issue a word of caution, you shouldn't wait until the last minute to book your plane ticket.

如果願意聽我提醒一句，你不應該等到最後一刻才訂機票。

● If I might issue a word of caution, there are 1,000 reasons for staying home during blizzards like this one.

如果願意聽我提醒一句，遇到這種暴風雪的時候，有一千個理由應該待在家裡。

說明 ▶ 本句型的主要子句通常是一個建議（如第一、二個例句），也可以是提出警告的理由（如第三個例句）。另外，wait until the last minute 是「拖延到最後快沒時間時才做某事」的意思。

Dialogue 簡短對話

A: If I might issue a word of caution, don't eat too much before the boat ride. The waves get choppy.

B: That's good to know, thanks.

A：如果願意聽我提醒一句，搭船之前不要吃太多，因為海浪波濤洶湧。

B：幸好先知道了，謝啦。

提出警告／告誡

如果要提出警告，有哪些好用的慣用說法呢？

➥ Keep your wits about you. 隨時保持頭腦清醒。／隨時保持警覺。

➥ An ounce of prevention is worth a pound of cure. 預防勝過治療。

➥ Keep a close eye on things. 隨時保持密切關注。

40 表達鼓勵與祝福
Encouraging and Wishing Luck

非正式

Do your best.　　　　　　　　　　盡力而為。

If anyone can pull it off, it's you. 句型1　　如果有人可以成功完成，那一定就是你了。

稍非正式

We're all behind you.　　　　　　　我們全都支持你。

I'm sure you'll do great. 句型2　　我相信你一定會做得很棒。

一般情況

Keep up the good work.　　　　　　做得很好，繼續加油。

Best of luck with the driving test. 句型3　　祝你順利考到駕照。

稍正式

I wish you all the best.　　　　　　祝你萬事如意。

You have my full support.　　　　　我全力支持你。

正式

I hope everything goes well with your permit application. 句型4　　我希望你的許可證申請一切順利。

I sincerely hope your partnership is successful. 句型5　　我衷心希望你們的搭檔合作能夠成功。

句型 1　**If anyone can..., it's you.**
如果有人可以⋯⋯，那一定就是你了。

Example 實用例句

- If anyone can pull it off, it's you.
  如果有人可以成功完成，那一定就是你了。

- If anyone can make it work, it's you.
  如果有人可以搞定，那一定就是你了。

- If anyone can fix the generator, it's you.
  如果有人可以把這台發電機修好，那一定就是你了。

  說明 ▶ 使用本句型時，通常表示對方非常有資格或能力完成某項工作。助動詞 can 的後面可以接以動詞為主的內容（如 pull it off, make it work, see it through 等），也可以接一件具體的任務（如第三個例句中的 fix the generator）。

Dialogue 簡短對話

A: How am I going to recover any data from the hard drive? The whole office was flooded, including the computer.

B: If anyone can do it, it's you. I've seen you work bigger miracles before.

　A：我要怎麼樣才能把硬碟裡的資料救回來啊？整個辦公室都淹水了，電腦也無法倖免。

　B：如果有人可以做到，那一定就是你了。我以前看你施展過更大的奇蹟。

　說明 ▶ work miracles 一詞源起於基督教，不過現在已經變成一個普遍使用的說法，意思是「完成一件神奇、了不起的工作」。

pull off... 成功完成（難事）	flood (v.) 使氾濫，淹沒
generator (n.) 發電機	miracle (n.) 奇蹟
hard drive 硬碟	

精進度 ★★ ☆ ☆ ☆

句型2 I'm sure you'll do...
我相信你一定會做得……

Example 實用例句

- I'm sure you'll do great.
  我相信你一定會做得很棒。

- I'm sure you'll do very well.
  我相信你一定會做得非常好。

- I'm sure you'll do a wonderful job.
  我相信你一定會表現得非常棒。

  說明 ▶ 本句型還有另外一個類似、但語氣比較強烈的說法：I have every confidence that you'll do...（我絕對有信心你一定會……）。嚴格說起來，第一個例句的 do 之後應該接副詞，不過在現代英文裡，do great 已經是普遍接受的用法，事實上，如果用 do greatly 反而極不尋常。

Dialogue 簡短對話

A: I'm kind of nervous about the presentation. Even my boss's bosses will be there.
B: Chin up. I'm sure you'll do a fantastic job.

　A：我對這場簡報有點緊張，連我上司的上司都會到場。
　B：打起精神來。我相信你一定會有很棒的表現。

  說明 ▶ chin up 是用來鼓勵別人面對挑戰時要奮發振作，字面上的意思是鼓勵人抬頭挺胸、不要顯露出沮喪的肢體語言，也可以用來安慰失敗或受到挫折的人。

精進度 ★★★ ☆ ☆

句型3 Best of luck with...
祝你……好運。

Example 實用例句

- Best of luck with the driving test.
  祝你順利考到駕照。

表達鼓勵與祝福

- Best of luck with finding a sound editor for your film.
  祝你順利為你的電影找到音效剪輯師。

- Best of luck with whatever you have planned after leaving the company.
  祝你離開公司後不管有什麼計畫都很順利。

  說明 ▶ best of luck 也可以替換成 good luck。with 的後面可以接一個簡短的名詞（如第一個例句）、動名詞（如第二個例句），也可以接名詞子句（如第三個例句）。

Dialogue 簡短對話

A: Best of luck with your interview.

B: Thanks. I really could use a break. Well, you know what they say: It's always darkest before the dawn.

A：祝你面試順利成功。

B：謝啦。我真的需要好運。嗯，你知道有句話是怎麼說的：破曉之前總是最黑暗的。

說明 ▶ 如果要強調即使是最糟糕的情況也會好轉，便可以像 B 那樣說 It's always darkest before the dawn.（破曉之前總是最黑暗的。／否極泰來。）相當常用。

 字彙 sound editor 音效剪輯師　　　　　　break (n.) 好運

精進度★★★★★

句型 4　I hope everything goes well with...
我希望……一切順利。

Example 實用例句

- I hope everything goes well with your permit application.
  我希望你的許可證申請一切順利。

- I hope everything goes well with the meeting.
  我希望會議一切順利。

● I hope everything goes well with the yard sale.
我希望庭院舊貨拍賣一切順利。

說明 ▶ 本句型另外有一個類似的說法：I hope there aren't any problems with...（我希望……沒有任何問題。）with 的後面通常接名詞。

Dialogue 簡短對話

A: I hope everything goes well with the musical. Break a leg!

B: Thanks. After all this rehearsing, I'm ready for the curtain to go up!

A：我希望歌舞劇的演出一切順利。祝你好運！

B：謝啦。經過這些排練之後，我已經準備好等著布幕升起！

說明 ▶ Break a leg! 的意思是「祝你好運！」，通常用於表演、音樂會、訪談之前，祝福即將上台的人好運。

字彙	permit (n.) 許可證 yard sale 庭院舊貨拍賣	musical (n.) 歌舞劇，音樂劇 rehearse (v.) 排練，預演

精進度★★★★★

 句型5

I sincerely hope...

我衷心希望……

Example 實用例句

● I sincerely hope your partnership is successful.
我衷心希望你們的搭檔合作能夠成功。

● I sincerely hope everything works out for the best.
我衷心希望一切都會有好結果。

● I sincerely hope the review board rules in your favor.
我衷心希望審查委員會做出有利於你們的裁定。

說明 ▶ 動詞 hope 的後面接子句。本句型另外有一個類似、但語氣比較正式的說法：It is my sincere hope that...。

Dialogue 簡短對話

A: Any day now, we should hear back from the bank about our loan application.

B: I sincerely hope they approve the loan. Your business plan is rock solid.

A：不久之後，我們應該就會接到銀行對我們貸款申請的回音。

B：我衷心希望他們會核准貸款。你的營運計畫堅若磐石。

說明 ▶ A 所說的 any day now 是「不久之後」之意。

字彙

partnership (n.) 合作夥伴關係	rule (v.) 裁定
work out for the best 最後完成得很好	in someone's favor 有利於某人
review board 審查委員會	rock solid 堅若磐石

相關表達　下面提供幾個可以用來鼓勵別人的慣用說法：

➥ If at first you don't succeed, try, try, (try) again.
如果一開始不成功，那就繼續嘗試。／欲得成功，貴在堅持。

➥ It's always darkest before the dawn.
破曉之前總是最黑暗的。／否極泰來。

➥ Break a leg!
祝你好運！

提醒他人
Reminding

非正式

Remember to call the plumber.　　　　　　記得要打電話叫水電工。

Make a note of the deadline.　　　　　　把截止時間記下來。

稍非正式

Don't forget to turn off all the lights. 句型 *1*　　不要忘記把所有的燈關掉。

You might want to make a mental note of it.　你可能會想把它記在心裡。

一般情況

I'll send you a reminder in a few weeks. 句型 *2*　我會在幾個星期後寄一封信提醒你。

Did you remember to send Mr. Harrison a thank you card?　你有記得寄謝卡給哈里森先生嗎？

稍正式

Please keep in mind that the marketing director likes to be called "Phil." 句型 *3*　行銷總監喜歡人家叫他「菲爾」，這一點請牢記於心。

We should all be aware of the cultural differences between some of the participants. 句型 *4*　我們都應該知道有些參加者當中存在著文化差異。

正式

I'd like to remind everyone that eating is not allowed inside the auditorium. 句型 *5*　我想要提醒各位禮堂裡面禁止飲食。

Could I please ask you to remember to activate the alarm when you go out?　可以請你外出時記得撥一下鬧鐘嗎？

句型 *1* Don't forget to...
不要忘記……

Example 實用例句

● Don't forget to turn off all the lights.
不要忘記把所有的燈關掉。

● Don't forget to upload the grades to the records department.
不要忘記把成績上傳到檔案處。

● Don't forget to apply two layers of varnish after you strip the wood.
拆掉木頭後不要忘記要上兩層亮光漆。

說明 ▶ 如果要讓語氣更強烈一點，可以將本句型改成 You mustn't forget to...（你不可以忘記……）。to 的後面接原形動詞。

Dialogue 簡短對話

A: Thank you again for keeping an eye on the house for us. Don't forget to feed the fish twice a day.
B: I won't. Your house and fish are in good hands.

　A：再次謝謝你幫我們看家。不要忘記每天要餵兩次魚。
　B：我不會忘記的。你們的房子和魚會獲得很好的照料。

說明 ▶ B 所說的 in good hands 是「受到很好的照料或關注」之意。

varnish (n.) 亮光漆，清漆　　　　　　keep an eye on... 留意…，看管…
strip (v.) 拆卸，拆開

句型 *2* I'll ... in a few weeks.
我會在幾個星期後……

Example 實用例句

● I'll send you a reminder in a few weeks.
我會在幾個星期後寄一封信提醒你。

- I'll remind you again in a few weeks.
  我會在幾個星期後再次提醒你。

- I'll drop you a note in a few weeks.
  我會在幾個星期後寫封短信提醒你。

  說明 ▶ 如果用本句型來表達，表示說話者會負責在未來某個時間發出提醒。in a few weeks 也可以替換成任何其他時間；或者也可以用 down the road（將來，今後）來表示未來某個未明確指出的時間。drop someone a note 是個非正式的說法，意思是「寄一個訊息給某人，寫一封短信給某人」。

Dialogue 簡短對話

A: I hope I can remember the date of Jamie's soccer game.
B: I'll remind you again the day before the match.
   A：希望我能記得傑米的足球比賽日期。
   B：我會在比賽的前一天再次提醒你。

 字彙 reminder (n.) 用於提醒的人或物   match (n.) 比賽

精進度 ★★★★☆

 句型 3

Please keep in mind that...
……這一點請牢記於心。

Example 實用例句

- Please keep in mind that the marketing director likes to be called "Phil."
  行銷總監喜歡人家叫他「菲爾」，這一點請牢記於心。

- Please keep in mind that this deep in the countryside, foreign visitors are rare.
  在這麼深入的鄉野間鮮少有外國遊客，這一點請牢記於心。

- Please keep in mind that all previous attempts to replicate the experiment have failed.
  過去所有複製這項實驗的嘗試都失敗了，這一點請牢記於心。

說明 ▶ 本句型用於向對方提醒或強調某個重點。keep in mind（牢記）可以替換成 remember，變成 Please remember that...。

Dialogue 簡短對話

A: Please keep in mind that Mr. Leary is sensitive about his age. So try not to bring it up.

B: Thanks for the reminder.

　A：賴瑞先生對於自己的年紀很敏感，這一點請牢記於心，所以盡量不要提到他的年齡。

　B：謝謝提醒。

replicate (v.) 複製
sensitive (adj.) 敏感的

bring up... 提起…

句型 4

We should all be aware...
我們都應該知道……

Example 實用例句

● We should all be aware of the cultural differences between some of the participants.
我們都應該知道有些參加者當中存在著文化差異。

● We should all be aware that the weather might force us to move the event indoors.
我們都應該知道天氣可能會迫使我們把活動移到室內。

● We should all be aware that it is a great honor to be invited to meet the conductor.
我們都應該知道能夠受邀與這名指揮見面是莫大的榮幸。

說明 ▶ 本句型的後面如果要接名詞，就要用〈be aware of + 名詞〉；如果要接子句，則要用〈be aware that + 主詞 + 動詞〉。

Dialogue 簡短對話

A: I wish we could take photos.

B: I'm afraid that won't be possible. We should all be aware of the taboo against photographing the ceremony.

A：真希望我們能拍照。

B：恐怕不可能。我們都應該知道這場典禮是禁止拍攝的。

字彙

aware (adj.) 知道的	conductor (n.)（管弦樂團或合唱團的）指揮
participant (n.) 參加者	taboo (n.) 禁忌
force (v.) 迫使	photograph (v.) 攝影，拍照
honor (n.) 榮幸	ceremony (n.) 典禮

提醒他人

精進度★★★★★

句型 5

I'd like to remind everyone that...
我想要提醒各位……

Example 實用例句

- I'd like to remind everyone that eating is not allowed inside the auditorium.

  我想要提醒各位禮堂裡面禁止飲食。

- I'd like to remind everyone that recording devices are strictly prohibited.

  我想要提醒各位嚴禁使用錄音或錄影裝置。

- I'd like to remind everyone that we need to meet back at the bus in 45 minutes.

  我想要提醒各位 45 分鐘後必須回到巴士這裡集合。

說明 ▶ 本句型通常用於對象是一群人的時候，remind 的後面一般會接 everyone, all the attendees（所有出席者）或 you all。that 的後面接子句。

Dialogue 簡短對話

A: I'd like to remind everyone that this is a working laboratory. So you shouldn't touch anything.

B: That's too bad. The mice are so cute!

A：我想要提醒各位這間實驗室正在運作中，所以不可以碰觸任何東西。

B：太可惜了。這些老鼠好可愛啊！

說明▶ 若用 working 來形容實驗室或診所，表示該實驗室或診所正在運作或執業中。

字彙

auditorium (n.) 禮堂

recording device 錄音、錄影裝置

prohibit (v.) 禁止，不允許

相關表達 **對於別人的提醒，有哪些常用的回應方式呢？**

➥ I'll keep that in mind.
我會記在心上的。

➥ Thanks for the reminder.
謝謝提醒。

➥ Thanks for reminding me.
謝謝提醒我。

➥ Please send me another reminder so I don't forget.
請再寄一封信提醒我，我就不會忘記了。

There's nothing I can do about it.

我無能為力。

Let's stick with the original plan.

我們就堅持按照原本的計畫吧。

I don't mean to be pushy, but a lower price point would benefit sales.

我無意施壓干涉,不過價格低一點會有利銷售的。

I can't budge on that issue. 句型 1

我在那項議題上無法讓步。

I must insist that we stick to the July 15 release date.

我必須堅持發售日期一定要在 7 月 15 日。

It's really the best course of action for everyone involved. 句型 2

這真的是對每名參與者都有利的最佳行動方案。

We feel very strongly about hiring an athlete to sponsor the line. 句型 3

我們強烈認為應該聘請一名運動員來代言這條產品線。

I hope you'll agree this is the best way forward.

我希望你會同意這是最好的方式 / 出路。

We can be flexible elsewhere; but in terms of packaging, we have a clear concept in mind. 句型 4

我們可以在別的地方有彈性,不過關於包裝,我們的心裡已經有明確的想法。

I'm afraid that on that point we're going to have to insist on a 60/40 profit split. 句型 5

恐怕在那一點上我們得堅持利潤六四拆帳。

句型 *1*　**I can't budge on...**

我在⋯⋯上無法讓步（或改變立場）。

Example 實用例句

● I can't budge on that issue.
　我在那項議題上無法讓步。

● I can't budge on any of those clauses.
　我在那些條款上無法讓步。

● I can't budge on the matter.
　我在這件事情上無法讓步。

說明 ▶ 本句型是表達立場已決的簡短說法，也可以改以 I haven't got any flexibility on...（我在⋯⋯上沒有任何彈性空間。）來表達。

Dialogue 簡短對話

A: Do you think we can do something about the issue of electronic distribution rights?
B: I can't budge on that matter. My hands are tied.
　A：你覺得我們可以對電子經銷權做點什麼嗎？
　B：我在那件事情上無法讓步。我無能為力。

說明 ▶ hands are tied 在字面上的意思是「雙手被綁住」，也就是「愛莫能助，無能為力」之意。

　budge (v.)（立場等）動搖，讓步　　　electronic distribution rights 電子經銷權
　clause (n.)（法律文書的）條款

句型2 It's really the best course of action for...
這真的是對……都有利的最佳行動方案。

Example 實用例句

● It's really the best course of action for everyone involved.
這真的是對每名參與者都有利的最佳行動方案。

● It's really the best course of action for both sides.
這真的是對雙方都有利的最佳行動方案。

● It's really the best course of action for all parties.
這真的是對各方都有利的最佳行動方案。

說明 ▶ 本句型用來說服對方，讓對方相信某個立場對各方都有利。course of action（行動方案，行動方針）有好幾種替代說法，包括 option（選項）及 solution（解決方案）。

Dialogue 簡短對話

A: I'm still not sure we need to relocate our operations overseas.
B: It's really the best course of action for all of us.

A：我還不確定我們是否需要把營運遷移到海外。
B：這真的是對我們所有人都有利的最佳行動方案。

字彙　party (n.)（法律協議或辯論中的）一方　　　overseas (adv.) 到海外；在海外
relocate (v.) 搬遷

句型3 We feel very strongly about...
我們強烈認為……

Example 實用例句

● We feel very strongly about hiring an athlete to sponsor the line.
我們強烈認為應該聘請一名運動員來代言這條產品線。

堅持立場

- We feel very strongly about choosing the project manager for the joint venture ourselves.
  我們強烈認為應該由我們自己來挑選這家合資企業的專案經理。

- We feel very strongly about the need for a clause guaranteeing a minimum order.
  我們強烈認為有必要簽訂條款來保證最低訂購數量。

  說明 ▶ 本句型清楚表示出說話者非常希望某件事朝某個方向進行。about 的後面接名詞或動名詞，其中以動名詞較常見。

Dialogue 簡短對話

A: We feel very strongly about using a cooking method with zero trans fat.

B: That might be tricky, but I think we can work it out.

 A：我們強烈認為應該使用一套完全不用反式脂肪的烹調方式。

 B：那可能會很棘手，不過我想我們可以想出辦法。

 說明 ▶ work something out 是指找出某個難題的解決方式或達成決議。

字彙	
athlete (n.) 運動員	clause (n.) 條款
sponsor (v.) 贊助，代言	guarantee (v.) 保證
project manager 專案經理	trans fat 反式脂肪
joint venture 合資企業	tricky (adj.) 棘手的

精進度 ★★★★★

句型 4

We can be flexible elsewhere; but in terms of..., we have a clear concept in mind.
我們可以在別的地方有彈性，不過關於……，我們的心裡已經有明確的想法。

Example 實用例句

- We can be flexible elsewhere; but in terms of packaging, we have a clear concept in mind.
  我們可以在別的地方有彈性，不過關於包裝，我們的心裡已經有明確的想法。

- We can be flexible elsewhere; but in terms of pricing, we have a clear concept in mind.

  我們可以在別的地方有彈性，不過關於定價，我們的心裡已經有明確的想法。

- We can be flexible elsewhere; but in terms of marketing, we have a clear concept in mind.

  我們可以在別的地方有彈性，不過關於行銷，我們的心裡已經有明確的想法。

  說明▶ elsewhere 可以替換成 in other areas（在其他方面），而 in terms of... 可以替換成 when it comes to...（一說到⋯⋯）。另外，we have a clear concept in mind 也可以替換成 our position is firm（我們的立場已定）。

Dialogue 簡短對話

A: In terms of wages, we were hoping to see some movement there.

B: We can be flexible in other areas; but when it comes to wages, our position is firm.

A：關於工資，我們希望看到一些變動。

B：我們可以在其他方面有彈性，不過說到工資，我們的立場已定。

說明▶ see (some) movement 意指在某個議題上看到調整或更動。

字彙		
elsewhere (adv.) 在別處	concept (n.) 概念，想法	
in terms of... 關於⋯	wage (n.) 工資	

精進度★★★★★

 句型 *5*

I'm afraid that on that point...
恐怕在那一點上⋯⋯

Example 實用例句

- I'm afraid that on that point we're going to have to insist on a 60/40 profit split.

  恐怕在那一點上我們得堅持利潤六四拆帳。

- I'm afraid that on that point our company has a set procedure.

  恐怕在那一點上我們公司有一套固定的流程。

● I'm afraid that on that point I haven't got any flexibility to make concessions.

恐怕在那一點上我沒有任何可以退讓的彈性。

說明 ▶ on that point 可以替換成副詞子句，具體講述在討論哪一件事，例如 I'm afraid that when it comes to the division of income,... （說到收入的拆帳，恐怕⋯⋯）。

Dialogue 簡短對話

A: Is there anything we can do about the issue of the franchise fee?

B: I'm afraid that on that point there's no room for negotiation.

A：關於授權費用問題，有什麼是我們可以做的嗎？

B：關於那一點，恐怕沒有協商的空間。

說明 ▶ there's no room for negotiation 是一個很強烈的說法，意思是「沒有協商或爭論的餘地」，表示立場已定，沒有任何可以更改或調整的彈性空間。

字彙		
profit split 利潤分配，拆帳，分帳	concession (n.) 讓步
set (adj.) 固定的	division (n.) 劃分，分隔
procedure (n.) 流程	franchise fee 授權費用
flexibility (n.) 彈性	negotiation (n.) 協商，談判

相關表達 當對方一直很堅持自己的立場時，可以用什麼說法來回應呢？

→ My hands are tied. 我愛莫能助。/ 我無能為力。

→ It's out of my hands. 這不是我能掌控的。/ 我做不到。

→ It's my way or the highway. 不按我的方式來就走人。/ 不聽我的就滾蛋。

說明 ▶ 這是非常大膽唐突的說法，有可能會被視為非常沒有禮貌。

進行猜測
Guessing

非正式

I'd wager (that) there are more than 50,000 people in the stadium. 句型 *1*

我打賭有超過五萬人在這座運動場內。

Is it a raccoon?

那是浣熊嗎？

稍非正式

I want to say the display case is acrylic. 句型 *2*

我會說這個展示櫃是壓克力做的。

The statue must be at least 20 meters tall.

這座雕像應該至少有 20 公尺高。

一般情況

There may be as many as 10 similar products on the market.

市場上可能有多達十種類似的產品。

I'd estimate the total cost will be 15,000 yen. 句型 *3*

我估計總成本會是一萬五千日圓。

稍正式

Somewhere between two and three kilograms would be my best guess. 句型 *4*

我猜介於兩到三公斤之間最有可能。

There's some speculation that the deadline will be extended.

有人猜測是說截止期限會延長。

正式

If I had to guess, I'd say most students would support longer vacations. 句型 *5*

如果一定得猜，我猜大多數學生會支持假期長一點。

At the risk of guessing incorrectly, I'd say the amplifier was probably made in Germany.

冒著猜錯的風險，我猜這台擴大機八成是德國製的。

句型 1

I'd wager (that)...
我打賭……

Example 實用例句

● I'd wager that there are more than 50,000 people in the stadium.
我打賭有超過五萬人在這座運動場內。

● I'd wager at least half the staff graduated from a top-tier university.
我打賭至少有一半的員工畢業於頂尖大學。

● I'd wager that most people will be willing to work longer hours for a higher salary.
我打賭大多數人願意延長工時來賺取更高的薪水。

說明 ▶ 本句型是一個比喻說法，說話者並不是真的要下注打賭。句型中的動詞 wager（打賭）可以替換成 bet，變成 I'd bet (that)...。

Dialogue 簡短對話

A: So, do you think we'll hit our sales target this month?
B: I'd wager that not only will we hit it, but we'll beat it handily.
　A：那麼，你覺得我們這個月會達到銷售目標嗎？
　B：我打賭我們不只會達到銷售目標，還會輕鬆超過。

 stadium (n.)（周圍設有看臺的）露天運動場　　work longer hours 工時較長
top-tier (adj.) 最高水準的，頂級的　　handily (adv.) 輕易地

句型 2

I want to say...
我會說……

Example 實用例句

● I want to say the display case is acrylic.
我會說這個展示櫃是壓克力做的。

● I want to say he's from Honduras.
我會說他來自宏都拉斯。

● I want to say the moisturizer is hypoallergenic.
我會說這個保溼霜是低過敏的。

說明 ▶ 語調是本句型很重要的一部分。如果要強調這是猜測，表達時句尾語調會上揚，就像問句一樣，顯示比較不肯定、猶疑的態度。相反地，如果要清楚表示這是很肯定的敘述，而不是猜測，重音就會放在 want 上。

Dialogue 簡短對話

A: What is this?

B: I want to say it's a key of some sort. Look at the ridges along the side.

　A：這是什麼？

　B：我會說這是類似鑰匙的東西。看看沿著這一面的脊柱。

---

acrylic (n.) 壓克力
moisturizer (n.) 保溼霜，潤膚霜
hypoallergenic (adj.) 低過敏的

...of some sort　某種的⋯
ridge (n.) 脊柱

進行猜測

精進度 ★★★☆☆

句型 *3*

I'd estimate...
我估計⋯⋯

Example 實用例句

● I'd estimate the total cost will be 15,000 yen.
我估計總成本會是一萬五千日圓。

● I'd estimate we'll lose three or four clients once the ad rates go up.
我估計一旦廣告價格上漲，我們會失去三或四名客戶。

● I'd estimate 60 or 70 respondents, total.
我估計總共會有 60 或 70 名受訪者。

說明 ▶ 動詞 estimate 的後面可以接子句（如第一、二個例句），也可以只接數字、日期等（如第三個例句）。

DIALOGUE 簡短對話

A: Roll-on Bus Lines' new routes are starting up next week. I wouldn't want to chance a guess about their impact on our ridership. What's your take?

B: I'd estimate we'll take a 5 to 10 percent hit in the first month. After that, it's hard to say.

A：動態公車線的新路線下星期會開始運行。我不想隨便猜測他們對我們的載客率會有什麼衝擊，你怎麼看呢？

B：我估計第一個月我們會有五到十個百分點的衝擊，之後就很難說了。

說明 ▶ A 所說的 take 是指「（某人的）觀點，意見」。另外，B 所說的 take a hit 是「蒙受損失，遭受打擊」之意。

字彙		
rate (n.) 價格，費用	chance (v.) 冒…的險
respondent (n.) 受訪者	impact (n.) 衝擊
route (n.) 路線	ridership (n.) 乘客量
start up 開始運轉	take (n.) 看法

精進度 ★★★★☆

句型4

...would be my best guess.
我猜……最有可能。

EXAMPLE 實用例句

● Somewhere between two and three kilograms would be my best guess.
我猜介於兩到三公斤之間最有可能。

● By June or July would be my best guess.
我猜六月或七月最有可能。

● The strike will end sometime this week would be my best guess.
我猜罷工最有可能會在本週某個時間結束。

說明 ▶ 本句型的主詞通常是一個時間、日期、數值或名字（如第一、二個例句），不過在口語上也可以用子句（如第三個例句），這時候通常會在主詞和動詞之間停頓一下。另外，如果要顯示對自己的猜測很有信心，便可以將本句型改成 ...would be a pretty safe guess.（你可以這麼認為……）。

Dialogue 簡短對話

A: Who do you think is going to be the new CEO?

B: A VP from the global planning department would be my best guess.

A：你覺得新的執行長會是誰呢？

B：我猜最有可能是一位來自全球企畫部的副總裁。

 CEO 執行長 (= chief executive officer)　　VP 副總裁 (= vice president)

精進度★★★★★

句型 5　If I had to guess, I'd say...

如果一定得猜，我猜……

Example 實用例句

- If I had to guess, I'd say most students would support longer vacations.

  如果一定得猜，我猜大多數學生會支持假期長一點。

- If I had to guess, I'd say the majority of shareholders will support the share buyback plan.

  如果一定得猜，我猜大多數股東會支持買回庫藏股計畫。

- If I had to guess, I'd say attendance at this year's harvest festival will be slightly down from previous years.

  如果一定得猜，我猜今年豐年祭的參加人數會比前一年稍微減少。

說明 ▶ 本句型以條件句 If... 開頭，其中 if 子句中的動詞用過去式，後面的主要子句則用 I'd... 或 I would...。另外，本句型還有其他類似的說法：If I had to make a guess, I'd say... 及 If I were to (make a) guess, I'd say...。

Dialogue 簡短對話

A: How much snowfall do you think we'll get this season?

B: The weather is so unpredictable these days, it's hard to say. If I had to guess, I'd say we'll get enough to keep the slopes covered through April.

A：你覺得這一季會下多少雪呢？

B：這年頭天氣很難預測，很難說。如果一定得猜，我猜會足夠讓山坡的白雪覆蓋到四月。

字彙

majority (n.) 絕大多數，過半數	harvest festival 豐年祭
shareholder (n.) 股東	unpredictable (adj.) 不可預測的
share buyback 股票回購，庫藏股	slope (n.) 斜坡

相關表達　如果不想胡亂猜測，可以怎麼說呢？

➥ I wouldn't want to chance a guess. 我不想隨便猜測。

➥ It's anyone's guess. 誰也說不準。／天曉得。

➥ Your guess is as good as mine. 我也不知道。

打斷別人說話
Interrupting

Can I (just) jump in here? 句型 *1*

我可以插個話嗎？

Sorry to interrupt you.

對不起打斷你。

I don't mean to be rude, but we're running out of time.

我無意無禮，不過我們快沒有時間了。

Excuse me, may I make a suggestion? 句型 *2*

不好意思，我可以給個建議嗎？

Pardon the interruption. 句型 *3*

對不起打斷一下。

If I can say something, I think there's another way we might look at the issue.

如果我有說話的餘地，我想或許可以從另外一個角度來檢視這個議題。

Before we move on to other business, I wonder if I could make a small point.

在我們繼續討論其他事項之前，我是否能提出小小的看法？

I apologize for cutting you off, but I have a plane to catch.

很抱歉必須打斷你，不過我得去趕飛機了。

If you'll allow me to cut in, I have some data that may be useful to the discussion. 句型 *4*

如果容許我打斷一下，我有一些資料可能對這個討論有所幫助。

I hate to interrupt (you), but can we go back to the sales figures for a moment? 句型 *5*

我不想打斷（你），不過我們可以回頭看一下銷售數字嗎？

句型 *1* **Can I (just) ... here?**
我可以……嗎？

EXAMPLE 實用例句

- Can I just jump in here?
  我可以插個話嗎？

- Can I get a word in here?
  我可以插句話嗎？

- Can I just say a word or two here?
  我可以說一兩句話嗎？

  說明 ▶ 本句型還有一個更正式一點的說法：I wonder if I can (just)...（不知道我可不可以……）。另外，jump in 是「打斷談話，插個話」，而 get a word in 是「插句話，插嘴」之意。

DIALOGUE 簡短對話

A: Can I just say a word or two here?
B: Sure, but if I could just finish this point first, it's really important.
　A：我可以說一兩句話嗎？
　B：當然可以，不過請讓我先把這一點講完，這真的很重要。

句型 *2* **Excuse me,...**
不好意思，……

EXAMPLE 實用例句

- Excuse me, may I make a suggestion?
  不好意思，我可以給個建議嗎？

- Excuse me, is it all right if I say something?
  不好意思，我可以說句話嗎？

- Excuse me, could I offer a slightly different perspective?
  不好意思，我可以提供稍微不同的觀點嗎？

說明 ▶ 使用本句型時，表示說話者期待對方做出回應，而對方的回應通常都是會簡短地表示同意。

Dialogue 簡短對話

A: So that's why I feel we're better off abandoning that particular sales channel.

B: Excuse me, may I offer some input before we make a final decision?

A：所以這就是我覺得我們最好放棄那個特殊銷售通路的原因。

B：不好意思，在我們做出決策之前我可以提出一些意見嗎？

字彙
perspective (n.) 觀點，思考方式	sales channel 銷售通路
abandon (v.) 放棄	input (n.) 投入物（指資訊、資源等）
particular (adj.) 特殊的	

精進度★★★☆☆

句型 3

...the interruption.
……打斷一下。

Example 實用例句

● Pardon the interruption.
對不起打斷一下。

● I apologize for the interruption.
很抱歉打斷一下。

● Sorry about the interruption.
對不起打斷一下。

說明 ▶ 進入辦公室、會議室等時，若發現有人正在開會、講電話或忙著做某事，通常會用本句型來表達。不過，也有可能對方什麼事也沒做，說話者只是為了表示禮貌而用本句型。

打斷別人說話

Dialogue 簡短對話

A: I'm sorry for the interruption. Have you got a minute?

B: Sure, come on in.

A：對不起打斷一下。你有空嗎？

B：當然有，快進來吧。

 interruption (n.) 打斷　　　　　pardon (v.) 原諒

精進度★★★★★

 句型 4

If you'll allow me to cut in,...
如果容許我打斷一下，……

Example 實用例句

● If you'll allow me to cut in, I have some data that may be useful to the discussion.
如果容許我打斷一下，我有一些資料可能對這個討論有所幫助。

● If you'll allow me to cut in, I think I can shine some light on the problem.
如果容許我打斷一下，我想我可以釐清一下這個問題。

● If you'll allow me to cut in, a study was just released that contradicts that claim.
如果容許我打斷一下，有一份剛公布的研究正好和那個主張互相矛盾。

說明 ▶ 句型中的動詞 allow（允許）也可以替換成 permit。另外，shine (some) light on... 是「對（某個問題）提出解釋、理由或細節」之意。

Dialogue 簡短對話

A: If you'll allow me to cut in, I may be able to explain what's going on.

B: Please, go ahead.

A：如果容許我打斷一下，我或許可以解釋到底發生了什麼事。

B：請說。

262

精進度★★★★★

句型 *5*

I hate to interrupt (you), but...
我不想打斷（你），不過……

Example 實用例句

● I hate to interrupt you, but can we go back to the sales figures for a moment?
我不想打斷你，不過我們可以回頭看一下銷售數字嗎？

● I hate to interrupt, but there's another possible reason for the air filter problem.
我不想打斷你，不過空氣濾清器的問題還有一個可能的原因。

● I hate to interrupt you, but I think we should focus on finding solutions, not assigning blame.
我不想打斷你，不過我想我們應該把重點放在找出解決方法，而不是咎責。

說明 ▶ 句型中的動詞 hate（厭惡）可以替換成 don't mean（無意），變成 I don't mean to interrupt (you), but...（我無意打斷〔你〕，不過……）。本句型還有另外一個類似的說法是 I'm very sorry for interrupting, but...（非常抱歉打斷你，不過……）。

Dialogue 簡短對話

A: Then, on the third day of our trip, we went up the Eiffel Tower. It was spectacular.
B: I hate to interrupt you, but I'm due in court in an hour.

A：然後啊，我們在旅行的第三天登上了艾菲爾鐵塔，景色非常壯觀。
B：我不想打斷你，不過我一小時後要到法院報到。

說明 ▶ due in court 表示預計以律師、證人、被告等的身分在法庭現身。

打斷別人說話

字彙   sales figures 銷售數字   Eiffel Tower 艾菲爾鐵塔

air filter 空氣濾清器   spectacular (adj.) 壯觀的

assign blame 歸咎責任，咎責   due (adj.) 預定到達的

相關表達   正在說話時如果被別人打斷，通常會怎麼回應呢？

↪ It's all right. 沒關係。

↪ Please, go ahead. 請說。

↪ If I could just finish this point first... 請讓我先把這一點講完……

表達同情
Expressing Sympathy

非正式

That's too bad. | 太可惜了。

I've been in your shoes before. Trust me, things will get better. 句型1 | 我以前也遇過跟你一樣的情況，相信我，事情會好轉的。

稍非正式

What a shame. | 好令人遺憾。

I'm sorry for your loss. | 我為你失去所愛感到難過。

一般情況

I know what you're going through. 句型2 | 我了解你受的苦。

I wish I knew what to say. 句型3 | 我不知道該說什麼才好。

稍正式

The fire at the processing plant was a real tragedy. 句型4 | 加工廠失火了，真的是個悲劇。

I can't imagine going through something so difficult. | 我無法想像經歷過這麼難熬的事情。

正式

I was sorry to hear about your sister's accident. 句型5 | 很難過聽到你姊姊發生意外的消息。

You have my sincere condolences. | 向你致上誠摯的慰問。

句型 *1*　**I've been in your shoes before.**
我以前也遇過跟你一樣的情況。

Example 實用例句

● I've been in your shoes before. Trust me, things will get better.
我以前也遇過跟你一樣的情況。相信我，事情會好轉的。

● I've been in your shoes before. It's tough, I know.
我以前也遇過跟你一樣的情況。很不好受，我知道。

● I've been in your shoes before. Don't worry. You're going to be fine.
我以前也遇過跟你一樣的情況。不要擔心。你會沒事的。

　　說明 ▶ 本句型是一個很常用的句子，意思是說話者也有類似的遭遇，後面通常跟著一句表達同情或鼓勵的話。in someone's shoes 字面上的意思是「穿某人的鞋」，實際意思則是「站在某人的立場，處在某人的境地」。

Dialogue 簡短對話

A: The typhoon blew over half the trees in our yard. The cleanup and repairs are going to cost a fortune.

B: I've been in your shoes before. It's a tough break.

　　A：颱風把我們院子一半的樹木都吹倒了，清理和修復要花一大筆錢。

　　B：我以前也遇過同樣的事，很倒楣。

　　說明 ▶ B 所說的 tough break 是指「倒楣的事，小惡運」；break 在此是名詞，意思是「好運，機會」。

tough (adj.) 難熬的；棘手的　　　　　　　　cost a fortune 花一大筆錢
typhoon (n.) 颱風

句型 2　I know...
我了解……

EXAMPLE 實用例句

● I know what you're going through.
　我了解你受的苦。

● I know how difficult this must be for you.
　我了解這對你一定很難熬。

● I know what it feels like.
　我了解這種感覺。

說明 ▶ 如果要向對方表示自己也有類似的經驗，以此來表達感同身受時，就很常使用本句型。本句型有另一個類似的說法：I have some idea...。

DIALOGUE 簡短對話

A: I can't believe someone stole my car. It's the worst thing that could have happened.

B: I know how you feel. The same thing happened to me a few years ago.

Ａ：我不敢相信竟然有人偷了我的車。這是我所發生過最糟糕的事情了。

Ｂ：我了解你的感受，幾年前我也發生過同樣的事。

句型 3　I wish I knew...
要是我知道……就好了。／我不知道該……才好。

EXAMPLE 實用例句

● I wish I knew what to say.
　我不知道該說什麼才好。

● I wish I knew how to respond.
　我不知道該如何回應才好。

● I wish I knew the right words to tell you.
　我不知道該跟你說些什麼話才好。

表達同情

說明 ▶ 如果要表達同情，有時候可以考慮像第一個例句一樣說 I wish I knew what to say.（我不知道該說什麼才好。），勝過一些陳腔濫調。

Dialogue 簡短對話

A: Because of our financial situation, we have to give up our house.

B: I wish I knew what to say. If there's anything I can do, please let me know.

　A：由於我們的財務情況，我們不得不放棄我們的房子。

　B：我不知道該說什麼才好。如果有我可以做的地方，請告訴我。

精進度★★★★☆

句型 4
...was a real tragedy.
……真的是個悲劇。

Example 實用例句

● The fire at the processing plant was a real tragedy.
加工廠失火了，真的是個悲劇。

● Leo and Kristen's breakup was a real tragedy.
利奧和克莉絲汀分手了，真的是個悲劇。

● Having to sell some assets to pay back creditors was a real tragedy.
必須賣掉一些財產來還債，真的是個悲劇。

說明 ▶ 並不是所有表達同情的情況都與人有關，也可能是物質或財務方面的損失。這個句型很適合用於人、意外、財產損失、生意失敗等。

Dialogue 簡短對話

A: The demolition of the old cinema was a real tragedy.

B: It certainly was. It was our oldest landmark.

　A：這座老戲院拆掉了，真的是個悲劇。

　B：確實是。那是我們最古老的地標。

精進度★★★★★

句型5

I was sorry to hear about...
很難過聽到⋯⋯的消息。

Example 實用例句

● I was sorry to hear about your sister's accident.
很難過聽到你姊姊發生意外的消息。

● I was sorry to hear about your father's passing.
很難過聽到你爸爸過世的消息。

● I was sorry to hear about what happened during the race.
很難過聽到比賽期間所發生的事情。

說明 ▶ 如果情況很嚴重或很悲慘，句型中的 sorry 也可以替換成 saddened（悲傷的），變成 I was saddened to hear about...。about 的後面可以接名詞（如第一、二個例句）或名詞子句（如第三個例句），通常是關於某個人或某個情況。另外，passing 是 passing away 的簡寫，是 dying 的委婉說法。

Dialogue 簡短對話

A: I was sorry to hear about the way the inspection officers treated you.
B: It's all right. They were just doing their job.

A：我很難過聽到調查官對待你的方式。
B：沒事。他們只是做他們份內的工作。

字彙
hear about... 得悉⋯，耳聞⋯　　　　inspection officer 調查官，檢查官

表達同情

↦ I'm here for you.
我在你身邊。

↦ What can I do to help?
我可以幫什麼忙呢？

↦ If there's anything I can do, please let me know.
如果有什麼我能做的，請告訴我。

非正式

I need to know when the next bus to Osaka leaves.	我得知道往大阪的下一班巴士幾點開。
Where is the subway station?	地鐵站在哪裡呢？

稍非正式

Does anybody know how to open the window? 句型 1	有誰知道要如何開這扇窗戶嗎？
Can I ask you what the price of this purse is? 句型 2	可以請問一下這只錢包的價格是多少嗎？

一般情況

Could you tell me which floor Dr. Olsen's office is on?	可以請你告訴我歐爾森博士的辦公室在哪一層樓嗎？
Sorry, would you mind directing me to the nearest elevator? 句型 3	不好意思，你介意告訴我最近的電梯怎麼走嗎？

稍正式

Do you think you might be able to show me how to operate the fax machine?	請問你可以教我如何操作這台傳真機嗎？
Would you happen to know Ms. Rice's cell phone number? 句型 4	你會不會剛好知道萊斯女士的手機號碼呢？

正式

I wonder if you might be able to tell me who that gentleman over there is. 句型 5	不知道你能不能告訴我那邊那位先生是誰。
I'm sorry to bother you, but I'm looking for the floor supervisor.	很抱歉打擾你，不過我要找樓層主管。

句型 1 **Does anybody know...?**
有誰知道……嗎？

EXAMPLE 實用例句

● Does anybody know how to open the window?
有誰知道要如何開這扇窗戶嗎？

● Does anybody know where the New Year's party is going to be held?
有誰知道新年派對要在哪裡舉行嗎？

● Does anybody know the combination to this lock?
有誰知道這個鎖的號碼嗎？

說明 ▶ 本句型用於對一群人提問時，另外也可以用 Do any of you know...?（你們有誰知道……嗎？）來詢問。和其他詢問資訊的句型一樣，動詞 know 的後面可以接名詞、名詞子句等內容。

DIALOGUE 簡短對話

A: Does anybody know if these cookies have peanuts in them? I'm allergic.

B: I made them. No peanuts, so enjoy!

A：有誰知道這些餅乾裡頭有沒有花生呢？我會過敏。

B：餅乾是我做的，沒有花生，請享用！

combination (n.) 密碼組合	peanut (n.) 花生
lock (n.) 鎖	allergic (adj.) 過敏的

句型 2 **Can I ask you...?**
可以請問一下……嗎？

EXAMPLE 實用例句

● Can I ask you what the price of this purse is?
可以請問一下這只錢包的價格是多少嗎？

- Can I ask you why the dental clinic is closed next Monday?
  可以請問一下這家牙科診所下個星期一為什麼休診嗎？

- Can I ask you where?
  可以請問一下在哪裡嗎？

說明 ► 如果要讓本句型更正式一點，可以把助動詞 can 改成 may，變成 May I ask you...?。Can I ask you 的後面通常接一個名詞子句（如第一、二個例句），不過有時候會把名詞子句的內容省略掉，而只留下疑問代名詞（如第三個例句）。

Dialogue 簡短對話

A: I have a quick question. Can I ask you who is in charge of overseas accounts?

B: That would be Ms. Brook.

A：我有個小問題。可以請問一下海外客戶是誰負責的嗎？

B：是布洛克女士。

說明 ► 針對別人的提問，常用〈That would be + 名詞〉來回答。

精進度★★★☆☆

 句型 3

Sorry, would you mind...?
不好意思，你介意……嗎？

Example 實用例句

- Sorry, would you mind directing me to the nearest elevator?
  不好意思，你介意告訴我最近的電梯怎麼走嗎？

- Sorry, would you mind telling me what floor the records department is on?
  不好意思，你介意告訴我檔案處在哪一樓嗎？

- Sorry, would you mind explaining how the game works?
  不好意思，你介意解釋一下這個遊戲怎麼玩嗎？

說明 ► 本句型有一個類似但比較正式的說法是 I wonder if you wouldn't mind...（不知道你介不介意……）。動詞 mind（介意）的後面接動名詞。

Dialogue 簡短對話

A: Sorry, would you mind spelling the company's name for me?

B: I'm not 100 percent positive how to spell it. I think it's "G-A-R-U-N-D-A."

A：不好意思，你介意把這家公司的名字拼給我聽嗎？

B：我不是百分之百確定該怎麼拼，大概是 G-A-R-U-N-D-A。

說明 ▶ 請求對方提供資訊或向對方提出請求時，通常會像 A 這樣在句尾加上 for me。

 positive (adj.) 有把握的，確信的

精進度 ★★★★☆

 句型4

Would you happen to know...?

你會不會剛好知道……呢？

Example 實用例句

● Would you happen to know Ms. Rice's cell phone number?
你會不會剛好知道萊斯女士的手機號碼呢？

● Would you happen to know his last name?
你會不會剛好知道他的姓氏呢？

● Would you happen to know how long the performance will last?
你會不會剛好知道這個表演會持續多久呢？

說明 ▶ 為了表達得更有禮貌、更客氣，通常會在 Would you know...? 中加上 happen to（剛好，碰巧）。本句型另有一個類似但比較不直接的說法是 Would you by any chance know...?（有沒有可能你剛好知道……呢？）。

Dialogue 簡短對話

A: Pardon the intrusion. Would you happen to know when the judging for the dog show starts?

B: Yes, it starts at 2:30.

A：抱歉打擾了。你會不會剛好知道這場狗狗大賽的評審何時開始呢？

B：我知道，兩點半開始。

intrusion (n.) 打擾，侵入　　　　　　　　judge (v.) 評審，評判

精進度★★★★★

句型5

I wonder if you might be able to tell me...
不知道你能不能告訴我……

Example 實用例句

● I wonder if you might be able to tell me who that gentleman over there is.
不知道你能不能告訴我那邊那位先生是誰。

● I wonder if you might be able to tell me her extension.
不知道你能不能告訴我她的分機號碼。

● I wonder if you might be able to tell me how to register for the promotional offer.
不知道你能不能告訴我如何登記取得促銷商品。

說明 ▶ 本句型另外有一個類似的說法：I wonder if you could please tell me...（不知道你能不能告訴我……）。tell me 的後面可以接名詞子句（如第一個例句）、名詞（如第二個例句），或名詞片語（如第三個例句）。

Dialogue 簡短對話

A: I wonder if you might be able to tell me when this yogurt expires.

B: Sure, let me check for you. It expires on the 23rd.

A：不知道你能不能告訴我，這盒優格什麼時候過期。

B：沒問題，我幫你看一下。23 日過期。

字彙 register (v.) 登記，註冊　　　　　　yogurt (n.) 優格
promotional offer 促銷商品　　　　　expire (v.)（期限）中止

相關表達 請求對方提供資訊前，可以先說什麼作為開場白呢？

→ May I ask you a question? 我可以問你一個問題嗎？

→ I have a quick question. 我有個小問題想請教。

→ Pardon the intrusion. 不好意思打擾了。

→ Can I please ask you something? 我可以問你事情嗎？

提出抱怨
Complaining

I'm very upset with the rental car you gave us. 句型1

我對於你租給我們的那輛車子非常火大。

There's a problem with the sink.

水槽有點問題。

We all think it's too dark in here.

我們都覺得這裡太暗了。

Something needs to be done about the public transportation in this town.

這個城鎮的大眾運輸需要做些改善。

I want to complain about the slowness of the service. 句型2

我要投訴服務慢吞吞。

Is there anything you can do about the mosquitoes in the shop? 句型3

對於店內的蚊子，你可以想點辦法解決嗎？

A few people have said something about a smell coming from the back room.

有一些人說過，裡面的房間有味道飄出來。

I hate to bring it up, but it's really cold in here. 句型4

我不喜歡提起這個，不過這裡真的很冷。

Normally I wouldn't say anything, but the soup is barely warm.

通常我什麼都不會說，不過這道湯幾乎是涼的。

Please don't take this the wrong way, but we can't hear ourselves over the music. 句型5

沒有冒犯之意，不過這個音樂讓我們聽不到自己的聲音。

句型 *1* I'm very upset with...

我對於……非常火大。

Example 實用例句

● I'm very upset with the rental car you gave us.
我對於你租給我們的那輛車子非常火大。

● I'm very upset with the e-mail response I got from your complaint department.
我對於你們客訴部門回覆給我的電子郵件非常火大。

● I'm very upset with the poor quality of the suitcase I recently bought.
我對於我剛買的手提箱其拙劣的品質非常火大。

說明 ▶ 本句型用於直接表達對某件事感到極度生氣、不滿意，另外也可以說 I'm not at all happy with...（我一點都不滿意……）。如果要表達更強烈一點，還可以說 I am livid about...（我對於……氣炸了。）

Dialogue 簡短對話

A: I'd like to make a complaint. I just received a set of glasses I ordered from your website. I'm very upset with the way they were packaged. Two of the glasses were scratched!

B: I'm very sorry, ma'am. I'll have a replacement set sent to you immediately.

A：我要投訴。我剛收到我從你們網站上訂購的一組玻璃杯，我對於你們的包裝非常火大，其中兩個玻璃杯刮到了！

B：非常抱歉，女士。我會立刻寄另外一組給您。

字彙
suitcase (n.)（旅行用的）手提箱
livid (adj.) 盛怒的

scratch (v.) 刮，擦
replacement (n.) 代替物

句型 2

I want to complain about...
我要投訴……

Example 實用例句

- I want to complain about the slowness of the service.
  我要投訴服務慢吞吞。

- I want to complain about the rude behavior of one of your salespeople.
  我要投訴你們其中一位銷售人員的行為很無禮。

- I want to complain about being kept on hold for nearly 30 minutes.
  我要投訴讓我在電話線上等了將近半個小時。

  說明▶ 本句型是相當直截了當的抱怨說法，也可以說 I'd like to complain about...。

Dialogue 簡短對話

A: Who's in charge here? I want to complain about the so-called "no smoking" section. It's right next to the smoking section, with no wall separating the two!

B: I'm afraid there's nothing I can do about it. It's always been that way.

　A：這裡的負責人是誰？我要投訴這個所謂的「禁菸」區就設在吸菸區的旁邊，又沒有牆壁分隔兩邊！

　B：恐怕我也無能為力，一直都是這樣。

rude (adj.) 無禮的	on hold 等候接聽（電話）
behavior (n.) 行為	in charge 負責，主管

句型 3

Is there anything you can do about...?
對於……，你可以想點辦法解決嗎？

Example 實用例句

- Is there anything you can do about the mosquitoes in the shop?
  對於店內的蚊子，你可以想點辦法解決嗎？

提出抱怨

● Is there anything you can do about all the children running around?
對於到處跑來跑去的小孩子，你可以想點辦法解決嗎？

● Is there anything you can do about the bicycles blocking the entrance?
對於堵在入口的腳踏車，你可以想點辦法解決嗎？

說明 ▶ 如果要對方對某事提出辦法或解決某事，便可以用本句型來表達；想要請對方解決的事放在 about 的後面。有一個更直接、更常見的說法是 Can you do something about...?（你可以對……做點什麼事嗎？）。

Dialogue 簡短對話

A: Is there anything you can do about that pounding jackhammer upstairs? It's really bothering us.

B: I can ask them to stop, but I'm not sure it will do any good. They're repairing a wall.

A：對於樓上轟隆隆的手持式鑿岩機，你可以想點辦法解決嗎？真的吵到我們了。

B：我可以去請他們停止，不過我不敢保證有用，他們正在修牆。

說明 ▶ B 所說的 do any good 是一個慣用語，意思是「有用，有效」，通常用於不確定某個做法是否有正面效果時。

| | mosquito (n.) 蚊子 | pound (v.) 連續重擊 |
| | block (v.) 阻塞 | jackhammer (n.) 手持式鑿岩機 |

精進度 ★★★★☆

句型 4

I hate to bring it up, but...
我不喜歡提起這個，不過……

Example 實用例句

● I hate to bring it up, but it's really cold in here.
我不喜歡提起這個，不過這裡真的很冷。

● I hate to bring it up, but the air in the lobby could be fresher.
我不喜歡提起這個，不過大廳裡的空氣可以更清新一點。

● I hate to bring it up, but there's a weird person going from door to door, looking in everyone's mailbox.

我不喜歡提起這個，不過有個怪人挨家挨戶查看每一戶的信箱。

說明 ▶ bring something up 是「提起某事」之意。另外，第二個例句中的〈could be + 形容詞〉是一個客氣的說法，暗指「不夠…」，舉例來說，如果向店員說 could be sweeter，言下之意就是飲料不夠甜，希望能再甜一點。

Dialogue 簡短對話

A: I hate to bring it up, but parts of the movie were out of focus.

B: Really? There may be a problem with the equipment. Thank you very much for letting us know.

A：我不喜歡提起這個，不過這部電影有些部分鏡頭失焦。

B：真的嗎？可能器材有問題。非常感謝你告訴我們。

 weird (adj.) 怪誕的，詭異的　　　　　out of focus 失焦，焦點模糊

精進度★★★★★

 句型 *5*

Please don't take this the wrong way, but...
沒有冒犯之意，不過……

Example 實用例句

● Please don't take this the wrong way, but we can't hear ourselves over the music.

沒有冒犯之意，不過這個音樂讓我們聽不到自己的聲音。

● Please don't take this the wrong way, but these chairs are rather uncomfortable.

沒有冒犯之意，不過這些椅子坐起來相當不舒服。

● Please don't take this the wrong way, but the last time I was at this store, there was a much bigger selection.

沒有冒犯之意，不過上一次我來這家店的時候，選擇多很多。

說明 ▶ 提出抱怨時為了表示客氣、禮貌，通常會以 Please don't take this the wrong way,... 的慣用說法來開頭，然後再表達負面的言論，這樣說的目的是不想冒犯對方或讓對方太過難堪。

Dialogue 簡短對話

A: Please don't take this the wrong way, but the last time we ate here, the salad was much larger.

B: We recently changed the portion size. I'll bring you some breadsticks, on the house.

A：沒有冒犯之意，不過我們上次來的時候，沙拉的份量大很多。

B：我們最近對份量大小做了更動。我拿些麵包條給您，老闆招待。

說明 ▶ B 所說的 on the house 是「老闆招待，免費贈送」之意，通常會在餐廳、咖啡店或其他小吃店聽到。

字彙 portion (n.)（飯菜的）一份，一客　　　　　breadstick (n.) 麵包條

相關表達　要詳細說明想抱怨的事情之前，會先說哪些話作為開場白呢？

↪ I'd like to make a complaint. 我要投訴。

↪ Can I speak with the manager? 我可以和經理談嗎？

↪ Who's in charge here? 這裡的負責人是誰？

表示歉意
Apologizing

非正式

My bad.

是我不好。

Sorry about that. I should have been more careful. 句型 *1*

很抱歉。我應該要更小心的。

稍非正式

Can you ever forgive me?

可以原諒我嗎？

I am so sorry. 句型 *2*

非常對不起。

一般情況

Please forgive me.

請原諒我。

I'm very sorry about the miscalculation. 句型 *3*

對於算錯這件事，我非常抱歉。

稍正式

I'd like to apologize for making you wait.

抱歉讓你等。

Pardon me for the intrusion. 句型 *4*

對不起打擾了。

正式

I must apologize for the appearance of my office.

我必須為我的辦公室外觀道歉。

Please accept my apologies for the problems with the shipment. 句型 *5*

對於出貨的問題，請接受我的道歉。

句型 1 **Sorry about that.**
很抱歉。

Example 實用例句

● Sorry about that. I should have been more careful.
很抱歉。我應該要更小心的。

● Sorry about that. I wasn't looking where I was going.
很抱歉。我走路時沒有看方向。

● Sorry about that. The umbrella slipped out of my hand.
很抱歉。雨傘從我手中滑落了。

說明 ▶ 說話者說完 Sorry about that. 之後，通常會接著責怪自己（如第一、二個例句），或是解釋、找理由等（如第三個例句）。本句型另外有一個類似的說法，不過比較簡短，也比較不正式，即 Sorry, man. 和 Sorry, buddy.（對不起，老兄。）

Dialogue 簡短對話

A: You forgot to add my presentation to the itinerary.
B: Sorry about that. It wasn't intentional. Give me five minutes, and I'll fix it.
A：你忘了把我的簡報加進旅行日程中了。
B：對不起。我不是故意的，給我五分鐘，我立刻修正。

slip (v.) 滑落	itinerary (n.) 旅程安排，旅行日程
presentation (n.) 報告，陳述	intentional (adj.) 故意的，有意的

句型 2 **I am ... sorry.**
……對不起。

Example 實用例句

● I am so sorry.
非常對不起。

- I am really sorry.
  真的很對不起。

- I am terribly sorry.
  非常非常對不起。

說明 ▶ 道歉時有時候可以用非常簡短的說法來表達，達到 short and sweet（即「簡短又明確，不廢話」）的效果。副詞的部分還可以用其他副詞來替換，例如 very 或 extremely。

Dialogue 簡短對話

A: Careful—you almost spilled paint on me!
B: I am really sorry. It was a complete accident.

　　A：小心──你差一點把油漆灑在我身上了！
　　B：真的很對不起，完全是個意外。

字彙	spill (v.) 使灑出，使溢出	paint (n.) 油漆

精進度★★★☆☆

句型3

I'm very sorry about...
對於……，我非常抱歉。

Example 實用例句

- I'm very sorry about the miscalculation.
  對於算錯這件事，我非常抱歉。

- I'm very sorry about all the problems with the booking.
  對於訂位出現的種種問題，我非常抱歉。

- I'm very sorry about this morning.
  對於今天早上的事情，我非常抱歉。

說明 ▶ about 的後面通常接很短的名詞（如第一個例句），不過有時候還是會接比較長的內容（如第二個例句）。此外，本句型也可以接一段時間（如第三個例句），通常這時候已經假定對話雙方了解彼此在說什麼，因此不需要明講問題所在。

Dialogue 簡短對話

A: I'm very sorry about misplacing one of your shirts. It won't happen again.

B: It's OK, I'm sure it will turn up. Anyway, in 20 years of getting my dry cleaning done here, this is the first problem I've had. That's a pretty good track record!

A：很對不起，我把你的一件襯衫放錯地方了。下次不會再發生了。

B：沒關係，我相信一定會找到的。反正，衣服在這裡乾洗了 20 年，這是第一次出現問題，算是很厲害的紀錄了！

字彙

miscalculation (n.) 算錯
misplace (v.) 放錯地方
turn up 出現

dry cleaning 乾洗
track record 紀錄

精進度 ★★★★☆

句型 **4**

Pardon me for...
對不起……

Example 實用例句

● Pardon me for the intrusion.
對不起打擾了。

● Pardon me for stepping on your foot.
對不起踩到你的腳了。

● Pardon me for not calling you earlier.
對不起沒有早一點打電話給你。

說明 ▶ 也可以只說 Pardon me. 即可。第一個例句中的 me for 可以拿掉，變成 Pardon the intrusion.。本句型也可以用於否定，像第三個例句一樣使用〈Pardon me for not + 動名詞〉。

286

Dialogue 簡短對話

A: I asked the other guy about this cell phone, but he didn't know anything about them.

B: Pardon me for that. He just started working here a few days ago.

A：我問了另一個人有關這支手機的情況，可是他什麼都不知道。

B：很抱歉。他幾天前才剛開始來這裡工作。

 intrusion (n.) 打擾，侵入　　　　　　　　step on... 踩到⋯

 句型 5

Please accept my apologies for...
對於⋯⋯，請接受我的道歉。

Example 實用例句

● Please accept my apologies for the problems with the shipment.
對於出貨的問題，請接受我的道歉。

● Please accept my apologies for everything that happened.
對於這一切所發生的事情，請接受我的道歉。

● Please accept my apologies for the long wait.
對於讓你久候一事，請接受我的道歉。

說明 ▶ 如果不想提到細節，只要說 Please accept my apologies. 即可。本句型也可以稍做修改，變成 Please forgive me for...（請原諒我⋯⋯），用於請求原諒。

Dialogue 簡短對話

A: Please accept my apologies for the spelling error on the poster.

B: That's all right. The important thing is we caught the mistake before the posters were put up.

A：對於海報拼錯字，請接受我的道歉。

B：沒關係。重點是我們在海報貼出之前就抓到了錯誤。

說明 ▶ B 所說的 catch a mistake 是「發現錯誤」之意。

表示歉意

287

相關表達 向對方道歉的同時，通常還會說些什麼話呢？

➥ It was a complete accident. 這完全是意外。

➥ I didn't mean it. 我不是有意的。

➥ It was senseless of me. 我完全沒有意識到。

➥ It won't happen again. 下次不會再發生了。/ 下不為例。

➥ It's my fault. 都是我的錯。

➥ I accept full responsibility. 我負起全責。

➥ The blame rests squarely on my shoulders. 一切都怪我。

➥ I didn't mean to... 我不是故意……

Never mind. 　　　　　　　　　　　　不要放在心上。

These things happen. It's OK. 句型*1*　　這是常有的事。沒事的。

Let's talk it over. 　　　　　　　　　我們來好好談一談。

It isn't worth arguing over. 句型*2*　　這不值得爭論。

I'd love to hear your point of view. 　　我很樂意聽聽你的看法。

Let's not let one small disagreement come between us. 句型*3*

我們不要讓一個小小的歧見橫亙在我們之間。

I apologize for the misunderstanding. 　我對造成誤會致歉。

I'm more than willing to sit down and talk about it.

我非常樂意坐下來談。

Thank you for letting me know your side of the story. 句型*4*

謝謝你告訴我你這方的說法。

If we talk things over, I'm sure we can work them out. 句型*5*

如果我們好好談一談，我相信我們可以找出解決辦法的。

句型 1

These things happen.
這是常有的事。

Example 實用例句

- These things happen. It's OK.
  這是常有的事。沒事的。

- These things happen. It's water under the bridge.
  這是常有的事。它是無法改變的既定事實。

- These things happen. I've already forgotten it.
  這是常有的事。我已經忘了。

說明 ▶ water under the bridge 是一個古諺，意思是「過去的事，過眼雲煙」，表示某件事已經是無法改變的既成事實，通常代表說話者現在感受到的問題已經過去，不該讓它繼續造成影響。

Dialogue 簡短對話

A: I can't believe we were given such short notice. Three days isn't nearly enough time to set up such a large banquet.

B: These things happen. Anyway, come on. We need to get started ASAP.

A：我不敢相信我們竟然這麼晚才得到通知，三天的時間根本不夠準備這麼大的一場宴會。

B：這是常有的事。反正，來吧，我們必須儘快開始。

short notice 臨時通知，緊急通知	banquet (n.) 盛宴，宴會
set up.. 準備…，安排…	ASAP 儘快 (= as soon as possible)

句型 2

It isn't worth...
這不值得……

Example 實用例句

- It isn't worth arguing over.
  這不值得爭論。

● It isn't worth fighting over.
這不值得爭吵。

● It isn't worth getting upset about.
這不值得心煩。

說明 ▶ 本句型用於試圖結束爭論來化解衝突的時候。如果要讓語氣更強烈一些，還可以再加入 certainly（無疑，當然）或 definitely（當然，肯定地）等副詞，例如 It definitely isn't worth...（這絕對不值得……）。

Dialogue 簡短對話

A: That business with Michael was ridiculous. He never should have been put in charge of the night shift.

B: Hey, no argument here. Try to put it out of your mind. It isn't worth getting upset about.

A：麥可那件事很荒謬。他不應該去負責晚班的。
B：嘿，同意。把這個拋到腦後吧，它不值得你心煩。

說明 ▶ A 所說的 that business 是指某一件事，這種說法通常帶有負面的含意。另外，B 回答 no argument here，表示同意 A 的看法。put something out of one's mind 則是「不要再想某事」。

字彙	worth (adj.) 值得的	ridiculous (adj.) 荒謬的，可笑的
	upset (adj.) 心煩意亂的	night shift 晚班

精進度 ★★★☆☆

句型 3

Let's not let ... come between us.
我們不要讓……橫亙在我們之間。

Example 實用例句

● Let's not let one small disagreement come between us.
我們不要讓一個小小的歧見橫亙在我們之間。

● Let's not let a simple misunderstanding come between us.
我們不要讓一個單純的誤會橫亙在我們之間。

化解衝突

Let's not let the idle gossip of one disgruntled employee come between us.
我們不要讓一個心懷不滿的員工毫無根據的閒言閒語橫亙在我們之間。

說明 ▶ 本句型用於試圖將大事化小來化解衝突的時候。come between... 是「挑撥……，妨礙……」之意。本句型還有一個類似的說法是 We shouldn't let...（我們不應該讓……）。

Dialogue 簡短對話

A: I can't believe you told Ms. Lawson that I'm an "amateur" artist. How am I supposed to get clients that way?

B: I'm sorry. It was a poor choice of words. Come on—we've known each other for 10 years. Let's not let a simple misunderstanding come between us.

A：我不敢相信，你竟然向洛森女士說我是一個「業餘」藝術家。如果這樣的話，我怎麼會有客戶上門？

B：對不起，那是用字不當。哎呀，我們兩個已經認識十年了，不要讓一個單純的誤會橫亙在我們之間。

說明 ▶ choice of words 是「用字，選詞」；poor choice of words 是「用字不當」之意。

字彙 misunderstanding (n.) 誤會	disgruntled (adj.) 心懷不滿的
idle gossip 毫無根據的閒言閒語	amateur (adj.) 業餘的

精進度★★★★★

句型 4 **Thank you for letting me know...**
謝謝你告訴我……

Example 實用例句

● Thank you for letting me know your side of the story.
謝謝你告訴我你這方的說法。

● Thank you for letting me know how you feel.
謝謝你告訴我你的感受。

● Thank you for letting me know about the problem.
謝謝你告訴我這個問題。

說明 ▶ 如果要順利化解衝突，讓對方知道你很仔細聆聽他／她的感受是絕對有必要的。本句型還有另外一個類似的說法：I appreciate your letting me know...（很謝謝你告訴我……）。此外，也可以用 I'm really glad you let me know...（很高興你告訴我……）來表達。

Dialogue 簡短對話

A: Thank you for letting me know what happened. Believe me, I was as surprised to hear about the problem as you were.

B: Well, I'm glad we could get to the bottom of it. Now let's just make sure it never happens again.

A：謝謝你告訴我事情的原委。相信我，得知這個問題，我跟你一樣驚訝。

B：嗯，我很高興我們可以找出問題的原因。現在我們只要確定下不為例就好了。

說明 ▶ A 表示和 B 有同樣的感受，表達出認同 B 的態度，以此降低彼此的緊張關係。另外，get to the bottom of something 字面上的意思是「到達某件事的底部」，其實就是指「追根究底找出某件事的真相，回到某件事的源頭」。

 story (n.) 對某件事的說法，辯辭

精進度★★★★★

句型 **5**

If we talk things over, I'm sure we can...
如果我們好好談一談，我相信我們可以……

Example 實用例句

● If we talk things over, I'm sure we can work them out.
如果我們好好談一談，我相信我們可以找出解決辦法的。

● If we talk things over, I'm sure we can come to an understanding.
如果我們好好談一談，我相信我們可以達成共識的。

- If we talk things over, I'm sure we can **arrive at a resolution**.
  如果我們好好談一談，我相信我們可以達成決議的。

  說明 ▶ 如果要順利化解衝突，提議坐下來好好談一談問題所在是相當標準的做法。

Dialogue 簡短對話

A: I've received five complaints about the stitching on these jeans. You're costing me customers.

B: I understand your concerns, and I do apologize. If we talk things over, I'm sure we can **straighten everything out**.

A：我收到了五則客訴，抱怨這些牛仔褲的縫線。你害我流失了客人。

B：我了解你的顧慮，非常抱歉。如果我們好好談一談，我相信我們可以把所有的問題都解決。

說明 ▶ B 使用了 straighten something out 這個說法，意思是「解決（問題或困難）；整頓（混亂的局面）」。

字彙

talk something over 仔細討論某事
work something out 把某事解決
come to an understanding
　達成共識，取得諒解

resolution (n.) 正式決定，決議
stitching (n.) 縫紉
jeans (n.) 牛仔褲

相關表達　遇到需要化解衝突的時候，有哪些說法可以使用呢？

↪ I understand your concerns. 我了解你的顧慮。

↪ I can explain everything. 我可以解釋一切。

↪ Things got out of hand. 事情失控了。

↪ I value our relationship/friendship. 我很重視我們的關係／友誼。

50 向對方道別
Saying Goodbye

MP3
50

非正式

Take care (of yourself).　　　　　　　保重。

Don't be a stranger.　　　　　　　　要常聯絡喔。

稍非正式

Keep in touch. I'm easy to reach via e-mail or phone. 句型 *1*

保持聯絡。用電子郵件或電話都
可以找到我。

I had a great time.　　　　　　　　我玩得很開心。

一般情況

It was good to see you. 句型 *2*　　能見到你真好。

Let's get together again soon.　　　我們很快再聚一聚吧。

稍正式

I'd better be going. 句型 *3*　　　我得走了。

I hope to see you again soon.　　　我希望很快就能再見到你。

正式

Thank you for taking the time to meet with me. 句型 *4*

謝謝你撥出時間和我見面。

I'm afraid I need to be on my way. 句型 *5*

我恐怕必須離開了。

句型 *1*

Keep in touch.
保持聯絡。

Example 實用例句

● Keep in touch. I'm easy to reach via e-mail or phone.
保持聯絡。用電子郵件或電話都可以找到我。

● Keep in touch. I'm free most afternoons after 3:00.
保持聯絡。下午三點過後我大多有空。

● Keep in touch. It would be great to share recipes again sometime.
保持聯絡。改天再一起分享食譜一定很棒。

說明 ▶ 說完 Keep in touch. 之後，通常還會提供自己方便或喜歡的聯絡方式（如第一、二個例句），或說明想要再次見到對方的原因或理由（如第三個例句）。Keep in touch. 也可以單獨使用，後面不必接任何句子。

Dialogue 簡短對話

A: Keep in touch. I'd love to talk to you about your research again.
B: My door's always open. Drop by anytime.
A: Sounds great. Bye now.
B: Bye.

　　A：保持聯絡。我想再和你聊聊你的研究。
　　B：我的大門永遠打開，隨時都歡迎你來。
　　A：太棒了。那就先再見囉。
　　B：再見囉。

 drop by 順便拜訪

句型2

It was ... to see you.
能見到你……

Example 實用例句

- It was good to see you.
  能見到你真好。

- It was a pleasure to see you.
  能見到你真高興。

- It was nice to see you.
  能見到你真好。

  說明 ▶ 本句型中間可替換的部分可以用形容詞（如第一、三個例句）或名詞（如第二個例句），在形容詞的前面可加副詞，例如 really good, so nice；在名詞的前面可加 such，例如 such a pleasure（很高興；很榮幸）。

Dialogue 簡短對話

A: It was such a pleasure to see you.
B: We should do it more often.
A: Definitely. Well, I'll see you later.
B: Cheers.
  Ａ：能見到你實在好高興。
  Ｂ：我們應該要更常見面的。
  Ａ：那還用說。嗯，那就再聯絡囉。
  Ｂ：再見囉。

句型3

I'd better be...
我得……

Example 實用例句

- I'd better be going.
  我得走了。

- I'd better be on my way.
  我得離開了。

- I'd better be leaving.
  我得離開了。

  說明 ▶ 本句型的前面通常會有一句鋪陳的話，例如 It's getting late.（時間已經很晚了。）或 Look at the time.（看看時間已經這麼晚了。）

Dialogue 簡短對話

A: Look at the time. I'd better be on my way.

B: So soon? Well, I'm glad we had a chance to get together.

A: Me too. It was really fun. Bye for now.

B: Bye.

　A：看看時間已經這麼晚了。我得離開了。

　B：這麼快？嗯，我很高興我們有機會聚在一起。

　A：我也是。真的很好玩。先再見囉。

　B：再見囉。

句型 **4**

精進度★★★★★

Thank you for...
謝謝你……

Example 實用例句

- Thank you for taking the time to meet with me.
  謝謝你撥出時間和我見面。

- Thank you for taking time out of your busy schedule.
  謝謝你百忙之中抽出時間。

- Thank you for scheduling this lunch meeting.
  謝謝你安排這場午餐會議。

  說明 ▶ 本句型用來表達對於對方抽出時間做某事的感謝。說話者除了很有禮貌地表達謝意外，還暗含另一層意思，即「希望結束這場會面」。

Dialogue 簡短對話

A: Thank you for inviting me to lunch.

B: My pleasure. I hope we can do it again sometime.

A: That would be great. Well, see you next time.

B: See you then.

A：謝謝你邀我共進午餐。

B：這是我的榮幸。希望我們改天再一起共進午餐。

A：那真是太好了。嗯，那就下次見囉。

B：到時見。

精進度★★★★★

句型 *5*

I'm afraid...
我恐怕……

Example 實用例句

● I'm afraid I need to be on my way.
我恐怕必須離開了。

● I'm afraid it's getting late.
我恐怕時間愈來愈晚了。

● I'm afraid I have another appointment.
恐怕我還有約。

說明 ▶ 道別通常有兩個部分，前半部分就像本句型一樣，為道別做個鋪陳，若沒有這個鋪陳，直接說再見就會顯得比較冷漠、不親切。後半部則簡單地說 Goodbye. 或 See you later. 之類的話。從上面三個例句可以知道，說話者在 afraid 的後面說出必須離開的原因或理由。

Dialogue 簡短對話

A: I'm afraid I need to be on the other side of town in an hour.

B: I understand completely. It was really good seeing you.

A: You too. Goodbye.

B: Goodbye.

　A：我恐怕一個小時之後得到鎮上另一頭去。

　B：我完全了解。能看到你真的很好。

　A：我也是。再見。

　B：再見。

相關表達　要和別人說再見，有哪些好用的說法呢？

➥ Goodbye. 再見。

➥ See you (later). 再聯絡。/ 待會見。

➥ Bye! 再見囉！

➥ Bye now. 先再見囉。

➥ Bye, bye. 再見。

➥ Have a good one. 再見囉。

➥ Take it easy. 保重囉。

➥ Cheers. 再見囉。

提升英語溝通能力，95% 的場合都能靈活應對

作者：濱田伊織

定價：350 元　　　　　　　　　　　　　　　　　　MP3

本書分成「和他人對話時的基本句型」、「以成熟態度回應對方的句型」、「站在對方立場發言的句型」三大部分，涵蓋感謝、道歉、請求、提議、拒絕、讚美、插話等場合及情境，收錄與主題相關的英文句型，並提供解說及豐富的應用語句。

如何提升英語溝通能力：關鍵句 1300

作者：崎村耕二

定價：380 元　　　　　　　　　　　　　　　　　　MP3

本書精選 1300 個溝通必備的英語句型，涵蓋「贊成、反對、指出錯誤、責備、交涉、表達意見、有技巧地討論、問題探討、論證、理解與誤會、道歉與解釋、遣詞用字」12 大主題 210 個情境，讓你進退不失據，完全掌握英語溝通的要領。

英文研究論文發表：口語報告指引

作者：廖柏森

定價：350 元　　　　　　　　　　　　　　　　　　MP3

本書收錄的英語句型，主要來自國際學術研討會、國內外相關的口語報告英文書籍、專業網站和語料庫，使用者若能參照本書所提供的英語句型，加上聆聽模仿 MP3 中的範例，就可在各種學術場合中，流暢地使用英語。

英文學術會議口語表達

作者：石井隆之

定價：380 元　　　　　　　　　　　　　　　　　　MP3

本書涵蓋各種國際學術會議場景，收錄研究發表者、會議主持人、小組討論成員、演說者、提問者等各種角色所使用的英文語句。另外，還針對社交場合提供應對例句，是研究人員和研究生事先準備的最佳參考手冊。

國家圖書館出版品預行編目 (CIP) 資料

看場合說英語：正式×非正式的 10 種說法 / 白安竹 (Andrew E. Bennett) 著；林錦慧譯. -- 初版. --
臺北市：眾文圖書，2015.07 面；公分
ISBN 978-957-532-465-0（平裝附光碟片） 1. 英語 2. 會話 3. 句法
805.188   104008561

SE063

看場合說英語：正式×非正式的 10 種說法

定價 350 元
104 年 7 月 初版 1 刷

作者	白安竹 (Andrew E. Bennett)
譯者	林錦慧
責任編輯	黃琬婷
主編	陳瑠琍
副主編	黃炯睿
資深編輯	黃琬婷・蔡易伶
美術設計	嚴國綸
行銷企劃	李皖萍・莊佳樺
發行人	黃建和
發行所	眾文圖書股份有限公司
	台北市 10088 羅斯福路三段 100 號
	12 樓之 2
網路書店	www.jwbooks.com.tw
電話	02-2311-8168
傳真	02-2311-9683
郵政劃撥	01048805

ISBN 978-957-532-465-0
Printed in Taiwan